Jennifer –
Happy 30
Birthday!
Su~ Rea~
Sierra
Hill

GAME CHANGER

Change of Hearts #1

SIERRA HILL

Ten28 Publishing

❀ Created with Vellum

To empowered and independent women everywhere who change the world and make it a better place to be.

The empowered woman is powerful beyond measure and beautiful beyond description.
Steve Maraboli

1

GARRETT

Your son has suffered major head trauma.

He may never be able to walk or talk again.

Those words said to me a little over two years ago from the Head of Pediatric Brain Trauma at University Hospital, are on a continual loop in my head this morning, as they are most mornings during our breakfast ritual.

Even after all this time, after all the specialists we've consulted, and the knowledge that it may never change for my boy, it fills me with rage and despair. The unfairness of it all is a kick in the nuts every time I think about the fact that he'll likely suffer from both physical and cognitive issues his whole life and may not grow out of them.

I stare across the table at Caleb, my nearly five-year-old son, who is having his morning meltdown over his cereal. Hands flailing in bunched up fists. Food flying, getting caught in his hair and across his cheeks and forehead. Loud screams from the top of his lungs, over what? Because he doesn't want the Cheerios this morning.

My eyes close and I take a gulp of my coffee, now cool from being neglected as I did a hundred other things this morning trying to get us ready for the day.

Why did this have to happen to us? Why can't he be a normal kid?

The minute the thought pops into my head, I curse myself and clench my teeth in fury at myself for thinking that way. Screwing my eyes shut tight, I try to scrub the thoughts from my head and focus on the positive. Focus on the things that are in my control.

Even on the worst days, I know I brought this on myself. It's my fault it happened.

Caleb, his reddened cherub cheeks, are streaked with big croc-odile tears that have been streaming down his face until about two seconds ago, and I immediately feel guilty. I love my son. He's the best thing that ever happened to me. But sometimes the people we love most cause us the biggest heartaches.

Caleb pushes the bowl of uneatened cereal away from him, threatening to topple it over off the table. "*Na-na-na-na-naaaaaa.*"

I sigh and count to five.

It's what I have to do every meal that I'm home, as we struggle through the same routine. The only things Caleb will eat without a hissy fit are chicken nuggets, sliced apple slices with the skins off and string cheese. And most of the time, I give in just to avoid this exact same standoff scenario that's happening right now.

"Caleb, we've talked about this. You have to eat what I give you so you can get the nutrients your body and brain need to help you grow big and strong."

His big blue eyes, fringed with the dark, long lashes he got from his mother, widen as he points his knuckled-fist hand toward me. "*Ooooh?*"

The word is uttered slowly, slurred and muddled, but I know he means me. I know he wants nothing more than to be big and strong like his dad. It makes my heart melt and turns my two-hundred-fifteen, six-foot-three frame into mush. And like every father, I want that, too.

"That's right. If you don't eat your food, you won't develop the muscle strength you need to play ball someday."

The words practically choke me as they leave my mouth, the lie so big it barely escapes my throat over my tongue and passed my lips.

I give him an easy smile, even though inside nothing about this is easy, and push his cereal bowl closer to him, picking out one of the berries I'd topped it with. He opens his mouth for the game we play, and I shoot it in his mouth with an exclamation.

"He shoots, he scores!" We both raise our arms in celebration, as he chomps on his raspberry with a wide grin.

"Okay, now you finish up while daddy gets ready. Remember, eat it all. You need it to grow big and strong." I emphasize this with a flex of my arm and bicep, which he does in return.

It's a lie. One that I tell him over-and-over again, day-in and day-out.

Because no matter how you slice it, the likelihood that my son will even ever be able to walk, let alone run, dribble a ball, or play any sport without assistance, is a pipedream. Sure, the doctors say there are chances this can happen, but every case is unique, every child is different.

Sucking in a deep breath, I exhale long and hard, letting go of the stress that's been simmering inside me since the moment I woke up this morning. Changes are coming, and with a kid like Caleb, who thrives on routine, this is going to be a difficult summer ahead of us.

My previous nanny, Delinda, retired after thirty-five years of teaching and caring for special needs kids. And because I'm a single, working dad, I need a replacement, at least for the summer, so I can coach the summer basketball camp I'm lined up to train.

The tension headache brewing at the base of my neck snaps and crackles, as I mentally steel myself to get through everything on my To Do list today. The first thing on the list is the interview with a potential summer nanny for Caleb. Brooklyn Hayes is a referral from one of my former college players, Lance Britton, who is also helping me coach the camp this summer. He highly recommended her, and her resume speaks for itself.

On paper, her credentials look stellar.

But as any parent with a special needs child knows, this job is demanding. It requires patience, strength, mental and physical, and a load of energy. I won't allow just anyone to take care of my son.

There are days when even I don't feel capable of being his father and wonder how the hell I've even come this far or how I even got here.

It's as far from my former NBA status as I can get.

And sometimes, in my weak moments when I just can't seem to catch a break, I wish for those days again. When I was living in the limelight and at the height of my pro-ball fame.

Back in time when I didn't have these responsibilities that aged me to the point of exhaustion.

It might make me a shitty father to think that way.

But then again, it's not far from the colossal dick I was back then.

Back when life was only centered on me. And I hurt all the ones around me.

2

It's not often I'm rattled or nervous.

But right now, my palms sweat, and I'll admit, I'm pretty damn nervous.

I usually exude confidence in everything I do. Even as a child, I thought I was capable of doing everything myself. If I had to guess, I'd say at least half my grade school teachers indicated that "Brooklyn can be strong-willed and bossy toward adults and other students."

I guess that's bound to happen when you're raised in an environment that pushes the *Lean In* mentality. Where women should never kowtow to male leadership or gender stereotypes. My mother, a successful psychologist, and a feminist to the core taught me to believe that I could do or become whatever I wanted in life.

Girl Power!

But that doesn't diminish my nerves as I stand outside the front doorway of Coach Garrett Parker's Scottsdale home.

Coach Parker is the Associate Head Coach to the ASU men's basketball team. The single father of Caleb. And, my potential new boss.

Breathing deeply, I do a quick assessment of my appearance, smoothing out the non-existent wrinkles in my casual, yet, comfortable interview attire. First impressions can make or break you, I've been told, and you should always dress to impress. Although, I can guarantee you that this job doesn't hinge on what I'm wearing.

What matters is how well I'll mesh with Coach Parker and his son, Caleb, and whether I can establish an immediate rapport with them.

If Coach even bothered to look through my credentials and resume, he'll probably surmise that I may be a bit over-qualified for the job. As a newly minted graduate of ASU, I now have my degree in Early Childhood Development and am enrolled in the graduate program to become a child psychologist. I'm not sure yet if I'll choose a clinical setting or something more hands on, but this summer job will be a great springboard to narrowing down my interests.

I've never met Coach before and don't know him, only what my friend Lance has mentioned. He's the one who introduced me to Coach via email a week ago and mentioned Coach's need for the summer nanny. Coach's emails weren't discourteous as we exchanged emails about the job, but he certainly didn't go out of his way to project any warmth or enthusiasm. He was blunt, to the point and didn't veer from the topic of his son.

Which is fine with me. I don't need to be friends with my employer. I just need a job.

Yet, it did pique my curiosity about Coach Parker's personality and what he would be like in person when I met him. I'd heard the rumors around campus about him, portraying my potential employer as an ego-driven, callously harsh, hard shell-to-crack, who is fiercely protective of his son and his personal life.

With all the negative shade thrown out about Coach Parker, you can see why I'm a little nervous as I stand outside his front door, hand poised at the ready to knock, trying to draw upon some of my reserved self-assuredness.

"It's now or never," I say out loud to myself, running my tongue over my front teeth.

My hand closes into a fist as my knuckles make contact with the door just as I hear a very loud crash from inside, followed by a piercing cry of a little boy.

My instincts kick in, and I double-rap on the door before testing the doorknob to find it unlocked. Opening it just a crack, I shout out, "Hello? Is everything okay in here?"

I wait at the threshold for a few moments, not hearing a response, only the continued cries of a sad kid, and then the soothing hushes from a deep, vibrato voice.

A voice that somehow reaches into my chest and splits it wide open.

"It's okay, buddy. Stop your crying, now. Let's get you cleaned up before Brooklyn gets here."

I pause in my tracks as I've by now taken a few steps in the entryway and turn to look into the kitchen. The first thing my gaze narrows in on is a very tall, fit man who has whipped off his T-shirt over his head and uses it to wipe away the mess the boy has made from the table in front of him.

Holy guacamole. I'm not normally at a loss for words, but it's as if my voice box is being strangled by a boa constrictor which is squeezing out every single drop of air from my lungs.

Coach's back is to me, so I have the pleasure of seeing every rippling muscle in his back flex and bow, as he single-handedly picks up his son from the booster chair in one arm and uses the other to efficiently clean up the mess. With his shirt.

And then my eyes lock on the sweetest, widest blue eyes I've ever seen. They stare back at me in confusion at first and then turn to startled fear.

"Aaaaaaaa," he wails, tears still streaming down his face and his arm flailing around like a windmill.

Realizing I'm scaring the shit out of him, I clear my throat, searching for my voice at the same time as I place a gentle smile on my face and give him a wave by wiggling my fingers.

"Um, hi, Coach Parker?"

Coach whips around, sending milk droplets and cereal O's scattering every which direction as he lets loose the T-shirt, grunting out a curse.

"Shit."

The expression on his face is not dissimilar to his son's, a little bit of surprise and confusion. But his transforms into something close to irritated alarm in a matter of seconds.

"How'd you get in?"

I'm taken back by the gruff accusatory tone and bite back my own immediate defensive response.

Glancing over my shoulder, I hook my thumb at the door behind me. "Sorry. It was unlocked and I wanted to make sure everything was okay."

Trying to be helpful, I bend down on one knee to pick up the discarded shirt. As I push back to my feet to stand, my gaze can't help but track the length of his body, all six-foot and more of him. The man is tall – obviously, given his former NBA career – but he's in better shape than David Beckham was in his glory days.

I've been around athletes my entire life. As a soccer player in high school and college, I dated a few football players and soccer players in my time, all who had pretty great physiques, and some very tiny brains. But that does not mean I'm immune to the mountainous man view of the incredibly fit body in front of me.

Garrett stands at least six-four, a smattering of light brown hair between his pecs, and a treasure trail of the same color and density leading into the waistband of his track pants, and abs that cry out to be touched and traced.

My fingers twitch from wanting a touch, but instead, I hold

out my proffered hand to him, the other still gripping the damp T-shirt.

Garrett eyeballs me like I'm a criminal that just broke into his house.

"Huh, I thought I locked that back up and had the security alarm on." He shakes his head as if to clear his thoughts. "Sorry, it's been a tough morning."

I hold my hands up. "No, my bad. I'm so sorry to have just barged in like that, but I heard all the commotion and did try calling out first. Anyway, hi. I'm Brooklyn Hayes. Nice to meet you, Coach."

Coach Parker shifts the boy in his arm, who squirms and mumbles gibberish, taking my hand in his warm, albeit a little damp, firm grip. The spark that exists between us shocks me so soundly that I'm rendered speechless for a second.

Retracting my hand, I shift on my heels and step back in hopes of regaining my balance that seemed to disappear from that simple touch. Realizing I still have his shirt in my grip, I hold it back out to him to take.

"Thanks," he says, adjusting his stance and slinging the shirt over a chair back. "Nice to meet you, too. Thanks for coming over this morning on such short notice. I'm Garrett and this is Caleb, my son. Why don't we go sit down so I can put Caleb down and I can grab a new shirt?"

I follow him into the adjoining room and am not disappointed with the view. There's a tattoo on his left shoulder, inked black and lined with perfect symmetry in the design. A Celtic symbol of some sort. I may also check out his ass as he leans over to place Caleb on the floor near the couch.

He suddenly turns back at me, as if where I've been staring has burned through his skin, and he catches me staring like I'm window shopping for Easter candy.

"Caleb, I'll be right back. This is Brooklyn and she's going to talk to us this morning. Why don't you show her some of your toys?"

Caleb blinks at me, gives me a shy smile and then buries his head into his dad's chest, hanging on to him for dear life. I feel the rumble of Coach Parker's laughter in my toes. It's a deep, warmth that moves between us like the current from the Southern California Pacific Ocean.

"Hi, Caleb. I'm so happy to meet you," I say in a soft voice, plopping my butt on the floor in front of him, crossing my legs, hands folded in the space between.

The boy peers up at me, letting Garrett go from the grip he'd had on his shoulders and cocks his head to check me out. He's adorably sweet, with the same chin dimple as his father, his hair only slightly lighter than Garrett's, and spindly legs and arms of a boy, no longer a toddler.

I wasn't sure what to expect upon meeting Caleb, considering I knew next-to-nothing about his condition from the brief emails I received from Coach Parker. All I knew was that Caleb was young, not yet school-aged, and had complications due to pediatric brain trauma. There was a mess load of potential issues that I could've walked into.

From just our brief interaction so far this morning, he appears to have limited mobility, based on the tiny walker that sits at the ready next to the couch and it appears he's unable to communicate very clearly.

I read up as much as I could in the last few days before coming over to learn about the impacts and effects of brain injuries on young children. If there is such a thing as typical, many kids under the age of four who have suffered neurological trauma due to abuse or falls or motor vehicle accidents, have noticeable speech and mobility limitations.

I don't know the details about Caleb's full condition, but regardless, it's exactly the reason I'm getting my Master's in Child Development and Psychology. To help assist in the counseling and development of their physical, cognitive and emotional state and to provide tools for parents in easing their burdens on managing life after an event like this has occurred.

Caleb purses his lips together and blows out a bubble, sounding something like "*Baaaaa.*"

I smile, nodding my head at what I assume is his attempt to say my name. I point to my cheek. "That's right. I'm Brooklyn."

Coach Parker eyes me warily with a half-smile that doesn't quite meet his eyes.

"As you can see, Caleb is working on developing his speech. He sees a speech therapist twice a week and that's one of the things I'll need this position to help with over the summer. But you're getting there, aren't you, buddy?"

The love that shines between both Coach and Caleb's faces is honestly the sweetest thing I've ever witnessed. There is something so pure and beautiful that radiates in their eyes, and it immediately shuts down all the rumors and hearsay that I've recently heard about the hard-ass coach.

He's not the self-absorbed asshole or 'has-been' pro baller that everyone says he is.

He's just a single dad, dealing with what has to be one of the most difficult of situations any parent must go through. A man clearly devoted to the health and well-being of his child. A man doing the very best he can to ensure his son is looked after and given every opportunity to thrive and live a good childhood.

And I want to be the one to help them both.

When Coach returns, he's wearing an ASU Sun Devils T-shirt and has a clipboard in his hands. I kind of want to laugh, because all he needs now is the coaching whistle to complete the outfit. But I keep my thoughts to myself and settle into his questions and stipulations regarding the position.

"Routine is extremely important to his development," he states adamantly, checking off from the list he's running through as we discuss Caleb's daily and weekly schedules. "I need someone who is consistent and won't deviate from the expected schedule."

"Got it. But sometimes kids need some freedom to just be kids and have fun, too," I counter back. "Regimenting a child's day without room for playtime or extra-curricular time can bring out unwanted behavioral traits."

Coach's stern gaze snaps to mine. "My child is not a dog. He's not going to be pissing in the corner if he doesn't get to play all day long. And he gets plenty of that with me. But when I'm not here, I expect things to go as I have planned."

Okay then. I didn't mean to rub him the wrong way with my opinion. But I've been taught it's better to speak up and challenge. Especially when it comes from a good place and I only mean well.

"Understood," I say more demurely this time. I don't want to start off on the wrong foot, or heaven forbid, sound too demanding or obstinate. I need this summer job. "You're right. I agree."

He nods briskly. "Brooklyn, I appreciate the fact that you have a lot of education involving childhood development. I read your resume and am very impressed. But here's the deal. I need someone who is going to listen to me and do things the way I say, for Caleb's sake. It's the only way this will work. Got it?"

Biting my tongue to keep myself from saying anything I'll regret, I acquiesce, smiling brightly.

"Got it, Coach. Message received, loud and clear. I want what's best for Caleb. And if you hire me, I'll make sure to do everything by the book."

3

GARRETT

"Mornin', Coach. How's it going?"

I lift my eyes from the roster I've been working on to see Lance Britton, my former player and now assistant camp coach, ambling through the doorway of my office. He's dressed in his usual attire – gray sweats and a T-shirt – looking healthy and happy.

"Hey, man. Glad you're here." I check the time on my watch and lift my chin with a teasing grin. "And on time, no less. I'm shook."

"Ah, look at you old man. Being all hip with the slang these days." Lance flips me off, plopping down in the chair in front of my desk.

"What can I say? I'm a working stiff now and need to impress my new boss. And surprisingly, I now enjoy mornings a helluva lot more when I don't have a head-crushing hangover." He chuckles good-naturedly, but I know the underlying message in his comment.

Lance says it in jest, but truthfully, he went through hell and back to get where he is today. Sober and alive. At the beginning of last season, his senior year on the team, Lance was really struggling in life, mainly with an addiction that nearly cost him everything – his relationship, his basketball scholarship and his life. Thankfully, he received a wake-up call and with the team's help and the love of his life by his side, he sought treatment to take control of his addictions.

And now he's married with a baby on the way and with a job this summer helping me coach this high school basketball camp.

"Hey, I wanted to talk to you about something before we start practice today."

Lance places his elbows on the desk, an eyebrow quirked up, leaning in to listen intently. "Yeah, what's up?"

Clearing my head of all the thoughts that have been swirling in my brain since meeting Brooklyn this morning, I relax back in my chair and rub my chin, the stubble rough since I didn't have time to shave this morning due to my rush. The bristles of my beard scrape against my hand. Add another thing to my ever-growing list of things to do.

Right between hire a replacement nanny and win an NCAA championship next season, hopefully setting me up for a future head coaching job someday.

When my career in the NBA ended abruptly, I had no idea where I was going or what I'd end up doing. The future looked so bleak two years ago, as I was dealt a hand that no gambler would ever want to bet on. A dead wife and a brain-injured child who would need constant medical attention and help. There was no way I was rebounding back into a spot on an NBA team roster, so I had to figure out a new plan and a new career.

Luckily, through my friend and former college teammate, Lucas, I found my way down to Tempe, Arizona and landed this coaching job.

Now I just had to figure out a plan for Caleb this summer.

"This girl you referred for the nanny position. Do you trust her?"

Lance's eyes narrow in question. "You mean Brooklyn? Hells yeah, I trust her. That's why I suggested her in the first place. I've known her for a long time, since our freshman year. She just graduated with her degree and played on the women's soccer squad. She's totally into kids with disabilities."

He stops abruptly, the look of guilt replacing his smile. "Fuck, I'm sorry, Coach. I don't know the politically correct term to use. I mean special needs kids."

Lance knows much, but not everything, about Caleb's disabilities, and has even met him a few times. I know he finds it awkward to talk about Caleb's limitations, as most people do when they first meet or see Caleb. He's not your typical four-year-old kid. He can't really walk or communicate, which makes people uncomfortable.

We've grown used to it, but it never gets any easier. The looks we get from strangers or even people I know.

Since joining the ASU men's basketball team staff, I've brought Caleb into the office and to games on a few occasions when my former nanny was able to swing it. Due to the walker, and sometimes the motorized wheelchair he uses, and his speech limitations, there are always misunderstandings of his condition and people are more apt to shy away due to ignorance and fear.

I've been asked if Caleb has cerebral palsy or is autistic or mentally challenged. Worse yet is when the ignorant mother-fuckers ask if my child is retarded.

It's those times that I want to throat punch them or grab them by the balls and spin them around before throwing them against a brick wall. But what can I do? There will always be stupid people who through their own limitations and ignorance don't know or understand.

Caleb is a brilliant, beautiful and sweet child but comes with limitations that other kids his age don't have. Every time I look at him, I'm racked with pain and guilt because he will never live an average or normal life. It will always be fraught with difficulties.

Regardless that I've been dealing with his condition for two years now, it hasn't gotten any easier. Not when his progress has moved slower than I've wanted. I'd hoped by the time he was ready to start school he'd be walking on his own and without assistance.

Maybe if I wasn't alone in this endeavor and Becca was still around, I'd have more patience. She was always the easy-going, laid-back, take-it-as-it-comes type of personality. But not me. I was born a competitor. Everything in my life, from childhood to adult, was something I wanted to achieve and win. If I wanted something bad enough, I made it happen. Perseverance, desire, and commitment.

Unfortunately, those traits don't necessarily translate when it comes to traumatic brain injuries and recovery in children. And it's given me more sleepless nights than I care to count.

That's why it's imperative that I have a nanny that I can trust and who will work with Caleb daily. Just as I do with my ball players, it's practice, practice, practice until you can do it without a second thought. And from what I could gather from my introductory meeting this morning with Brooklyn, she's equipped and educated to do that.

But she also struck me as highly-opinionated and defiant. Or at least, that was my first impression of her.

Sliding my foot over my bent knee, I dismiss Lance's concern over the proper term. "It's cool, man. Everyone has different preferences. Physically challenged, disabled, differently abled...special needs. It all works. Anyway, about Brooklyn. We met this morning and I think she brings a lot to the table and is willing to work through the summer and maybe even into the fall with my variable schedule requirements and out of town demands."

Lance nods and gives me the thumbs up. "That's great. So,

what's the problem? Seems like a good gig. And how about a 'Thanks, Lance, for brokering this deal.'"

I let out a short laugh because although Lance isn't a dad yet, he does have one on the way, and he'll learn soon enough that being a father means that no one is ever qualified or trustworthy enough to care for your child.

Sometimes I wonder how I'm even qualified to be Caleb's father or how I've made it this far without making every mistake in the book. Being a parent is the hardest thing in the world. And being a single parent to a special needs child? Well shit, that only triples the anxiety that comes along with the job.

Out of the corner of my eye, off to the side of my desk, I notice the picture of Caleb and me from last Father's Day. It was taken nearly a year ago after we'd just moved to Phoenix from Indiana. I'm carrying him on my back, his arms loosely swung around my neck and he wears a gigantic, baby-toothed smile across his face.

He doesn't remember what it was like before the accident. Before our worlds were irrevocably changed. He doesn't even remember his mom, Becca, who cared for and loved him like her own.

In that picture, he didn't know that he was the only reason I got myself out of bed some days. The only thing that continued to push me to do anything after what happened in the accident.

Before Caleb was born, my life centered around three things - me, myself and I. I had no cares in the world, an exciting NBA career that brought me celebrity and money, as well as notoriety. Looking back on life before and the way I was with Becca, how I took her for granted and didn't count myself lucky to have such a beautiful and honest woman in my life, I can now say what a selfish asshole I was. And how I didn't deserve any of it.

And then Caleb came into my life — my perfect little boy - who I had to fight tooth and nail for. Who Becca and I did everything for.

Until that night that sent my life reeling, spiraling like the sieve down a drain, leaving me a widowed single father, alone to raise this special little boy.

Shaking off my dark thoughts, I return my attention to Lance. "I need to be certain she's the right fit. I don't want someone breezing in and then realizing the work is too hard or too much to handle and then leave us high and dry. Caleb already lost his mother, then I had to uproot him from his home, so I want him to have some stability in his life again, even if it's just for the summer. If you have any reservations about Brooklyn, now's your chance to let me know. Otherwise, if you endorse her, then I'll give her a chance."

Lance nods emphatically, his longish hair dipping over his eyebrows. He's still so young. Barely twenty-three. Although I'll be thirty this year, I feel like I've lived two lifetimes with everything that's happened. The before and the after.

"Absolutely, Coach. She's a hundred percent legit. No reservations whatsoever." And then he surreptitiously glances back and forth in my small office, as if someone might be spying on us and with a low whisper acknowledges what I'd already had on my mind. "She's not too bad on the eyes, either. Am I right?"

He wiggles his eyebrows knowingly.

A laugh bursts free from my lungs and I roll my eyes at his distasteful, but wholly accurate, comment.

Of course, I'd be dead not to have noticed how attractive Brooklyn is. How could I not? She's tall, maybe five-eight, with an athletic frame – not overly curvy, but in all the right places. Athletically fit, with toned shoulders and legs that go on for miles, like an Arizona highway.

Her long, dark-blonde hair was pulled back into a high-ponytail that swung from side-to-side when she walked. And yes, I noticed her firm ass in those black-yoga-type dress slacks as she walked ahead of me or stooped over to pick up a toy for Caleb.

"Dude, you're a married man. You shouldn't be noticing other women."

Shrugging a shoulder with an innocent smirk, Lance stands up and grabs the roster from the desk, giving it a cursory glance and then turning toward the door.

"Hell yeah, man. I might be crazy in love with my smoking hot wife, but I ain't blind. Brooklyn Hayes is one fine-looking nanny. So be careful with that."

He leaves me with a wave of his hand as he disappears out the doorway and down the hall, I'm left to wonder how I'll survive the summer with the spirited, intelligent and hot as fuck Brooklyn Hayes as my live-in nanny.

It's going to be hard as hell.

4

"I'm gonna miss you this summer, boo."

My roommate, Peyton, plops down on my bed, shoving over a pile of clothes with a pouty-whine. I look up from my suitcase I've been trying to pack with all the necessary summer essentials and give her a slight frown.

"It's not like I'll be going far. Just a few miles away and I'll see you on weekends as much as possible. I mean, I do get days off once in a while, you know."

I make a face and close the top of the smaller of the two cases, successfully zipping it shut with a "*Yes!*" a la Napoleon Dynamite.

After accepting Coach Parker's offer for the live-in nanny summer position, I'd mentioned the idea of subletting my share of the apartment out to another girl this summer, so I wouldn't leave Peyton high-and-dry without me. She admitted to me once how she hates being alone and needs the company to make her feel better. So, we agreed to post a Room for Rent on the college boards so she'd have a roomie while I was away.

Although, it's not like I'm moving out of state and I'll still have days and evenings to myself most of the time. I made it a point to negotiate that into the agreement, along with a two-grand salary bump over his original offer. Coach can't be hurting for money, considering his former NBA contract and I know he won't find anyone else with my abilities this late in the game.

That's not me being cocky. It's simply the fact that I know I'm a good hire for Coach Parker and his son and he's lucky to land me. And my mother, a leader in the fight for women's rights, taught me long ago that women need to continue to fight for equal pay and never accept anything less than what we're worth.

Peyton picks up a T-shirt from the pile I had neatly stacked on the bed and examines it with distaste. We've been a great match as roommates over the last three years, originally meeting in an undergrad lecture our sophomore year in college. We get along famously, our personalities meshing well, except for the one small difference when it comes to fashion sense and style. Or rather, Peyton says I have no style whatsoever.

It's true, I really don't care much about fashion. I'm a sporty, tall girl and aside from a few skirts and one pair of heels hidden in the back of my closet, there's never been a reason for me to worry about dressing up or trying to impress anyone outside of my circle. All that's mattered to me is achieving good grades, doing my best for my club and team, and working toward my Masters and maybe a Ph.D. in Child Psychology some day.

Yes, definitely following in my mother's footsteps.

"So, tell me about the elusive Coach Garrett Parker. Is he as hot up-close-and-personal as he is down on the basketball court sidelines?" She sighs dreamily, a faraway look in her eyes. "He is so hot in that gray suit. And that scowl of concentration across his face? Oooh, makes me wonder if he wears the same expression when he fucks."

She turns over onto her back and laughs huskily, toying with my shirt in her hands.

Honestly since attending the senior night basketball home game together this past March, all Peyton could talk about the entire game was how handsome the Associate Head Coach was, and how much she loved a man who hid all their assets under a well-tailored suit. While I agreed with her assessment at the time, noting that he did look very handsome, I was more into the game happening on the court to be gawking at the sidelines.

There is no doubt that Coach Parker wears that suit of his quite well. But now that I've seen him in person, wearing nothing but a T-shirt and track pants that showed off his toned, muscular frame, I'd say that is much more appealing to me.

And even more appealing? Those few minutes in his kitchen when he was bare-chested. Holy hell, I nearly tripped over my tongue and my own feet at the sight of his impressive torso and defined ab muscles that screamed, *"Hey ladies, this ain't your typical dad-bod."*

So yeah, I can understand Peyton's attraction to Coach Parker, even if it's absolutely, one-hundred percent off-limits and nothing I can do about it now that I'm his employee. I take my job seriously and am a professional. My focus needs to be on my career and fulfilling my obligations, not getting involved with a hot sexy single dad.

Plus, he most likely has a girlfriend. No man that good-looking would be without female attention.

"Listen, get that shit out of your head right now. Coach is my new boss and I can't have you all googly-eyed over him. Otherwise, you're never getting an invite to visit me."

She blows a raspberry between her lips and I snatch the T-shirt out of her hands with a growl, placing it in the second open suitcase at the end of the bed.

"Come on, Brooklyn," she hums breathlessly. "Just admit it one time. You think he's hot, don't you? And if you didn't work for him, he'd be exactly your type. Tall, smart jock, even a little broody."

She gives me a haughty wink, which I respond to with an overly-dramatized sigh.

"Sure, fine. Whatever. If things were different and I just met him like at a bar or a party somewhere, yeah. I wouldn't hesitate. But that's not how this is. So, you can just scrub those thoughts right out of your sex-crazed, overactive imagination and help me figure out what else I need to bring with me."

Peyton jumps off the bed and rushes to my open chest of drawers, whipping out all my thongs and sexy, non-sports bra essentials. She dangles a lacy-white bralette in the air and whistles.

"This...you definitely need *this* one."

I grunt with annoyance. "No, I definitely do not. I need to be comfortable because this job will be very physical and will require me to get down on my hands and knees a lot."

Wrong thing to say.

Peyton tilts her head and pops her hip to the side, twirling the lacy bra in her fingers.

"Exactly my point. We've all heard the stories about daddies falling for their nannies. It's so classic. Jude Law. Rob Lowe. Gavin Rossdale. Men just can't help themselves when a hot young thing is under their roof. It's just man vs. nature."

"Stop with the clichés, Peyton. I mean it. You're making my job sound sordid and sleazy. You know I'm not like that. I'm not becoming a nanny to land a rich guy. And Garrett is dealing with some pretty big life shit. I mean, his wife died and he's raising his disabled son on his own. I can tell you one thing for certain, and that's, that Coach Parker is not looking to hop into bed with a nanny and complicate his life any further."

Peyton remains silent, her only non-verbal response is through the lift of her eyebrows and tightly pursed lips. A look that says, "*Yeah, right.*"

Sometimes Peyton's take on life is skewed and a bit

pessimistic. Most likely due to the way her mother was nearly beaten to an inch of her life less than a year ago.

I, on the other hand, had a pretty great childhood growing up, with loving parents who doted on me and my brother, Brayden. Although they divorced soon after I turned five, both my mom and my dad had an active role in raising me and Brayden, who also happens to be my older autistic sibling. My compassion toward those who are made uniquely different from others is definitely a result of my upbringing and living with a brother who faces challenges every day of his life.

Which is precisely the reason that I want to work in the field of child development.

I finish up my packing and take a look around my room one last time.

"You already heard from someone about the room and are meeting her today?" I ask, looking to change the subject from my sleeping arrangements over the summer to hers.

Peyton claps her hands excitedly and pirouettes on her tiptoes. Former dancer-style. And then she swings her arms wide in overly-dramatic style.

"Not a girl...his name is Kyler Scott. He's one of my classmates in my art and design program. He's going to be a famous designer someday. I can't wait for you to meet him, he is absolutely fabulous. Maybe *he* can change your mind about your dismal wardrobe."

I snort. "Highly unlikely. But we'll see."

5

I'm literally dragging from exhaustion as I flop down on the couch, throwing my feet over the edge and heaving a gigantic sigh of relief.

I don't even remember being this tired when I played back-to-back NBA games on the road. But this level of tired is from entirely different reasons. My body is drained from dealing with hormonal, angsty teen boys all day on the basketball court and then coming home to parent a hungry, grouchy kid who has trouble communicating what he wants and needs.

Even in the midst of my exhaustion, both experiences still bring me a tremendous amount of joy, especially coaching these talented kids who want nothing more than to someday play professional ball. Coaching is such a unique experience, tapping into my knowledge of the game and my expertise to share that with these kids. But damn, it's hard some days.

I check the time on the microwave clock and feel a sense of

relief. I have a twenty-minute window to take a quick nap before Brooklyn arrives. Yes, I said nap.

After calling to offer her the summer job, we agreed that it would be best for her to start tonight, while Caleb was in bed, so I could go through our routine and daily schedule without interruption. I'd show her around the house and provide her with all the emergency contacts she might need in my absence, as well as talk through Caleb's requirements.

My former nanny, Delinda, retired in May, right after my school basketball season ended. She'd been caring for other people's children for over thirty-five years and was in her mid-sixties. She earned her retirement and I didn't begrudge her one bit for leaving, but it sure put me in a tough bind going into the summer. She'd given me plenty of notice, and I'd worked with an agency to find someone to replace her, but no one fit the bill for what we needed.

While I'm cautiously optimistic about Brooklyn and having her endorsed by one in my inner circle, she's still going to have a steep learning curve. This job requires not only a plethora of physical strength and endurance but an over-abundance of patience and empathy. Even I've struggled with patience with Caleb on a regular basis. Without meaning to, and through no fault of his own, Caleb demands a lot and takes a lot out of you, mostly because of his inability to communicate.

Closing my eyes for just a moment, I allow myself to remember how easy things were six years ago.

Pre-Caleb. Pre-accident. Pre-fucking everything.

My life was fucking fantastic. I was at the top of my game as a new player in the NBA. After I finished my college career with the Indiana Hoosiers, I was drafted in the first round by the Chicago Bulls, but after the first season, I was traded to the Indiana Pacers, which was actually perfect because it brought me back home. And Becca was just finishing school.

Becca was my college sweetheart. We met halfway through my

junior year through my younger brother, Thad, when they were both Freshmen. Becca was the classic girl-next-door. Sweet brown eyes, a smile that lit up the room, and curves everywhere. She was kind-hearted, loved by everyone and kept me grounded.

But we were both realistic about the facts of life related to an NBA career. Having a long-distance relationship and the infrequency of togetherness could be a hardship. Becca and I decided to wait on marriage until she was done with school and ready to make that type of commitment.

Turns out, I apparently was the one not ready.

In true form, I was the epitome of a cocky-rookie player. It's true what they say about celebrity and fame. It warps your sense of right and wrong and makes you believe you're untouchable.

And because of that belief, my life derailed during a period of time when Becca broke it off with me, and I made one of the worst mistakes of my life. It's during that time when I turned into one of those cliché players who slept with a different girl in every city. It was fun for a while until I realized how shallow I'd become. How lonely and miserable I was without Becca.

"Baby, please. I need you. I miss you," I'd begged, desperate to have her back in my life. "I can't do this without you."

She stood in front of me, her eyes cast downward, still redrimmed from attending my brother, Thad's funeral. I'd taken a short leave from my basketball schedule to be by my brother's bedside, as we knew the time was drawing near. My mother was inconsolable, as was Thad's new wife, Addison, already in her third month of pregnancy.

We hadn't been given much time after learning of Thad's diagnosis. It was Stage 4 osteosarcoma, spinal cancer, and inoperable. Even going through treatments wouldn't have guaranteed any more time for him, and would've reduced his quality of life. Becca and Thad had been close, she and Addie had been like sisters, and Becca was there with my family while I was off playing ball.

It was a terrible time in my life and one of the most difficult losses to experience. Thad was younger than me and we didn't share the same dad, but we'd always been close. While he was talented in other ways outside of sports, we had a deep brotherly love and connection. Losing him was hard and made me rethink everything I knew about what I wanted out of my life.

"Garrett," she'd replied, lifting her gaze up to mine. "Are you sure this isn't just your grief talking? You've suffered a huge loss and maybe you think you need me because of the hole in your heart left from Thad's death?"

Yes, she was right that my heart felt so empty, heartbroken and shattered, but I still knew I loved her and needed her in my life.

"Becca, I love you. I want to start a life with you. Buy a house and settle down. Start our own family."

Her eyes glistened with misty tears, as they trailed down her cheeks. I bent down and softly kissed away one of the fallen tears.

"I want that, too, Garrett. But I don't know if I'm made to be a WAG. I'm not like them."

By them, she was referring to the wives and girlfriends of my teammates, many who had been cheerleaders or models, and women she shared nothing in common with. Becca was raised on a small dairy farm in southern Indiana and never planned on living a lifestyle like I was offering.

I'd held her hands, hoping she'd feel the connection we had strong enough to fight against her resistance.

"You aren't like them and that's what I love. You're everything to me and I will do everything I can to make you happy. I promise."

That promise was short-lived. We got back together, got engaged, bought a house and had just moved in together, the beginning of our future together, and then the ball dropped.

That's when I got the call from Penelope Slattery. My one-night stand from a road game in Pittsburgh two months earlier.

Life changed in the blink of an eye.

It only felt like seconds, but I must've fallen asleep because a knock on the door jars me awake. I look around the room through sleepy eyes and a groggy head.

Swinging my legs over the side of the couch, I slip on my Nike slides and head toward the door.

Passing the hallway mirror, I flick a glance at my reflection and notice my hair is in complete disarray. As I open the door to reveal my new nanny standing on the front stoop, I comb my fingers through my hair, smoothing down the errant strands of my short dark hair.

"Brooklyn, hi. Come on in." I greet her with a smile, reaching to grab one of the handles of the suitcases at her sides to help carry them in. I'm a chivalrous guy. But just as I do, her hand lands on top of mine at the same time, our fingers colliding in a battle of wills. "Here, let me help you with that."

At the same time, she waves me away, "It's okay, I've got it."

I raise my hands in surrender and allow her entry. Although I was raised to be a gentleman, I'm also a supporter of female equality and believe wholeheartedly that women can do anything a guy can do. If she wants to carry in her own bags, by all means, who am I to argue. Brooklyn has already proved to be a strong, independent woman and I admire that about her.

She steps into the foyer, clearly struggling with excursion as she carries the luggage and a large bag over her shoulder, dumping them on the floor by her feet.

"Good grief, it's still hot as blazes outside."

Closing the door behind us, I lock and check the latches, verifying they are locked. "Yeah, that's definitely taken some getting used to since I've moved here. Where I grew up, it was hot and humid in the summers, but not this kind of heat."

"Where are you from originally, again?" She fans herself with a hand, wiping away droplets of sweat trickling down her temple.

"I'm from Indiana. How about you? Have you lived here all your life?"

She shakes her head. "No, I'm from the San Diego area. Carlsbad, actually."

"That's a beautiful area. The ocean is always nice."

Turning to the security panel on the wall, I point to the electronic keycode. "While we're here, I want to show you how to turn on the security system using the code."

Brooklyn takes two steps toward me, inches from the wall, awaiting my instructions, and all I can do is breathe in her sexy, fresh scent and want to fall to my knees and drink her in.

Sucking in a deep, solid breath, I clear my throat. And my thoughts.

My house is a large 4-bedroom rambler in an older Scottsdale gated community subdivision. I chose the house for a variety of reasons, mainly so that my mom could visit me during the winters and have her own wing at the back of the house. It's also in a well-renowned school district and I'm hoping that will come in handy when Caleb begins kindergarten in the fall.

If he goes to school at all.

And lastly, the neighborhood is fairly secure, with a security guard on duty at all times. This was a plus, not knowing if the troubles I've had in the past with Penelope are over or not. I wasn't going to take any chances.

Brooklyn turns her full attention on me and the expression of interest on her face does something indescribable to my loins. My cock instantly responds, growing stiff behind my zipper, as I watch her full lips part and her eyes flash a curiosity that has me wondering if it's the same look she'd have if I were on top of her, slamming home.

Fuck, get those thoughts out of your head right now.

She's not here for me. She's here for my son.

"I had this installed when I first moved in last year. It's not so imperative now, but I did have some overly eager *fans* who didn't understand personal property or space."

This was part truth and part lie. It wasn't just a fan. It was Penelope. Too much had gone down to not consider her a possible threat to my son.

"I can imagine," Brooklyn agrees with a nod of her head.

"People are just weird sometimes. I had an old boyfriend who struggled with boundaries."

A lift of my eyebrow invites her to go on, but she dismisses me with a wave.

"Sorry, old news. Go on."

I continue, typing in the code. "It's a combo of my wife's and Caleb's birthdays. 608802."

Brooklyn sucks in her bottom lip between her teeth, titling her head up to look at me. Her eyes are a soft silver-gray that holds a myriad of questions in them. I narrow my eyes, neglecting to discuss the fact that I just mentioned my wife when she clearly isn't around anymore.

She takes the cue and repeats the number, committing it to memory.

"It's also important for Caleb so he can't just roam around outside. While his mobility is slightly hampered, he can scoot around with his walker pretty damn fast when he wants. And his chair is motorized and he's just like any other boy his age. He gets curious and doesn't think before he acts. Fast is the name of the game."

This draws a laugh from Brooklyn and fills me with a remarkable and inexplicable delight. Her laugh lights up something in my chest that over the last two years has been dormant. Dim and dark.

She covers her grin with fingers to stifle the laugh.

"I have an older brother who is just the same. He got this three-wheeled tricycle when we were kids and I don't know how many times he wiped out at the bottom of the small hill in our cul-de-sac. And honestly, he wasn't the only one who liked to go fast. I was kind of a speed demon. My parents were scared to death I'd get in an accident once I got my driver's license."

And then she stops, a horrified look forming across face, painted pink with embarrassment, her forehead pinched at the connection between her comment and Becca's accident.

It's no secret and I'm sure something Brooklyn would know had she even done one simple Google search on my name. All the national papers and news stories were chock-full of coverage when Becca died. It wasn't about her accident, so much as the aftermath and the fact that it happened to an NBA player.

"Oh my God, I'm sorry. You do not need to worry about that now. I promise. I'm a very careful driver. You do not need to worry about me driving with Caleb."

There's a moment of pause between us and I know I should reassure her that what she said is no big deal.

Because it really isn't. I know she didn't mean anything by it.

It's only a big deal because of how I got to where I am now. Changing my direction and the rules of the game entirely.

6

Not even ten minutes on the new job and I've already stuck my frickin' foot in my stupid, dumb-ass mouth.

What was I thinking, mentioning a car accident? The one thing he hasn't outright mentioned, but that I heard through all the rumors floating around campus and the high-profile media that seemed to be everywhere when Coach moved to town. I didn't know anything about him before he started as the new Associate Head Coach, but it was everywhere. Talk of the town.

Luckily for me, Coach let my comment slide on by and we moved on to other things, such as the tour of the house. He guided me toward the back of the house where my room will be, allowing me time to put my bags away before meeting him back in the kitchen.

As I walk into the large, country-style kitchen, equipped with one of those impressive round, hanging pot racks over the center island, a thought pops into my head. Does he even cook?

Never one to keep my mouth shut, I blurt out the question before I can think better of it and stop myself.

Reaching my hand above my head, I trace the copper bottom of the pan with my finger, the movement having a pendulum effect.

"Do you cook often, Coach?"

Garrett looks up from a sheet of paper he's making notes on, the curvature of his mouth tilting upwards, drawing my attention to his lips.

The movement of his full mouth, adorned with the right amount of stubble, sends a frisson rippling through my entire body before landing in my belly. Kicking and dancing like it was at a country bar.

He leans the length of his body against the counter and crosses his arms over his chest, the movement accentuating his biceps, probably built and maintained through years of sports strength-training, that bulge under the material of his shirt. I can't help but stare, secretly imagining the feel of those arms wrapped around me.

"Only if you count putting a frozen pizza or chicken fingers in the oven as cooking," he answers with a soft chuckle.

My head tips down toward the floor and I cover my eyes in mock disapproval.

"I'll give you a little credit there," I chuckle, returning my gaze to his brown-sugar colored eyes. "Lucky for you and Caleb, I'm an excellent cook."

His laugh is harsh and sharp. "Good luck with that. I'm lucky if I can get any vegetables passed his lips. I don't know how my wife did it, but she could get him to eat anything. But that was before..." He stops and the air in the room seems to stop moving. The weight of his words are heavy and oppressive. Sorrowful and fraught with pain.

"I'm sorry for your loss, Coach."

Without realizing it, my arm automatically extends to touch

his muscled shoulder. I feel him tense where my fingers lightly graze the soft cotton of his T-shirt. He seems so stoic. Unmovable and impenetrable, yet just underneath the surface is something sad and sensitive. There's a tick in his jaw and he stares down at where my palm has landed as if it was a bug that he wants to smack away. I immediately drop my arm back to my side, taking a step back into neutral territory.

I have to say, I'm not used to someone so bottled up. I want to dig and investigate, try to figure out what makes him act the way he does. I want to delve into his psyche and identify the inner-workings of his brain so I can help.

But the way he tends to shut down makes me wonder how we'll end up getting along this summer. Will I be in his way? Will he be sick of me within a week?

It's too early to tell, but for now, I need to remind myself to keep to general topics and not – I repeat – NOT bring up his wife.

Coach clears his throat, seemingly more comfortable now that I'm not in touching distance to him.

"Caleb originally had difficulty with some foods and textures, and developed an affinity to chicken nuggets, apples – but only if they're cut in a specific wedge shape – and he loves string cheese. Let's just say, dinnertime is sometimes like going into battle."

I keep my hand at my side, careful not to reach out and touch him again, even though it's my natural tendency to want to do so.

"Coach, take heart. You're not alone. I know exactly what you're dealing with because my brother, Brayden, is autistic, and has food aversions, as well. There's something about the texture of certain foods that can be a real deal-breaker. But we learned through trial-and-error the best way to get him his nutrients, and I bet I can employ some of those same tricks on Caleb."

He stares at me skeptically, but it morphs into something akin to a challenge, as his eyebrows shoot skyward in a dare.

"Hey, if you can get him to eat the right foods, more power to ya. I can use all the help I can get."

His eyes leave mine and he seems to shut down again, turning back to the notepad on the counter.

"Speaking of food, let's go over his schedule."

"You got it, Coach."

"Brooklyn," his voice is tentative, a little hesitant, which comes as a surprise to me. "You can call me Garrett. I'm not your coach. You're in my home, not my basketball court."

No, you're just my hot boss.

I shift on my feet, feeling my face flush just slightly at that thought, laughing uncomfortably. "Oh, of course. Garrett. I've just never heard anyone else call you by your first name. Only Coach."

I say his name, letting it roll off my tongue, allowing the taste of it to swirl around on my tongue, the sweet texture of it reminding me of melted chocolate.

"I can assure you, I wasn't born Coach. Just Garrett."

He gets back to the tasks at hand, discussing Caleb's daily schedule and the routines he wants me to adhere to.

"Most weeks I'll be here for his breakfast and home in time for dinner by six. I'll let you know if something comes up and I'm running late. I have your number and will text or call. I'll expect you to do the same. You don't have to constantly communicate, but I do want to hear throughout the day how he's doing, especially after his weekly speech therapy and occupational therapist appointments. He also starts equestrienne therapy in a few weeks."

I nod in earnest, a massive smile lifting the corners of my mouth. "That makes me so happy to see kids around horses. I interned at an equestrian camp for kids my last semester and saw it do wonders for kids with physical and emotional challenges. I can't wait to see Caleb riding."

A thought crosses my mind, then, as I look around the house in search of a four-legged creature.

"What's the matter?" Garrett asks, a crinkle in his forehead.

I consider whether to say anything but figure I should at least mention it in case he hasn't considered it before.

"Well, I was just wondering if Caleb had an emotional support or service dog? They really are such great companions and help for disabled children."

A scowl forms and a dark flash of something appears in Garrett's eyes, turning his brown into a black abyss.

"No. We don't have a dog. And we aren't getting one, either."

The asperity in his tone has my curiosity piqued. And instead of backing down, it only urges me on. I don't know Garrett well enough yet to determine where my boundaries are, but as a headstrong woman, I don't back down even when I should.

"Dogs can be such great companions for kids. They love unconditionally and encourage children with special needs to step outside their comfort zone when it comes to their development."

Again, another resounding "*No.*"

I hate failure. It's not an option for me.

"I'm happy to look into a canine companion program for you. In fact, I can just add it to my list right now..."

"Brooklyn, listen. I said no dog. Are we going to have a problem with this?"

By this, I can only assume he means my insubordinate behavior.

His face flushes with color, and it seems I've found what button to push to piss him off.

And while I'd love to continue to argue the merits of service animals, I also know when to employ common sense and know it's not good form to push your boss on your very first day.

But Garrett can rest assured I won't drop it entirely and upon the next opportunity, I'll be sure to bring it up.

Raising my hands in surrender, I take a step back, having not realized how close I'd gotten to Garrett's side once again, and I provide him some room to stew.

"You're the boss," I say with an overly bright tone and smile on my face. "As far as the schedule goes, everything seems very manageable. How about after hours, like evenings and the weekends you're home? Do you want me out of the way so you can spend alone time with Caleb?"

Garrett rubs a hand over his roughened chin and shrugs thoughtfully.

"Up to you. I guess I hadn't thought that far in advance, yet. My former nanny didn't live with us and it was only me and Caleb in the evenings and weekends, except during basketball season when I traveled." A crease forms in between his dark-brown eyebrows as he thinks this over some more.

"I don't want you to feel like you can't have a life outside of the house, so you should feel free to come and go as you please. But I will need to draw a line regarding, um, well, having people *over*. I'd obviously ask you respect that you're living in a house with a young child in it and be considerate to that rule. No parties or *sleepovers*."

Garrett clears his throat and I want to laugh at his implication. I kind of want to mess with him because he's being so serious, but think better of it. I've never even had parties in my own apartment with Peyton, with the exception of a few of my friends for movies or game night.

"No problem. No sleepovers for me, I swear." I stick my fingers up in the Scout's Honor. "I've given up on dating, anyhow, so you don't have to worry about me sneaking anyone back."

Garrett tilts his head to the side, an incredulous look on his face.

"You don't date?" And then, as if rethinking this, he backpedals on the question. "Never mind. Forget I asked that. None of my business."

And because I can't help myself, I ask, "How about you?

Anyone in your life that might not like another female in her territory?"

Yes, I did just imply that his potential girlfriend would be jealous of me living in Garrett's house. But come on. It's a reasonable possibility that any woman he'd be dating, whether model-perfect or not, could be a little jealous to have him sharing his house with a younger, single woman. Even if it is just me and I'm not that kind of girl.

He coughs into his hand. "I don't date, either."

Hmm. Questions, questions and more questions swirl uncontrollably around in my head, dive-bombing my mouth, readying their escape to find the answers to this perplexing and complicated man.

Even though I really, really want to know the answer to that, I keep my trap shut for the first time on the job and avoid the temptation of peeling back the layers of Garrett Parker.

There'll be time enough for that later on.

7

GARRETT

I can't sleep.

Rolling over on my back for the hundredth time in the last hour, I stare up at the ceiling, groaning over my inability to wipe free the images of Brooklyn in bed in the room down the hall from my head.

She's close enough that when she opened the bathroom door earlier tonight, the scent of her intoxicating lotion or hair product came wafting down the hallway at me, giving me all sorts of NSFW ideas. Her scent still lingers in the air, permeating my bed sheets that cling to my body, hard and needy.

Fuck, why did I think it was going to be easy living with this woman?

I'm half-tempted to call up Delinda to ask her to come back out of retirement, ready to pay whatever salary she demands just so I don't have to wonder about the sexy-as-fuck grad student sleeping just twenty-feet down the hall from me.

It was hard enough to sit through dinner with her the second night and then have her watch as we walked through Caleb's bedtime routine, as she stood at my side or behind me the entire time, interacting and asking me questions so she could become comfortable with Caleb.

It was goddamn torture and I brought it on myself. I only have myself to blame. I almost wish she wasn't working out as well as she is, because then I could have an excuse to get rid of her.

Instead, she's already bonded with Caleb in a way I haven't seen him take to another person, or woman, since Becca. That right there says something. It tells me I should run and hide.

If there were any doubts at the beginning that she wouldn't be able to handle Caleb's needs, they've all been buried after watching her over the last week show how she effortlessly can manage herself. Caleb took to her immediately, squealing with joy when she played boats with him in the tub.

We were right in the middle of bath time a few nights ago when I got a phone call from Coach Welby that I had to take. I'd been a little reluctant to leave them alone, but I'd left my phone on the kitchen counter, so I had to hand over the reins. The beauty in that proposition was that Brooklyn was there for me and gave me the freedom to do what I had to do. To balance my child's needs with my work demands.

For the first time in two years, I wasn't alone.

My phone call only lasted less than five minutes, as Coach Welby had asked a question about the recent recruiting report I'd put on his desk. But by the time I'd ended the call and walked back toward the bathroom, I heard the sweet voice of Brooklyn, pitched high with an overly-exaggerated perkiness, as she sang a bath song to Caleb.

My breath nearly stopped at how overcome with emotion I'd become. It was a fucking bath time song, yet it dredged up nostalgic memories of how once Becca was the one to sing my son a song. It hit me square in the chest, and then for some reason, it turned into bitter anger. It pissed me off that Becca wasn't the one here with me and Caleb.

I nearly flew into the bathroom in a rage, ready to drag him out of the bathtub and tell Brooklyn to leave us alone.

That is until I turned the corner and saw the two of them together. I stood at the doorway just hidden out of sight, my heartbeat kicking in my chest like a horse's hind leg, hands binding into fists at my side, my guarded rage thawing. What I saw and heard filled me with a strange form of consuming need and hunger for this beguiling woman.

"When I take a bath, I wash my face, wash my face, wash my face."

Even though slightly offkey, her voice seemed to cast a magical, melodic spell over Caleb, who had quieted down except for the occasional splashing of hands in the water in time with her tune.

Brooklyn sat on the side of the tub, leaning over the edge to manage the washing part, pulling back every time he splashed her. I'd finally gotten smart after struggling over a year with this task. As Caleb grew bigger and heavier, it was killing my back to try and hold him upright while I bathed him, ending up with a kinked and sore back every time. So, I purchased him a bath seat specially designed for kids with disabilities.

Soft cushiony-material that washed up easily along with a rubber harness to keep him from falling over face-first and prevented back strain for me. At first, Caleb wasn't thrilled about being harnessed up, but with Brooklyn's lighthearted song and playful atmosphere, she successfully navigated the chore of bathing my son within an hour, where it took me a good week to get him to learn to enjoy himself.

She smoothed a washcloth over Caleb's sweet, wet face as he blew his raspberry bubbles. "That's it, buddy. We need to wash our face and then we get to play with the colored duckies next. We can count them, and you can tell me their colors, okay?"

A delighted squeal emitted from the back of his throat, followed by exuberant gibberish.

I watched with rapt interest as she turned the usual chore of bath time into a fun, new experience, as she sang and made a game of getting him clean. God, how easy it is for her. It seems to come so naturally, where I struggle to be a good parent.

Maybe I'm not father material? While I love my son with all my heart, honestly, when this happened, I wasn't ready to raise him on my own. It was Becca's territory and I just followed her lead. Without her in our lives, I've fumbled and stumbled to learn what works and what doesn't, never really knowing if it's the right way or not.

It's pretty easy to see that Caleb has already fallen for his beautiful, sunny-dispositioned nanny. And it's no secret as to why.

After putting him to bed every night, that's when the discomfort seems to creep in between Brooklyn and me. It's been the most difficult part of this whole new living arrangement. While Caleb has fared just perfectly – better than I had anticipated – it's taken Brooklyn and me a little more time to gain that comfort level around each other.

Perhaps it would easier if I didn't find her so incredibly sexy.

Earlier tonight, while standing in the hallway outside of his room, Brooklyn shifting from one foot to the other in front of me, and me doing some weird shuffle myself, it became increasingly unclear as to how we're ever going to make this work.

I feel so out of my depth when she's around. Like a stranger in my own home. As if I'm tiptoeing around the complexities and unfamiliarities of a new relationship.

Which is crazy, since she's not my girlfriend or even my lover. She's my nanny.

It's rare for me to feel uncomfortable around a woman. I'm not saying I was a ladies man in my prior life, but I could certainly hold my own in a conversation with a beautiful woman. I knew how to put the moves on when the moment called for it. Or flirt with the opposite sex, charming the pants off a girl.

But Brooklyn is a rare and different breed altogether. Aside from her beauty, she's not only sweet and strong but sophisticated and scholastically brilliant, as well. That much is already apparent by the way she speaks and talks about her childhood development educational experience.

Honestly, that first night when she asked me about a dog for Caleb, I knew she meant well and provided some very relevant facts about it, which I can't deny, but there's no way I'm ready and able to get a dog. Not now and maybe not ever.

It wasn't just my wife that I lost the night of the car accident, but also my chocolate lab, Ollie. I'd had him since he was a puppy and he went everywhere with Caleb and Becca. He'd sleep at the end of Caleb's bed when he first came to live with us after we were granted sole custody. He was the best dog in the world, and I still had residual sadness over losing both my loves that night.

Yet, I acted like an ass toward Brooklyn, and instead of explaining my reservations, I just shut down, ending the conversation with my tone and grumpiness.

She didn't deserve it. Brooklyn is amazing and I've already seen changes in Caleb that I hadn't noticed before.

And then there's also the part of her being stunningly sexy. I about bit my tongue as I stood behind the corner the other night watching like a fucking creeper as she leaned over the bathtub to wash Caleb's back. The smooth cheeks of her ass peeked out from under her denim shorts, taunting me like a devil with a promise.

Because at that moment, I promised to give my soul for a chance to touch that ass with my bare hands someday.

And now I'm plagued with those unruly thoughts as I shift in bed uncomfortably, throwing the sheet off my legs, my erection tenting my briefs. Maybe I just need to go out on a date and get laid like my friend, Lucas Mathiasson, suggested the last time we hung out. He's actually the reason I moved down to Phoenix and accepted the job as Associate Head Coach at ASU. We attended college together in Indiana and after graduation, when I went onto the NBA, he came down here to grad school, then got his Ph.D. and is now a professor of art history. He also happens to be Caleb's godfather, since my brother had already been dead for a few years before Caleb was born.

The last time I was with Lucas, I was *this* close to going home with a woman and probably could've fucked her against the wall in the bathroom if we'd had time. But instead, I got a call from my babysitting service indicating that Caleb was running a fever. That was two months ago.

Being a single father sure can complicate a guy's sex life.

Needless to say, I'm feeling all kinds of horny and in need of release as my hand slides down my stomach and under the stretch of the waistband, finding my aching, neglected cock. I wrap my fingers around my shaft and stroke it hard from root to tip.

Perhaps I should feel guilty over the impure, lustful thoughts I've been having about Brooklyn, but right now, I just need relief and I don't care how I get it. I'll worry about reality and the psychological implications of me jerking off to images of Brooklyn's naked ass later.

My imagination takes off as I continue to stroke myself, conjuring up sexual fantasies about Brooklyn knocking quietly on my door.

She pads in on her bare feet and slowly undresses in front of me, as I lay outstretched and naked on my bed.

"I know you want this," she'd murmur, climbing on top to straddle me, her firm breasts falling over my face just in reach of my mouth. Her hands would wander over my shoulders, down my contoured torso and underneath the sheet where she'd trace the V at my pelvis, as I'd arch into her aching for her touch.

"Yes, I want you, Brooklyn. I want you to ride me hard so I can see your tits bounce. And when you come, you'll say my name like a prayer."

Her body would feel so warm, so welcoming as my cock slides through her wet heat, impaling her in the perfect spot that makes her back arch, thrusting forward with a moan of pleasure. My mouth would suckle the hardened peak of her nipple, dusty rose and ripe, her moan of satisfaction eliciting an animal-like growl from deep within my chest.

My cock strains, pulsing in my hand that begins to move with more fervor, with less precision and more friction, as I feel my balls draw and tighten up. Hot semen pours over my clenched fist as I imagine shooting my load inside her tight heat.

It's then, as the ringing in my ears quiets down and I lay listless against my pillow, that I hear a creak outside my bedroom door.

Surging from the bed and to my feet, my instincts kick in and I grab my shorts from the floor, tucking my still semi-hard dick in my shorts and fly to the door, ready to protect my home from an unknown invader.

My mind races, the adrenaline thumping in my ears, as a hundred different scenarios rush through my head, most prominently an intruder situation. I grip the door handle and swing it wide only to find a very alarmed and stunned Brooklyn standing outside my bedroom door.

Sheer panic threads across her face, her wide-eyed stare immediately causing me guilt.

"Brooklyn, what are you doing up? Is everything okay? Is Caleb okay?" My voice is raspy and a bit harsher than I mean to sound, but goddamn, she can't be sneaking around in my house at one a.m. in the morning.

And by the way, I just orgasmed thinking about you coming into my bedroom and stripping. Not feeling guilty over that at all.

"Yes, I'm so sorry," she mutters, instinctively wrapping an arm around her middle. The other hand holding a cup of water. "I was just in the kitchen to get some water and I thought I heard something and thought it might be Caleb."

My gaze flicks down the hallway to his halfway open doorway and then back to Brooklyn, who I now see is wearing pajama shorts and a cropped cotton tank. I inwardly cringe, knowing now that I won't ever be able to expunge this from my memory.

"He's fine. I'm fine. Jesus, you scared me. Go back to bed."

She nods, biting the edge of her lower lip, and turns slowly to walk back down the hall into her bedroom. Hesitantly she peers over her shoulder and I see the flash of something in her eyes before she disappears out of sight.

And then it dawns on me that perhaps I wasn't as quiet as I'd thought, and maybe she heard me jacking off and may have even overheard my climax.

Shit, I'll have to be mindful of that possibility in the future.

8

I try to keep my embarrassment in check this morning as I finish making breakfast for Garrett and Caleb. Not a lot embarrasses me these days, but I can't help but feel my cheeks flush the minute Garrett walked into the kitchen.

Damn if the memory of what I heard last night coming behind Garrett's door doesn't get me hot, the evidence of that effect leaving a wet spot between my legs and a blushed speckled red over my cheeks.

There is no doubt in my mind that what I overheard was Garrett getting himself off as I tiptoed as quietly as I could as I passed by his doorway into the kitchen. The low vibration of his moans, and the slap of skin from the other side of the doorway had me skittering to a stop in the middle of the darkened hallway, my search for water now secondary to the interest in listening to his sexy sounds.

But on my return trip, glass in hand, I couldn't help myself. It sounded so damn hot, I put my ear to his door and listened like a guilty-pervy interloper as he orgasmed, unseen on the other side of the wall. My body heated and reacted, requiring that I hold a hand over my mouth and clench my thighs together to stop the ache building between my legs.

It certainly wasn't the first time I'd heard sex noises from someone other than me and my partner. Living in a college dorm and with roommates for years, you get used to the creaking of beds, the husky moans of couples getting it on and the heavy pants and screams of climaxes.

But stumbling upon my new hot boss having an intimate solo session with himself? It's enough to make me blush like a virgin bride on her wedding night as Garrett sits down at the table, freshly showered, hair still damp and slicked off his forehead, the smell of his aftershave clinging in the air.

"Good morning," I greet, staring into the frypan as I finish cooking the scrambled eggs and bacon. "I wasn't sure if you were a breakfast eater or not, so if not, don't feel obligated to eat it. But I know you have a long day ahead of you."

Before we went to bed last night, Garrett mentioned that this week's training schedule would be long and nothing short of grueling, informing me ahead of time that he'd likely not be home each night before Caleb went to bed. Ensuring me that if I had any problems, I shouldn't hesitate to call him. What we didn't talk about, though, was his breakfast needs and whether he expected that I was to only make it for Caleb or for him, as well.

"Oh, thanks. It smells great, but you don't need to worry about me. But since you went to the trouble, I'll stick around for a few extra minutes."

"Good morning, buddy. Give me some skin, little man."

Peering over my shoulder, I see Garrett bend down, planting a gentle kiss across Caleb's forehead and then hold his palm out to give his son a high-five. Grinning like a lunatic down at the eggs, I hear Caleb making his happy noises of contentment, trying so hard to express himself in a way his father will understand and be proud of.

It breaks my heart that Caleb can't communicate with us using speech. Which reminds me that I want to talk with his speech therapist later this week to see what tools he's been using with Caleb so I can continue working with him outside of his appointments. I've been doing some reading at night before bed on traumatic brain injuries in young children, and with Caleb's abilities, I think he can really make some progress in this area, given the right tools, and lots of time, practice and patience.

"Looks like Caleb had a good night's sleep. And how about you? Did you get what you needed last night?"

I nearly drop the pan I hold in my hand at his question. Holy shit. Did he know what I did after I shut my bedroom door? After he'd gotten me so worked up, I had to take care of myself with my own fingers?

I turn at the sound of his voice and realize he's suddenly appeared at my side at the counter, opening a cupboard above his head to pull down some plates.

Just the close proximity of this man sends tingles dancing up and down my spine. Like there's this electric force field that activates anytime he's within a few feet of me, turning me stupid. It's so difficult not to find this man attractive, and to keep my feelings in check where he's concerned. It doesn't seem to even matter to me anymore that he's my boss and that I shouldn't be crushing over him like this. It goes up in flames like I did last night.

Did I get what I needed, he asked. Well, I guess technically you could say, yes. It took me mere seconds to bring myself to climax, no BOB required.

My hands shake and the words come out in a husky whisper. "Um, get what I needed?"

Garrett tilts his head, staring at me as if I've grown two heads, his eyes lingering on my face for a beat.

"Yes, when you came down to the kitchen last night. Did you get what you needed?"

"Yes. I did. And I have to say, that mattress is like heaven. Sure, beats the lumpy twin I have in my apartment."

I feel it before I even see the change, but his entire demeanor tenses up. Dishing up the food, my eyes wander to his face, taking in the tightness of his jaw and his lips pursed tightly. I fight my intuition and snatch my hand back before reaching out to touch his shoulder, remembering to keep my hands to myself. Whatever I just said has turned his bright mood, sour. It was obviously the wrong thing.

"Everything okay, Garrett?"

He shakes his head as I hand him a plate full of food.

"Yeah, it's stupid really. It's just that the guestroom bed used to be mine and Becca's. I should've gotten rid of it when I moved down here but I couldn't because you're right, it's a great bed. Becca said the same thing about it the first night we slept on it."

His laugh is forced and humorless.

Well, fuck a duck.

I'm sleeping in his old marriage bed. One he slept in with his dead wife. No wonder he doesn't want to sleep on it anymore.

Just when I thought this morning couldn't get any more awkward than it already is, I've gone and inadvertently stuck my foot in my mouth. Again. Why do I seem to continue to do that?

Hoping to change the subject off of anything having to do with his previous life, I sit down with my own breakfast and ask about his summer camp.

"How's your summer team looking, Coach?" I give him a playfully crooked smile, which he returns with a grin.

"They're looking good. I have hopes that we'll see some All-Stars come out of it." Shoveling a forkful of eggs into his mouth, he moans around the utensil. "Jesus, these are so good. How can eggs taste this good?"

I wink. "A good cook never divulges her secrets."

Garrett glances over at Caleb who babbles loudly. "Did you hear that, buddy? Brooklyn has a secret and she's not sharing. You remember what we do to extract secrets out of people, don't you buddy?"

Caleb laughs and giggles, his smile contagious and filled with innocent excitement.

Garrett quirks an eyebrow at me and then turns on Caleb, throwing his arms up and growling like a monster before tickling Caleb's ribs and underneath his chin, all while he laughs maniacally.

"We use the tickle monster to get those secrets out of you, don't we?"

I begin to laugh as they play and rough house, until Caleb's little voice breaks up the laughter.

"Babababababa!"

And before I even know what's happened, Garrett turns toward me and with the speed of a Ninja, starts tickling my side. Throwing back my head in laughter, I wiggle in my chair, until I can't take it anymore and I jump up on my feet, making a run for it and hiding behind Caleb's chair.

"Caleb," I shriek. "Help me. The Tickle Monster is going to get me!"

Caleb seems to love this game and is screaming in delight at the top of his lungs, spurring Garrett into action.

"We have to tickle it out of her, Caleb!"

And then he's chasing after me, as I run around the table and the sounds of our laughter fill the spacious kitchen, once filled with two lonely boys.

We're huffing and out of breath when Garrett finally grabs hold of me in his huge wingspan and swings me off my feet, his arm firmly planted around my stomach. It's only as our laughter dies down and we catch our breath that we simultaneously realize what a compromising position we're in.

The thick warmth of his arms and his solid chest against my

back feels impossibly good. While his impressive height has the top of my head barely touching the bottom of his chin, his breath leaves warm paths of air at the nape of my neck, sending shivers down my spine. The scent of his minty breath and his spicy after-shave has my body coming alive, hot with want.

There's a moment Garrett's hesitation makes me wonder what he's thinking. Does it feel good to him, too? Or is this just a game to make Caleb laugh and it means nothing to him?

My thoughts shake free the minute Garrett tenses, the ripples of his muscles flexing and then going lax as he drops me to my feet, taking a gigantic step away.

He mumbles an apology, his voice cool and crisp like his after-shave. "Sorry. But I need to get going. Thanks for breakfast."

Garrett picks up his plate of mostly uneaten food and sets it in the sink before placing a gentle, lingering kiss on his son's head.

"Bye, buddy. I'll see you later tonight. Be good for Brooklyn today, do as she says and we'll see about going to the park later tonight. Okay?"

Caleb's face lights up and he bangs his tiny four-year-old fist on his table. "Yaaaaaaayaaaaayaaaa."

Garrett's smile vanishes as he peers at me just outside the kitchen.

"I'll see you later. Call if you need anything."

And then he leaves me standing in the kitchen wondering how the hell I'm going to deal with his awfully erratic mood swings.

Just when I think we're making progress, he closes down again, shutting down like a power outage.

9

GARRETT

The hallways of campus are fairly deserted during the summer months, although the summer session is in full swing.

Knowing Lucas will likely be in his office this time of the morning, I make the trek from the athletic center over to the art history building and head to the second floor. Making a sharp right at the top of the stairway, I locate the hallway running down into the faculty office corridor and get to the office marked Art History Department. Finding Lucas's door slightly ajar, the name placard stating The Doctor is In, I laugh and give a quick rap with my knuckles.

"Enter," he says, his voice low and sounding distracted.

"Well good morning to you, too."

I find him with his nose buried in a book, an open MacBook on the side, and a pencil in his mouth. So typical of Lucas.

His head pops up in surprise and the pencil falls from his mouth.

"Garrett. What the hell are you doing here?" He bellows out his surprise, standing from the chair and moving around the desk to give me a slap on the back, bro hug. "You didn't call. Is everything okay?"

Lucas gives me that look of concern I've seen on many occasions in the past ten years. He's been with me during the best of times and also during the worst, where I wasn't sure how I'd go on. When we lost the NCAA championship our senior year. When I met, dated and then broke things off with Becca. When my brother died. And then everything that happened after Caleb's birth and Becca's death.

I can honestly say I've never had a better friend. He's been my rock. My friend to the end. And I love him like a brother.

I give him a shake of my head, hoping to convince him I'm all right. Even if I'm not sure whether I am or not.

"Yeah, man. Everything's good. I mean, as good as they can be, I should say."

He plants half an ass against the table, crossing his legs at the ankles and folding his arms across his chest. For a professor and history buff who is never without a book and never went into a museum he didn't like, he's still very athletic in his build. We played college ball together and although he doesn't play now, he still gets outdoors a lot. Hiking, climbing and off-road biking.

"Caleb doing okay? Is he getting excited for his birthday? Because I found the best birthday present for him just last week. Dude, it's perfect."

I tilt my head and grunt suspiciously. "You remember that I can veto anything that's too loud, too fast and too expensive, right? Sometimes Uncle Lucas's judgment isn't the best when it comes down to a kid with a disability."

He snorts. "I have no idea what you mean, bro. I do extensive research on these things."

Lifting a brow, I show him no mercy. "So, you're using the

NASA space station jungle gym you bought him last year as proof that you employ common sense when buying my son gifts?"

This high-tech set up he purchased and tried assembling for Caleb for his fourth birthday last year was a mess. It was two-stories high and was definitely not something he could access with his mobility limitations.

Lucas frowns, the corners of his mouth curling down and his shoulders sagging with a sigh.

"Fine, I'll admit I got a little over excited by the whole NASA thing and thought maybe Caleb would grow into it. Epic failure. But this time, I know it'll be a success," he confirms with a jab of his dress shoe toe into my shin. I lean down to rub the spot and look back up at him.

We're such a sharp contrast in style and lifestyle. Except for the suits I wear on game days, my typical uniform is track pants or shorts and tees. Lucas, however, was raised wealthy and with some pedigree, and he always looks the part. I'd give him hell if he wore the elbow-patched tweed jackets, but his fashion sense is a much higher grade. Today it's a button-down shirt, with sleeves, rolled up to expose his forearms, and gray dress slacks.

"Spit it out. If it's not Caleb, what is it?"

Bending at the waist, my legs spread wide, I lean down and plant my elbows on my knees and rest my head in my hands.

"I make poor choices, Luc. And it's always getting me into messy situations."

"I'm not sure I'm following you. What poor choices are we talking about?"

I tip my chin up and give him that look that says, *'Do I really need to spell this out for you?'*

Lucas patiently waits for me to explain.

"I hired a summer nanny."

His smooth forehead screws up tight and then relaxes. "That's right, Delinda retired. But it's a good thing, right? Otherwise, you would've had a tough summer trying to juggle Caleb and the basketball camp. And your mother would have had to come down."

Giving myself a moment, I lean back into the chair and close my eyes, picturing the beautiful nanny living in my home, taking care of my son and making me think and do things I shouldn't be thinking or doing.

Like this morning. What the hell was I thinking to start that game with Brooklyn? What on earth prompted me to tickle or touch her like I did?

Christ almighty, I'm a fucking idiot.

"Yeah, I hired a grad student to watch over Caleb this summer. It's been a week and Caleb already loves her. She's such a natural with him. Not at all squeamish or bothered by the things outside the norm that she needs to do to care for him. She's perfect."

"Mmm-kay," he stalls, moving to the chair next to mine to sit down. "Sounds like a great hire, then. So, what's the problem? What am I missing?"

I let out a long-suffering sigh. "She's a *live-in* nanny."

Lucas still has an '*I don't get it*' look on his face.

"And...?"

"And, I may not have only jerked off while thinking about her last night, but I also touched her inappropriately today."

"Oh, Jesus." Lucas's head rears back and his hands shoot up to his ears, covering them like one of those Hear No Evil, Say No Evil, Do No Evil monkey emojis.

"I don't want to hear any of this, bro. That way I don't have to testify against you if she decides to sue."

"Fuck man, it wasn't like that. At least, I don't think it was," I mutter, confusion over what transpired between us this morning clouding my head and tripping me up. "We were playing a game with Caleb over breakfast. And I may have tickled Brooklyn in the process and picked her up and held her. But it wasn't sexual in any way. I swear."

And it wasn't. Or didn't start out that way.

But I can't lie. I liked the way her body felt pressed against mine. Her feminine scent and curves did all sorts of crazy things to my libido. That's why I had to get out of there as fast as I could and left before I even finished breakfast. I know based on the look she gave me when I left abruptly that she was confused by my sudden departure, and I feel bad about that. But if I hadn't left when I did, I was bound to do something I'd regret.

And therein lies the problem.

If my thoughts are this inappropriate so soon after hiring Brooklyn for this job, what's going to become of me as the summer progresses? After seeing her day-in and day-out? Finding her bent over my son's bathtub with her ass half-exposed every night. Or opening my door to see her standing in a darkened hallway in her teeny-tiny pajamas, her pert nipples poking through the cotton material, as if begging me to pluck them or suck them into my mouth?

"Did you say her name is Brooklyn? As in, Brooklyn Hayes?"

"Yeah."

He purses his lips and nods as if he understands all my problems.

"I can see the attraction. She's beautiful and intelligent. Great smile. Great ass."

I give him a mock look of horror. He's always been pretty nonchalant about women, leading me to believe he might be confused about his sexuality and preference.

"Have you slept with her?" I ask, jealousy taking flight in my caveman brain.

"Hell no," he bellows incredulously. "She interned for Professor Wilson in the psychology department a few semesters ago. I think she was a child psychology major. Anyway, I met her at some function and afterward Wilson couldn't say enough glowing things about her. You definitely got a good one there, G. So, here's my advice."

I lean in, hoping he'll bestow on me some brotherly counsel that will be the answer to all my problems.

He pats my knee and smiles. "Keep your dick in your pants. Problem solved."

Asshole.

10

BROOKLYN

After a dramatic outburst of tears and begging from Peyton, I finally agreed to go out with her on Friday night to a summer block party.

It's an annual event held around the university the last weekend in June where two city blocks are cordoned off and filled with food trucks and carnival games and lots of beer gardens for festival goers. We've gone together the last two years and there was no way I could back out on her, even though I tried my hardest.

I've been working with Garrett and Caleb for nearly a month now feeling my way through the daily routines (and occasional mishaps and landmines) of their life, getting accustomed to living with them. Although Garrett told me right from the start that I was free to come and go as I please on weekends (minus the sleep-overs) I still felt weird leaving them to their own devices on a Friday night.

Walking down the hallway toward the front door, I hear

sounds coming from the living room where Garrett and Caleb are hanging out, both on the floor playing with Legos.

Garrett takes a double-take as he looks up from his structure, a small frown crinkling the edges of his mouth, and then returns his gaze to the building.

"I hope it's okay, but I'm going down to the festival tonight with my friend Peyton. I won't be out too late."

"I said it was okay. You have a right to a life." His voice is gruff and with a bit of sarcasm.

Pausing for a moment, I'm uncertain how to respond. The last few days I thought things were pretty good between me and Garrett. It's not like we've been sharing intimate details about our lives, but we have some good conversations in the evening after I've finished up the dinner clean-up as he's put Caleb to bed.

In fact, just last night we ended up watching the Arizona Sun's game on TV together, me rooting for the Suns and him cheering on the Pacers, his former team. I'd asked him what it was like to in the spotlight like that and the pressure that came with NBA stardom.

He'd lifted a shoulder noncommittally. "At first, I ate it up. I was pretty cocky as a rookie and would spout-off to my team-mates and talk a lot of smack to other players. I cringe at some of the locker room interviews I did back then. I was such a conceited ass."

I'd laughed, not because I agreed with him, having never seen those interviews, but I couldn't reconcile the Garrett he was describing with the Garrett I'd become familiar with. Even though all the rumors circulated around campus since he joined the coaching staff indicated that he was an arrogant, self-centered prick, I just didn't see it.

What I saw was a reserved man who cared about two things – his son and his players.

But what I hadn't learned yet was what caused that reservation and the turmoil that seemed to lie just underneath the surface.

I don't immediately respond to his barbed remark about having a life, wondering if he just had a bad day with the team, and lean down and place a kiss on top of Caleb's damp, just bathed head.

"I'll come in and kiss you good night when I get home, Caleb. And maybe I'll win a fun prize for you at the carnival game."

He babbles excitedly and flaps his arms, which I take as a sign of interest.

Garrett sits just at my side and I notice he gives a surreptitious glance at my legs, starting at my sandaled feet and working up to the hem of my jean shorts. When he finally lifts his chin and our eyes meet, his flicker with a dark, mysterious gleam before he looks away, returning back to the Lego blocks.

"Okay, I'll see you both later. I hope you have a good night."

Keeping his head down, he responds. "Yeah. You, too."

I leave out the front door and get to my car, wondering why he is being so surly all of a sudden. Maybe I should've asked if they wanted to come along? The street carnival would've been fun for Caleb, with all the people and games and lights and music, except it's a Friday night and would be way past his bedtime.

I'm nearly ready to go back inside to invite Garrett when my phone rings and I see it's Peyton.

"Heya, babes, I'm just about ready to leave," I answer.

"Awesome. I'll be there in ten and will meet you by the Banana-Split truck. I've been starving myself all week just so I could indulge."

Something akin to fear creeps into my chest like an overgrown vine. "Peyton, I hope you don't mean that. You can't starve yourself like that."

Since living with Peyton in the same apartment for the last several years, I'm well aware of her past issues with food. Specifically, her eating disorder that began when she was twelve and she finally got a handle on last year with the help of a counselor and group therapy. It was alarming to see her drop two sizes in a manner of months the first year we roomed together, but I just figured she was stressed out over school. Turns out, it was much deeper than that.

Peyton scoffs in my ear. "I don't mean it literally, Brook. I'm healthy, I swear."

"Okay, good," I acknowledge, turning the corner out of Garrett's cul-de-sac. "I'll see you soon."

As I end the call, I worry about how Peyton is doing without me now and if she and the new roommate get along as well as we do together.

Which leads me back to wondering what I may have done to rub Garrett the wrong way tonight. Everyone has their foul moods from time-to-time, and it was an especially long week for him. Maybe he was hoping I'd be around to pick up the slack so he could rest tonight.

Dammit, now I feel guilty for leaving him tonight because being a single-parent has got to be difficult and I'm sure he could use all the help he can get. But on the other hand, I deserve that time off, too. It was in my contract and I'm not beholden to him every waking hour.

I can't say I haven't been curious about his personal life, though. It surprises me that a gorgeous man like Garrett hasn't found love again. Or doesn't even date. As far as I know, he doesn't go out with anyone. I haven't seen him with anyone, at least.

None of my business, I remind myself, as I pull into a parking spot along the street a few blocks away from the carnival. As I start the trek to our meet-up spot, my phone vibrates with a text notification in my pocket. It's probably Peyton again telling me she's there.

As I glance down at the phone, I'm surprised by not only who it's from but the content of the message.

Coach Parker: I'm sorry for my piss-poor mood tonight. Have a fun time. You deserve it.

My heart thumps at the sweet apology.

And then the next text solidifying just how truly sweet he is.

Coach Parker: I really appreciate you, Brooklyn. Thank you for being so great with Caleb.

And then he sends the cutest picture of Caleb, smiling huge for the photo in front of the finished Lego building he erected.

I sigh at his words of appreciation and adorable photo but am a little disappointed that it didn't include Garrett.

But just the fact that he was thoughtful enough to send the compliment and the fact that he expressed his appreciation in this manner has my insides tingling with deep, warm gratitude.

And maybe a little of something else.

11

GARRETT

I know I was a first-class asshole to Brooklyn before she left earlier tonight. She didn't deserve my hostility or frustration.

The heat and exhaustion from the week had really done a number on me and all I'd really wanted to do when I came home was to grab an ice-cold beer and plop on the couch to watch a game on TV. Instead, Brooklyn let me know after dinner that she was meeting up with her friend Peyton.

And goddamn, the minute she walked into the front room with her hair down in curled waves, a light amount of make-up adorning her eyelashes and cheekbones, and those short shorts, I turned into a jealous beast.

In my mind, Peyton is a dude she's meeting. One of those names that can go either way. Peyton Manning, etc. The thought of her going out on a date with some dude named Peyton just riled me up, even though I have no right to feel jealous or proprietary over Brooklyn. She's simply my hired help. My son's nanny.

A woman, who only after a month, has quickly become indispensable to me.

And, I like her a damn lot.

Over the last month, she's impressed me with her incredible knowledge and expertise in how she manages Caleb and his special needs. She's sweet but firm. Nurturing but not a pushover. I like that about her.

There have been a few instances where she pushes back a bit more with me, especially when it comes to that damn service dog. I don't know how she does it, but at every turn, she has a way of fitting it into the conversation.

For instance, when we went to a park last weekend with Caleb, it was doggie heaven. She'd say, "Oh, look Caleb. Isn't that dog so sweet?" or "It would be so fun to watch Caleb run around with a dog, wouldn't it, Garrett?"

I'd bite my tongue or roll my eyes at her comments, and either snap back or ignore it altogether.

But the thing is, I know she's not wrong. I've thought about it considerably, especially after she keeps nudging me about it. I've even Googled the local canine companion services to find out what their selection criteria might be. I'm not a complete ogre in this arena.

Now it's become almost fun to banter back and forth with her over it. To wind her up and watch her go. She's pretty cute when she gets all animated and worked up over the subject matter.

Not to mention, sexy as fuck.

Finding her attractive and wanting to fuck her is highly inconvenient. I'd hoped as the summer progressed it would get easier. That I would become desensitized with having her in the house, in my personal space and being around her. Every day and every night.

It also doesn't help that we've established a new norm in the evenings. After Caleb is in bed, Brooklyn will bring a book, her favorites are the John Sanford thrillers, and sit on the couch as we watch a basketball game or other sporting event on TV together. I enjoy those nights and have become accustomed to her presence.

Therefore, that's the real reason I was so pissy tonight when she went outside the norm. I felt left out of her life.

Deciding I need to do something to shake up my routine and have my own life, I take Lucas up on his offer and make arrangements to go out tomorrow night.

Caleb plays quietly on the floor next to me as I grab my phone and call Lucas up.

When he answers, he does so with a loud ruckus voice. "Yo, G!"

In the background, I hear metal clanging and loud grunts of excursion. "Hey man, did I catch you at a bad time?"

He sounds out of breath. "Nah, man. I'm at the gym just finishing up. What's up?"

"Checking in to see if you want to go out tomorrow night? I really need a break from my scene." I say this last part with my hand covering my mouth and in a low tone, so Caleb doesn't overhear me.

I feel guilty over saying it, and even just thinking it, but every single parent needs a break now and then, right? Even if it's just for a few hours. We need it for our sanity.

I realize I'm a lucky son-of-a-bitch to have live-in help. There are plenty of single parents out there who struggle to manage a household and hold down day jobs with no help whatsoever. But I can't help feeling the way I do.

There are days I miss Becca so much. She was a hell of a mother to Caleb. Even though he wasn't her biological son, and he came into this world under a cloud of indiscretion, she made the ultimate sacrifice to be his only true mother when Penelope, Caleb's birth mom, gave up her parental rights when he was still a baby and Becca adopted him as her own.

I've made a lot of mistakes in my life, but marrying Becca was not one of them. The unfairness of it all is that Caleb will never know his true mother or know what it feels like to have both parents in his life, racks me with guilt every day.

And Penelope will never be that person.

She was a one-night mistake that had a lifetime of consequences.

Lucas responds with a laugh. "Absolutely, bro. I'm here to help. How does eight tomorrow night work? How about that new place, Gravel, on Second Ave?"

"Perfect, man. See you then."

I'm about to say goodbye when I hear a weird noise. I'd moved around the corner just for a second while I was on the phone to be out of earshot but still close enough to Caleb if something happened, but I became distracted by my conversation with Lucas.

The sound coming from Caleb is alarming. I rush around the corner to find that he's fallen on his right side and is convulsing.

"Fuck," I roar. "Luc, call 911. Caleb is seizing!"

I drop the phone and fall to my knees alongside my son who is in a state of seizure.

His little body is tense and quaking, his muscles spasming and twitching, his eyes rolled back into his head.

The instructions given to me by his physicians and therapists at the onset of his condition immediately come to mind, as I thwart off the panic by recalling the steps required to handle this emergency. I grab a throw pillow from the couch, hoisting his head gently with my hand and sliding it under his head, keeping him on his side so he doesn't choke on any spittle or vomit.

It punches a hole in my gut to see his little limbs seize and quake like this, turning him into an immobile statue and me into a helpless father. When we first came home from the hospital after the accident, the doctor's prepared me for the worst and the inevitable. Seizures are common in children who've had traumatic brain injuries, yet they couldn't tell me when or what might trigger a seizure. It was anyone's guess what could bring one on or when they might happen.

We've been lucky because he hasn't had one in the last six months. As he's grown older, the frequency has declined. The very first one he had happened two weeks post-accident, and was mild, but caught me off guard, extremely uncertain how to remain calm when my son was seizing uncontrollably. It was alarming, to say the least.

Since that time, he's experienced four different episodes, each one in varying degrees of seriousness. There is no rhyme or reason and no predictable pattern to what might prompt them, but I've been keeping a journal of when they occur and trying to pinpoint anything of statistical relevance.

All I can do is ensure he's lying on his side, with his head protected and ensure there's nothing obstructing his mouth or any hard objects in his way that might cause him more harm. I hold his head, whispering words of assurance to my son as I wait for the paramedics to arrive.

"You're gonna be fine, Caleb. Daddy's here and loves you. You're doing great. I'm so proud of you, buddy. You're getting so smart and learning so much every day. You amaze me, Caleb. I don't know what I would do without you."

Leaning over my young son's quaking body, I plant a kiss on the top of his head, sweeping the now sweat-drenched hair from his forehead, and close my eyes against the pain of seeing my son in this condition. And I worry.

I worry that someday this will happen when I'm not around. That it will happen when he's at school and the kids won't understand it and will tease him and make fun of him. They'll be cruel and mean because they're kids and Caleb will be different than them.

So many worries enter my head as the blaring sounds of an ambulance become louder and louder in the distance the closer they get and they're soon right outside my house.

I can see the lights flashing from the front window from my spot on the floor and wave them in as they knock and announce their arrival.

"We're in here," I say, directing them into the house. "I think it's near the end."

Caleb slowly comes around, his big blue eyes opening wide, as tears flow down his flushed cheeks. He blinks at me with no understanding of what's happened, or who the two paramedics are at his side, but I comfort him with my hand on his arm as they take his vitals.

"You're okay, Caleb. You just had a seizure. You're okay now. The paramedics are just going to check things over and make sure you didn't hurt yourself."

As the aides take his vitals and ask me questions, Caleb begins to cry out of fear and I know exactly how he feels. My adrenaline has slowly worn off and I'm trembling and exhausted. Just like when I used to play ball, the adrenaline is the boost that drives you to win and to push through the fear of failure. But once that rush of excitement and anxiety wears off, you come crashing down in the inevitable freefall.

That's when only sex, or a fight, or a very stiff drink can alleviate the aftershock.

And I'm not in the position to have any one of those at the moment.

12

It's a little after midnight as I unlock and enter the front door, finding the house interior is dark and quiet as I walk inside.

I left Peyton a little while ago at the block party listening to a live band with a couple of our classmates we'd run into earlier in the evening. We'd known Jake and Conor since our sophomore year and although they are great guys and I know Peyton hooked up in the past with Jake, I've never had any interest in Conor. He's asked me out on multiple occasions, all of which I've declined.

But tonight after a few beers in the beer garden, he got a little handsy, prompting me to take my leave.

As I softly toe off my sandals and pad into the kitchen to get some water, I pull out my phone to use as a flashlight. It's then that I notice I have seven queued texts and two missed calls. My heart is in my throat with alarm as I scroll through the texts and notice they are from Garrett.

To my utter horror, a string of them lights up across my screen, one after another.

Urgent! 911.

In case you get home and we're not there, taking Caleb by ambulance to Children's Hospital.

In the ER now waiting.

Still waiting.

Hello? Brooklyn, are you getting these?

I hate to ask, but can you pick us up? No car. Brought here by ambulance.

NM. Home now.

Oh shit. My heart sinks down to my toes as I read and reread them, and the urgency involved in them. They were all sent within a three-hour period. A panicky sickness sloshes around in my stomach and I want to heave at the distress that I can feel through these messages.

Oh my God, I've failed them already in my first month on the job. Garrett tried notifying me for over three hours and never heard back from me. He is going to think I'm the most unreliable nanny in the world. He'll never trust me again.

I wasn't intentionally ignoring my phone, but it was so loud at the block party, with voices of the crowds, singing and live music, I just couldn't hear my phone after I put it in my purse once I met up with Peyton. And because of that oversight, I've fallen down on the job.

My shame and panic have distracted me until the clank of a glass against the table grabs my attention. Clutching my heart, I gasp loudly, whirling around to see a dark, imposing figure at the table.

"Garrett!" I practically wail, rushing to the table and dropping to my knees next to his chair without thought.

I touch his thigh, my hand cold against the heat of his leg. His muscle flexes and tenses under my palm.

"Oh my God, I'm so sorry. I'm so very sorry," I repeat, unsure of what else I can say.

"Where the hell were you? Why didn't you respond?" His

voice is razor-sharp, like a crack across the face with a palm and his eyes flash dark. "I tried for hours, Brooklyn."

The scent of bourbon or whiskey fills the small space between us, giving me reason to believe this isn't his first drink.

Of course, he would have a drink. Who wouldn't under that level of stress? He must've been out of his mind with crazy worry about Caleb. And he was alone and had no one else to go with him or be by his side for support.

I lift the phone in my shaking hand as if its presence clears things up and provides evidence to exonerate me. "I know. I'm so sorry. I couldn't hear anything. I didn't even think to check until I got home."

He bristles with anger. "Jesus Christ, Brooklyn. I was out of my fucking mind with worry. Not only was I worried about my son, but I had to wonder why you weren't responding and if you were in a ditch somewhere or died in some fiery car accident."

Tears prickle at the edge of my eyes as I hear the pain and panic laced through his words and my body slumps to the floor, hand still gripping his leg. His own hand suddenly lands on top of mine, tentative at first, but then squeezing hard, as if to emphasize how much this ordeal cost him.

I look up into his face with pleading eyes, the words tumbling out of my mouth as the tears stain my cheeks. "Please tell me Caleb is okay. Is he home now? Is he asleep? Can I go see him?"

I begin to stand, but his grip on my wrist and his authoritative command keep me rooted there.

"Stay," he demands. "I'm not done with you yet."

I gulp. Here it comes. This is it. Garrett's patience with me is gone and he's going to fire me right now.

What will I do? I need this summer job and the hands-on experience for grad school next year. And I've already developed such a bond with Caleb and care for him so much, I don't want to leave him. There's so much more progress that can be made and I know I can help him if I have a little while longer.

Garrett gets to his feet, towering over me as I lift my chin to look up at him. There's an electric current crackling between us, made up of fear, frustration and something else entirely. Something dark and forbidden.

I wet my lips and swallow as he pulls me up to stand. Garrett steps into me and I instinctively back up. Glancing down, I see his palm still clamped around my wrist, feeling my blood rush to the site where he holds me. I'm rooted to the floor, unable to move further, my back now up against the kitchen wall.

His voice rasps as his eyes volley between my eyes and my mouth. My lungs drag in the air that doesn't seem to circulate or oxygenate. I'm literally breathless. I force out a gasp as our bodies physically collide and his voice cuts through the silent darkness.

"Do you know what you did to me, Brooklyn? You made me fucking worry about you."

My breath is caught in my throat. My senses suddenly overwhelmed with everything Garrett. His smoky, bourbon scented-breath, the hard resistance of his muscular thigh positioned between mine, and the empty ache inside me that needs to be filled.

"I don't *want* to care about you."

My nipples pebble with desperation and need. In need of his touch. His kiss. His body.

His murmur is so low it's barely audible. "But I do."

He's a breath away from me, our eyes locked in some sort of battle of wills. A battle to hold out. To not give into this contagious energy between us. Unable to hold off any longer, I throw my arms around his neck, stretching up on my tiptoes, as my heart beats so hard it could smash through my ribs.

My hands coast over the ropey muscles in his neck, staring into his eyes that have turned dark and heavy with arousal.

"Don't," he hisses, his gaze latched onto my parted mouth, but I don't listen.

Our lips collide in a hungry, desperate kiss. My lips part and his tongue slips into my mouth, demanding something my body is eager to give.

The groan that escapes his throat fills me with such hungry need. As if he feels the same way, one hand slides down the curve of my waist and behind, grabbing my ass to tug me closer. The fullness of his erection presses snugly in the cleft of my shorts where I've come alive and hot with want.

Garrett's other hand cups my jaw, tilting my head so he can deepen the kiss. I clutch at his neck to give myself more leverage. To take what I want from him. To give him what he needs.

I've never experienced a kiss this passionate or desperate before. Garrett kisses me as if I am the air he needs to breathe. The sustenance he requires to live.

Our kiss deepens as I part my mouth wider, to allow his tongue to roam free, as he licks and sucks every part of my mouth.

Crazy, desperate desire awakens and sparks like a dormant sleeping dragon low in my belly. Our breaths turn into pants and turn ragged as he plunders my mouth and claims me.

Needing friction where I've grown wet and desperate for release, I lift my leg, wrapping it haphazardly at his hip, as his arm drops to secure it in his hold.

He breaks away, mumbling against my lips. "This is too good. You feel so fucking good."

A small helpless noise falls from my mouth as I clutch at his shoulders to find purchase, bucking my hips against his, the wet, sensitive flesh underneath my panties seeking out and demanding more friction.

All I can think about is getting Garrett's hands on my naked body. Having him slide his cock inside me and taking me right here, against the kitchen wall. Letting him have me as a way of slaking his need and finding relief inside me. I want to give that to him because in doing so, I'll get it in return.

Something broken inside him speaks to something desperate

to help inside me, complementing us physically and connecting us emotionally.

I've wanted this generous, sexy, devoted man since we first met. That first day when he single-handedly cleaned up the mess with his shirt and held his son in his arms.

I want to fix what's broken in his life. Repair the loneliness that has deconstructed this once great ball player.

Moving my hands up to his head, I spear my fingers through his short, soft strands, tugging and eliciting a grunt of approval.

"*I*-I want you inside me. I want to make you feel good."

I don't know what happens, but one second his hands are roaming my bare leg and the next thing I know, my feet have hit the ground, my arms are left dangling at my sides and Garrett has taken two gigantic steps away, panting like he's just won in OT, and glaring at me as if he just learned I had the Ebola virus.

He's retreating. His face turns white, his mutinous glare turning into a scowl.

No, no, no. Not yet.

His gaze hardens on me with an accusatory look that fills me with shame as he rakes a hand through his messed-up hair.

"No. This can't happen. I'm going to bed."

Before I can even work my mouth open to say '*wait*,' Garrett's grabbed the bottle of booze and his glass and in three long strides, is halfway down the hallway to his bedroom, where the soft click of the door is the only indicator that the night is over.

Leaving me alone and questioning all my morals.

13

Rolling over in my sweat-drenched sheets, I'm careful not to jostle the 40-ton boulder that is my aching head and stare blurry-eyed at the clock and then the photo on the bedside table.

Ten-thirty a.m.

I've slept in when I should be out taking care of Caleb.

The photo of Caleb is pre-accident, taken two years ago, just before the accident on Mother's Day, when Caleb was two and still in diapers, running around like a maniac. Becca and Caleb had flown out to see me in LA that weekend while I was there for a game against the Lakers and we'd gone out to Laguna Beach. The picture is the two of them out on the beach making a sand castle, happy smiles, and sand for miles.

There are so many mistakes I've made in my life, having Caleb and fighting for him was not one of them. And marrying Becca wasn't either. She took on the role of mother to my son without batting an eyelash and was a natural, unlike his birth mother,

Penelope. Caleb loved Becca something fierce and lit up anytime she was around. I don't blame him. She was an angel.

Or, she is an angel.

Although I'd made a life-altering choice the night I slept with Penelope, and it caused over a year of heartache and legal battles, the day Becca adopted Caleb as her own was the best day of our lives. And for a little while, our life was picture perfect, just like this photo.

But then the accident happened. Caleb's needs came first. I had to end my ball career and find an alternative career. And then the letters, texts, and calls began. Penelope wanted back in.

I wasn't nervous at the onset or overly concerned about Penelope. She was unstable, yes, but I didn't think she would have the funds or the desire to go back to court. She'd originally voluntarily given up her rights – for money – but it wasn't a bribe. It was all done through the legal process. The initial lawyer on the case told me I had nothing to worry about.

When I moved to Phoenix, that's when things started to get a bit dicier. Penelope became a little more aggressive in her attempts at wanting to see Caleb again. She'd claimed to have changed and cleaned up her act, realizing she missed her son.

Per my attorney's advice, I didn't respond to any of her attempts. No sense opening the door a crack only to get it kicked open.

Slowly I stumble out of bed and lumber to my bathroom, turning on the shower before taking a piss. My balance is a little compromised from last night's binge, the bourbon seeping out of my pores.

I sigh loudly as I step under the hot deluge of the shower, scrubbing a hand over my face, hoping it'll relieve the tension and erase the memory of that kiss last night with Brooklyn.

Hangover or not, just the memory of her taste and the sexy sounds she made when we kissed fills my cock with blood, as it thickens with lust. I grab the bar of soap and lather up, avoiding my groin area for now with the hope that my hard on will simmer down.

No such luck. It strains and bobs between my legs, as I glare down at my offending erection that has a tendency of getting me in trouble.

The same dick that nearly got me into a hell of a mess last night.

Had Brooklyn not spoken the words she said, I would've had her naked in ten seconds flat and fucked her hard against that wall. No question about it.

Her body was eager and hot, and her supple mouth sent me into another world. That kiss vaporized every worry and frustration I'd ever had. Colored my dark thoughts with a bright, cheerful hue. Her kisses consumed me. And their decadence started a blaze I almost couldn't contain.

I'd been sitting there in a dark, bitter place before she got home, fuming over every bad thing in my life. My anger had hit a tipping point through all the drama leading up to her return. From Caleb's seizure, the hours of wait time in the Children's ER, the unreturned texts and calls from Brooklyn. It was the perfect storm leading me to a frenzied state of irritation. I felt ignored by her lack of response and insignificant to Brooklyn, who was on my mind constantly.

The moment she came home, I lost all control and could barely see straight through the cloudy haze of bourbon and lust.

I'd already lost one woman I cared about deeply. Not hearing from Brooklyn led me to the edge of insanity and I did a piss poor job of handling emotions when she finally entered the kitchen.

It wasn't Brooklyn who I was irritated with, per se. It was the entire night's circumstances culminating in a ball of anxious fear that drove me to a point of no return, and I pounced. My body knew, even if my brain didn't, that I needed a release only she could give, and I almost let that happen.

Let me make you feel good.

It was those words – the same words that Penelope used the night I fucked her and subsequently impregnated her – that threw a proverbial bucket of cold water in my face and tossed me back into reality.

Usually, when said by a beautiful woman to a man, it's the perfect aphrodisiac and come on. But not for me. When she murmured those words, they spun me up and shook free the memories of a night and time in my life I'd much rather forget.

Hot water scalds my back as I press my hands to the wet shower tile, my head bent in agony. I know I need to grow a pair and go out to apologize to Brooklyn for my behavior and promise her it'll never happen again.

Instead, I'm hiding out in my room while she has probably already fed and taken care of Caleb without so much as a word of complaint. It's also a Saturday, technically her day off, yet I'm exploiting her graciousness by sleeping in.

Christ, I'm such a bosshole.

I finish my shower and get dressed, taking a handful of Advil while draining my water glass. It's quiet in the house as I head out to the kitchen, as I search around the house to find them not inside as expected. It's fairly quiet, just the low hum of the dishwasher running and the sound of the sprinkler system on its automated time cycle out in the backyard.

And that's when I hear the gleeful howl of Caleb and my eyes dart to the kitchen window overlooking our backyard.

Brooklyn is in a bikini, holding my son in her arms as she jumps up and down in the shallow end of the pool, spinning and dancing him around in pirouetting twirls.

Lord help me. She's wearing a bikini.

Slipping my flip-flops on, I head out the sliding door and without a second thought, head out to meet them.

Brooklyn's mid-twirl when her smiling eyes land on me and when they do, she drops them demurely.

"Sorry, did we wake you?" she asks, brushing away strands of wet hair that are stuck to her temple.

I move toward them, shaking my head and shifting my gaze to Caleb, who is wearing his floaties and a life vest, like I advised Brooklyn. I keep my focus on him and away from the tops of her breasts that appear above the water line as I answer her.

"Not at all. I'm so sorry I overslept because it looks like I'm missing out on all the fun out here."

I remove my slip-ons and take a step into the pool, the warm water lapping at my ankles from the waves they've been making. Pulling the neck of my T-shirt over my head, I sling it over to the side of the pool and then submerge under the water.

I pop back up over the waterline and throw my hands in the air, like a sea creature breaching, and growl like a monster as Caleb giggles and screams, splashing water everywhere.

I reach for Caleb, pulling him out of Brooklyn's arms, the touch of her skin against mine, even for that second, sends promises of unfulfilled pleasure skittering down my spine.

Kissing his neck, I soak in the scent of his wet toddler flesh and then blow a raspberry against his cheek, his laughter floating through the air.

It took a long time for that laughter to return to our household. Kids are resilient, but even Caleb experienced the grief of losing the only mother he ever knew.

Brooklyn pauses in front of me, sweeping her arms out over the water, making rippling waves appear between us. The sun has tinted her skin a golden-brown, and I can't help but admire her flawless curves and full breasts in the bright orange bikini top.

My mouth goes dry for wanting to touch.

"Thanks for letting me sleep in. I'm sorry about that."

"No worries. I was up early anyhow. Couldn't sleep." Her comment is laced with the underlying meaning as her lashes flutter, the silver in her eyes shining like a silver coin.

Then she moves to swim around us toward the stairs, taking

each one with fluid ease, grabbing for a towel hanging over the edge of one of the lawn chairs.

As she turns her back to dry off, it gives me the excruciating sight of her ass in that bikini. Lord help me, I'm done for. Her body is tight and lean, sculpted in all the right places with curves for days.

Her back is to me when she speaks. "I need to go shower and then have some errands to run today."

Brooklyn's confidence seems to have wavered, avoiding eye contact with me altogether. I'm to blame for that. Goddammit. I'm not used to women's emotions that I steamroll over them.

"Brooklyn, wait," I beg, wishing I could reach out and touch her. To prove my sincerity. To connect like we did last night. "I'm really sorry about...well, I was a wreck and probably still in shock. I was inappropriate and out of line. I'm very sorry for my behavior."

She holds the towel around her waist in a tight grip, as if protecting herself from me. The shiny tint in her eyes making way to a darker flash something else. Regret, maybe.

"It's fine. It was totally my fault for coming on so strong. It's a bit of a personality flaw. I'm known to be a little impulsive at times." She laughs at her self-deprecating remark, waving a hand in the air before turning inside.

Opening the slider, she peers back over her shoulder at Caleb and me, still standing in the water with a soaking wet son, who is now squirming for me to let him swim.

"I'm going to stop at Target, so leave me a list of grocery items you want for the week and I'll get them today."

"Thanks, will do."

Jesus, dude. Say something else, you idiot.

"Oh, Brooklyn, that reminds me. I'm going out tonight with a friend. Do you mind watching Caleb, or should I call a sitter?"

Her face blanches a bit, the tanned color giving way to a paler hue. But then her gaze lands on my boy in my arms and her smile returns warm and receptive.

"Sure thing, I'll be here. Caleb and I have some PAW Patrol shows to catch up on tonight, don't we, C?"

He shakes his head emphatically and tries to work his mouth to get out his words. I look down at his sweet face for only a moment, and then back to where Brooklyn was, but she's now disappeared in the house. And I fear I've fucked up this situation beyond all repair.

14

BROOKLYN

It's just after ten p.m. and Caleb has long been asleep in bed. Although he took his usual afternoon nap, I think the swim time earlier this morning, on top of the "studying" we did this evening, really tuckered him out and he zonked quick after bath time and a bedtime story.

He and I have been working on practicing his speech and enunciation, as well as using the new speech app I downloaded on his iPad that I asked Garrett to buy for Caleb. His speech thera- pist had recommended it to help Caleb in learning how to communicate wordlessly. Although I know he tries so hard and has the intellectual capacity, the brain trauma he experienced really impairs his speech function.

In the evenings, we've been using cuddle time on my lap to learn how to use the app, identifying pictures with words and then forming sentences from the images. He clicks the images in sequence and then it "speaks" for him.

Along with that, we're working on pronouncing his "words."

The poor kid puts so much effort into sounding out words when we read together and gets easily frustrated when they just won't come out right. In fact, the other night, he had a full-on meltdown, which thankfully only lasted an hour. But during that time, he kicked and screamed and threw a bloody tantrum and nothing I could do or say was going to make a difference.

I can't say I blame him. After what happened last night between me and Garrett and our awkward discussion this morning, I'd love to have a pity party and a little tantrum, myself.

Instead, I plop down on the couch, queue up my latest Audiobook, and open up the pint of mint chocolate chip ice cream that I bought for myself this afternoon.

Taking the first bite, I nearly orgasm over the creamy cold deliciousness and dig in for more goodness when Garrett's home phone rings. After my complete failure to respond to his messages, I waste no time, dropping my spoon back into the tub and jumping off the couch, nearly tripping over my feet in haste to grab the phone off the charger. As I pick up the receiver, I drop it on my foot.

"Shit."

I'm a little out of breath, though, when I finally answer it. "Hello, Parker residence."

There's a beat of silence and I repeat my greeting.

"Hello, this is the Parker residence. Can I help you?"

A female voice sounds on the line, a smoky-tint to her words.

"Is Garrett home?"

My intuition is on high-alert as if to announce that this voice brings danger. Stupid, really, but I've become very protective of my employer and his son.

For more than one reason.

"Um, who may I ask is calling?"

She sighs heavily, expressing the ridiculousness of my request through her snide tone.

"This is Penelope."

My brow creases, as I try to figure out why that name sounds familiar. I know it's not Garrett's mother, because her name is Corinne and I've spoken to her already a few times on the phone.

To my knowledge, he has no other family member or sisters that might call, and it's not the neighbor, Marilyn, who I met a few weeks ago at her garage sale. My only logical conclusion is that this is a woman Garrett's dating, even though I haven't seen him go out on a date in the month and a half I've lived here.

"Penelope? Do you have a last name?" I ask politely. Professionally.

She practically snarls at me like a rabid dog. "Oh, for Christ's sake. It's Penelope Slattery. Caleb's mom."

The few spoonfuls of ice cream I swallowed before answering the phone threaten to curdle and come right back up the way they came. *His mother?* I thought his mom was Becca and she's dead. My confusion has stopped me short and I plunk down heavily on the kitchen stool, mouth dropping wide open.

"I, um, I'm sorry, Caleb's mother?"

"Are you an idiot savant? Who are you and why are you acting so dumb? Please just get Garrett on the line. This is urgent."

I may not be dumb, but I am dumbfounded, as I shuffle around to the junk drawer and pull out a pen and paper. Again, my gut intuition says something isn't right about this situation. Not once has the name Penelope been uttered in this house by Garrett. Meaning one of two things.

She's either lying and is some sort of stalker fan.

Or, she is Caleb's mother but there's a reason why she's not in the picture.

"I'm sorry, Penelope. But Garrett is not home at the moment. I can take down your name and number to have him call you back. That's the best I can do."

"You still haven't explained to me who you are and what business you have watching my son while his father is *obviously* too busy partying on a Saturday night to be home with our son, leaving Caleb to someone with half a brain."

Oh, lady. You're messing with the wrong nanny.

She has no clue just how devoted a father Garrett is to his son. This woman has absolutely no right to call him out for enjoying some well-deserved downtime. No right, whatsoever.

"Excuse me, *Penelope*, but I happen to know Caleb's mom passed away several years ago. And this *half-brained nanny* has never heard of you, *Penelope*. I don't need to explain the reasons why Mr. Parker has entrusted me with his son's care for the evening so he can have a much-needed break from being a single father. I can assure you that I will take down your name and number, but what Garrett chooses to do with it is his business."

I think I've stunned her with my straight-up, no-nonsense retort and the idea fixes a victory smile across my face.

She stammers slightly before relaying her number to me, which I write down in neat, punctuated penmanship, doodling a little devil-face next to her name. What can I say? She's the devil's spawn if you ask me.

When she finally spits out a goodbye and hangs up, I reread her name several times and then decide I need to investigate this woman to see just who the hell she thinks she is.

Google is my best friend. But I don't forget the ice cream.

15

Damn, I needed that.

Spending time with Lucas tonight was something I didn't realize I missed until we got to talking and all my cares and my problems just seemed to melt away.

I'm not saying it was better than sex, but it came a close second in terms of diffusing my pent-up frustrations. Life has become so complicated in the last year, and even more so with all the changes recently in my household.

On top of which, the most recent doctor appointment with Caleb's specialist wasn't as hopeful as I'd wanted. While he's tracking better with his motor skills, his cognitive development is far more slow-moving and delayed. The doctor was still cautiously optimistic about his prognosis and progression, but Caleb still struggles with so much.

All I want is for him to be able to walk, run and talk like other kids and not have to face a life full of difficulties and challenges. I'd give everything I had just to make that happen for him.

As usual, during our three hours together, Lucas was able to cheer me up as he regaled stories of our college years together. He's a good friend. But was evasive, as always, when I asked him how things were in the dating department.

He'd been dating an airline attendant for the past two years and had just come off a messy break-up with the one he thought he was going to marry.

"I'm done, man. I'm going the celibate monk route for the next fifty years," he laments, raising his hand in the form of a Stop. "It's just not worth it, ya know?"

And boy, did I.

I'd given my heart and my life and watched it crumble in a stolen moment. I decided after Becca died, I was done. I didn't ever want to fall in love again or have to care about someone so much that it shattered me to lose them.

Granted, losing Becca the way I did was a pretty tragic event. A death I'm to blame for. Although I wasn't even in the same state the night the collision happened, it was my phone call to Becca and the subsequent argument that distracted her. They say she was going too fast around a curve and veered into the other lane when she was hit by the oncoming truck.

My fault.

"I'll drink to that, bro." I lift the beer glass to toast to his martini, his eyes crinkling in the corners.

He scans my face skeptically, tilting his head as if assessing who I am.

"Something happened with your nanny, didn't it?"

I'm shocked by his spot-on analysis. Jesus, I knew he was smart, but not a mindreader, too.

"How the fuck did you come to that conclusion? I haven't even said a word about her all night."

Lucas tips his head forward and gives me a pointed look.

"Exactly. It's *because* you haven't mentioned her that I know you're hiding something. Spill it, bro."

"What are we, like twelve-year-old's telling each other our secrets?"

He lifts his shoulder in a shrug. "Nope. Just thirty-year-olds who go way back. Now tell me what's going on."

After ordering another round of beer for me and his cocktail, I tell him the story of what happened the night before in my kitchen and our awkward interaction this morning and the brief goodbye when I left to go out tonight.

He considers my plight thoughtfully, assessing the potential havoc it could create in my household and the problems it might cause with Caleb if Brooklyn left us.

"But on the other hand," Lucas ruminates, scrubbing a hand over his chin. "It could work out great. She's a genuinely nice person. Seems to care a lot about your son. And she kissed you back and asked you to fuck her. Why not pursue that? You're both consenting adults and there's no contractual obligation for you to keep your hands off your nanny. I don't see a true downside."

"I see. So, if the roles were reversed and you had a student that you were attracted to and vice versa, you'd be okay with that relationship?"

His eyes narrow on me and then he laughs. "Totally different scenarios. I have to consider my reputation and my position of authority as a professor of a public university, as well as the potential for a conflict of interest. Plus, young twenty-year-old chicks don't do it for me."

"Hmm, not all college students are twenty-years-old chicks. I'm sure there are plenty of college women who could easily debunk that theory for you."

"Maybe, but it doesn't matter anyway," he says adamantly, pointing a finger at his chest. "Monk status. That's me."

We laughed and had another drink together until we decided the bar was getting too loud and crowded on a Saturday night, and we took our old thirty-year-old asses out of there.

Now as I walk into a fairly dark house, the discussion with Lucas runs on repeat in my head as I wonder just what might happen if I started something with Brooklyn. It's obvious we have a mutual attraction to one another. She matched each one of my kisses with an intensity of her own, not backing down or shying away with her touches and comments. She's the one who kissed me first.

She asked me to fuck her.

I doubt Brooklyn has ever said something she didn't mean. She's too smart. Too confident in what she wants and what she's after in life to be anything other than authentic.

She's a woman who balances her nurturing side with a sexual heat that smolders underneath the surface. Brooklyn has never come off as a flirtatious or overtly seductive woman. She's never openly flaunted her body or sexuality with me, but it exists in everything she does.

Brooklyn possesses a natural softness in her mannerisms. She does everything with a shine and a sparkle. It's no wonder that Caleb has fallen in love with his nanny. And there's no doubt it's part of the reason she's captured my interest and pulled me into her captivating warmth.

I come to a stop in the living room where a table lamp glows yellow, where Brooklyn is curled up on the couch, her hands stacked together underneath her cheek. Her legs, partially covered with a quilted throw, stretch out along the cushions, her light-pink painted toes peeking out from under the blanket. One of Caleb's stuffed toys is cuddled between her arms, snuggled into her breasts.

She looks content and beautiful as she surrenders to sleep.

I gaze down at her sleeping form for a few minutes, listening to the soft wisps of her breath and watch the rise and fall of her chest with each slow intake of air into her lungs. My feet move in her direction on their own accord. My desire to make sure she's comfortable is overshadowed by my greedy impulse to touch her.

Sinking quietly to my knees on the floor beside her, I tenderly stroke the side of her cheek with my thumb, her rose-petal softness overwhelming my senses. A sweet mewling noise escapes her lips and I halt my movement. She's quiet again, and I continue tracing a line across her cheek, down her neck and sweep away the hair that's fallen across her neck. Her scent surrounds me and has me aching for a taste of her skin. To gorge myself on her fragrance of lilac and linen.

Brooklyn slowly stirs awake, her eyes peeling open, lips parting and the tip of her pink tongue peeks out to wet her bottom lip. I stifle a groan.

"*Mmm*. That feels good." The lazy, lethargic grin she gives me is my undoing.

It's sweet torture, but I allow my fingers to trail the silky slope of her shoulder and down over the curve of her waist and hip where her shirt rises up. I sweep over the surface, back and forth, back and forth, until I can't take it anymore and I slide my hand underneath her shirt where a strip of skin appears. My fingertips brush over the soft surface there, extracting another moan from Brooklyn, this time longer and louder.

My cock thickens against my pants zipper, straining upward as if a marionette on a string, the sound of her pleasure is music to my ears. And to my dick.

I lean over her, my lips finding the patch of warmth at the hollow of her neck. A now familiar scent of sun and crisp linen fills my nostrils and rushes to my stiffening cock.

A shot of lust ricochets through my body when she rolls over onto her back, her hand lassoing around my wrist to relocate my palm to her breast.

Oh fuck. This is going to happen.

"Are you sure, Brooklyn?"

She pushes up to her elbows, bracing herself against the cushions so her face is inches from mine.

She brushes a kiss at the corner of my mouth, her lips tilting up in a *'come hither'* smile.

"Yes. I want this, Garrett."

16

I was dreaming about Garrett.

In my dream, he held me pressed against the kitchen wall just like the other night, his hand down my panties, fingering me to orgasm as he handed out open-mouthed kisses all over my body as if they were candy.

And then suddenly, as if I'd manifested it into happening, my sex-filled-dream became something real, as a living, breathing Garrett began touching and kissing me with such unbelievable tenderness that I could no longer contain my husky moans of pleasure.

His own smoky voice filters through my sleep-dazed consciousness and my body awakens to a flood of heat and desire.

"Let me make you feel good, Brooklyn. It's all I want to do."

Garrett's hand that I had transferred to my breast with a naughty grin, kneads and plumps my flesh, a thumb skimming over the rounded peak of my nipple, eliciting a sharp fissure of pleasure between my legs.

I smooth a hand over his jawline, the texture of his whiskers rough against my palm. I shiver as my lips meld with his. Hard. Intense. His tongue plunges into my mouth and I suck on him ravenously, with a hunger that's been building for weeks.

We move together, our mouths connected, tongues dueling greedily, as I shift into a sitting position, Garrett's hand sliding down the material of my tank to expose my breast. He cups it in his hand, plumping the flesh in his palm with just the right amount of pressure that could get me off with little to no more effort than that. I make sounds like I've never made before, moaning and keening for something just out of reach.

When his wet mouth finds my nipple and he suckles it between his teeth, rolling the tip of his tongue over the delicate flesh, I cry out for mercy. For more. My overly sensitive skin basking in every touch of his mouth, his hands, his body.

Garrett snickers, a sexy smirk twisting across his lips and his eyes cut to mine before he goes in for the kill and laves my entire breast with the flat of his tongue. My body jerks skyward, hips punching forward as he sweeps a hand underneath my rear and pulls me forward, my knees spreading wide as he nestles me against his firmness.

Just like the other night, his hard bulge strains beneath his jeans and beckons me to grind against him wantonly, as he continues to bite, nip and savor my breasts.

I reach between us, rubbing my palm over his erection, applying firm pressure as I graze over the imposing thickness.

Nimbly, I unbutton his fly, sliding my hand into the waistband and hitting the motherlode. My fist conforms around his cockhead and I squeeze, his groan of pleasure confirming what I'd already hoped. That he likes my boldness.

I'm not a shy lover. My experience isn't vast but the men I've been with in college have taught me enough of what I need to know. But there isn't always a one-size fits all answer, so it's also my policy to ask.

"How do you like it?" I ask with a hard pull of his flesh as he jerks in my hand.

"Anything. Hard and fast is good."

Testing the waters, I allow my hand to slip further down where there's less give in the material, to the curve of his balls, cupping their weight in my palm and scoring them lightly with my short fingernails.

He simpers with flat-out pleasure. "Oh shit, yes."

While I've distracted him for only a moment, his focus returns to the task at hand and he works to extract my shorts and panties from me, pulling them over my hips and down my legs. Having to adjust my position, I shift my knees and lift my ass, allowing him room to divest me of my clothes.

Garrett backs up onto his heels, surveying the property between my legs like a man looking over his choices at a buffet. Hungry and undecided as to what he wants. Ready to fill his plate with everything and gorge until he gets his fill.

With an appraising glance, his eyes grow dark, indicating he likes what he sees. With one hand on my kneecap, he nudges my legs open. The other cups my mound, a finger tracking the small patch of landing strip at my pelvis, sending zinging pulses of pleasure through my body and drenching me with wetness.

"I'm going to put my mouth on you," he vocalizes in a low, sexy timbre. "And I'm not stopping until you're either screaming my name or God's."

My head involuntarily drops back against the couch as he drags his knuckles over my inner thigh, his thumbs digging into both thighs before he leans in and breathes me in. He's barely touched me and I'm nearly convulsing with riotous pleasure as his lips curl around my clit and he sucks.

I was already wet and pliant for him, but the minute his mouth lands on my center, and he opens the folds of my core with his fingers, I'm seconds from coming. It won't take much more than that.

I hear myself cry out a plea of something. What, I don't know, but it's all irrelevant because Garrett seems to know exactly what I need and want.

He vacillates between using soft, feather-light strokes of his tongue and fingers to torturing me with long, hard pulls of my clit between his teeth, and then soothing the sting with caresses and the plunge of his tongue inside me.

I'm stretched out wide, Garrett's head between my legs, my hand on top of his head, undulating my hips as I buck and grind against his face. The stubble of his beard abrades my sensitive inner thighs, only heightening the tension that rises and builds, coiling low in my belly, like a Cobra ready to strike.

My voice is a strangled whisper. "I'm close. Garrett...so close. Just a little more..."

But I can't finish the sentence as he locks his lips around my clit and sucks hard, two fingers entering me and curving upward to find the sweet spot that sends me to oblivion.

"*Ommmmmigod*, Garrett..." I scream out in pleasure as I'm rocked with one of the longest, deepest, purest orgasms I've ever had.

My entire body tightens and strains against the radiating vibrations of my release, rocketing me up to the heavens and then slowly returning me to earth with a floating glide of triumphant relief.

When I finally find the strength to open my eyes and lift my head, which feels heavy and weighted, Garrett is wiping a hand over his mouth with one hand and stroking his cock in the other.

Holy hell, that's so hot.

"You planning to hog that all for yourself?" I ask with the tilt my head, giving him a taunting smile as I slide my fingers between my legs where he'd just been. "Or are you going to fuck me?"

I gasp loudly when he grabs my leg and yanks me off the couch and we tumble to the floor, Garrett landing on top of me.

"You're a naughty little tease, aren't you?"

And then he's plunging inside me, hard and deep, until I practically see stars.

17

GARRETT

When I was playing professional basketball, I'd get in the zone, where everything else shuts down and goes quiet in your head and the only thing that matters is the game.

Dribble, run, pass, shoot, block.

Repeat.

The same thing happened the moment I walked in and saw Brooklyn stretched out asleep on the couch. The minute our mouths connected, and we kissed, any and all rational thought I may have had flew out of my head, leaving me on a runaway train with a one-track desire. To get inside Brooklyn.

The only things that would've stopped me would have been the word 'No' or Caleb's cries from his bedroom. Thankfully, neither happened and I was on a mission to devour Brooklyn and bring us both to orgasm.

As soon as she came on my tongue and I felt her spasming release, I couldn't hold back any longer. My cock needed relief, so

I took matters in my own hand. And this time, when she asked me to fuck her, I didn't think twice.

My cock nestled into the juncture of her thighs as I landed on top of her on the floor, her heat so intense there was nothing that could stop me from burying myself inside her.

I swallow her gasp with a searing kiss, my tongue sweeping through her mouth, her salty honey taste still on my lips as we explore the feel of each other in this position.

"Brooklyn," I grit her name out through my teeth, the pleasure so exquisite it has me shaking and ready to come soon. "You okay?"

The heels of my palms press into the rug next to her ears, as I lift myself over her, inviting her to open her eyes to look at me. I don't know what I expect to find when she opens her silvery-green irises to me, but it fills me with a happiness I haven't felt in years.

I experiment with a slow thrust, groaning from the tight heat that sheaths my aching cock. Her arousal on my tongue was consuming, but the slick wet slide of her pussy is magical. This woman has cast a spell over my life in every way.

She lifts her head, lips meeting the curve of my neck as she bites my flesh before teasing the sting with the tip of her tongue.

"Yes," she says breathlessly. "Don't hold back. Take me there again."

Who is this girl? My God, she's fucking perfect in every way.

I let out a soundless laugh because she has no idea what she's in for. I'm a competitive person, it's made me a good ball player and now a decent coach. I thrive on the win, my determination to exceed goals propelling me to victory. And damn, if she wants me to make her come again, then by God, I'll make it happen.

Brooklyn's tank top still covers her deliciously full breasts, and I want to feel everything. I want to make her wild with desire as I play with her nipples and sink into her heat.

I shift to my knees, the move extracting my dick from her entrance. She stares at me as if I'm crazy.

Removing my T-shirt over my head, I flick my chin for her to do the same. I discard my shirt to the side and help her divest her tank when her arms get tangled in the material, extracting a disgruntled gripe.

"Here, I got you." I reach over her head where her arms outstretch and tug the shirt off.

We're now completely naked, our bodies exposed in intimate knowledge of one another, and the sheer connection we share is combustible and explosive. I slip a hand in hers, holding it above her head, interlacing my long fingers through her delicate ones, holding her in place as I dip my mouth to her exposed breast.

Everything about Brooklyn is sweet, but her rosebud nipples are a delicacy. She squirms beneath me, lifting her hips off the floor to connect once again with my throbbing cock. Using my teeth to score lightly over the pebbled tip, I guide my cock back inside, as she opens for me further.

I want to watch her tits bounce as I fuck her. To see the fluid movement and jiggle of her perfect breasts – plump, full and pert. Freeing her wrist from my grasp, I tilt her hips up with my hands underneath her ass, as I push back on my heels, leaving her feet planted on the floor. Repositioned now, it allows me to go so much deeper, the tip of my cock hitting her in a place I know she likes each time I plunge deep. With every surge of my pelvis, I make contact with her sensitive clit, grinding my hips in a slow rotation, the move drawing out a gasp.

"There, there, there."

My hands clutch her firm ass, drawing her into me with each thrust so she can grind against my lap. She's soon panting heavily, her rocking hips and parted lips a sure sign she's close.

My balls begin to tighten, drawing up to signal my impending orgasm, slapping against us both, the sounds of our panting breaths mixing with the tension of our climbing need.

Her pussy clenches around my cock, and I use my thumb to circle her clit until she detonates and comes apart.

"Garrett..."

I see the moment she lets go, her mouth opening in a gasp, an elongated moan slipping past her lips and her body tensing as her eyes snap shut.

"Open your eyes. Look at me. I want you to watch as I fuck you."

Her body undulates and shakes uncontrollably in my grip, her eyes hooded with desire.

My release barrels out of nowhere, overtaking my stability, requiring that I lay her flat so I can thrust wildly with abandon as I pump faster and harder inside her. The tingling sensation starts in my toes, climbing up through my legs into the base of my spine, my thighs, and ass tightening, balls contracting with warmth as I reach the point of desperation.

"I'm coming..."

The spasms of release send me to the moon and back, my entire body seizing and contracting as I pull out and shoot my release across Brooklyn's smooth abdomen.

Recovery comes slowly, as my heart rate and breath become more regulated, the sweat beads drying across my back, as I succumb to relaxation and roll to my side.

"Holy shit," I murmur, my eyes drifting closed in post-coital bliss. But that feeling doesn't last long, as reality comes racing back swift and fast.

I just fucked Brooklyn.

My son's nanny.

A woman I employ and need to keep employed through the remaining summer.

I have no idea what this might mean for her.

What if she wants something more from me than just sex?

I can't do a relationship. I won't ever go through that again.

On top of these worries, we had unprotected sex. Although I

pulled out at the last minute so I didn't come inside her, we didn't discuss protection. We didn't discuss anything.

Jesus, there I go again. I've already made this mistake once before. I'm not ready to make it again. I like Brooklyn. A lot. I care about her. But I can't give her a commitment right now.

All of these thoughts run through my head and put an immediate damper on the experience we just shared, turning it into a minor panic attack for me.

Even though Brooklyn assures me with her words, it still sends prickles of fear through my head.

"Garrett, I'm on birth control. I should've let you know that."

I roll to my back, scrubbing a hand roughly over my forehead, my now flaccid dick plopping limply against my thigh.

A metaphor for how quickly this could change the atmosphere between us and how easily it could deflate our working and living arrangement.

"Totally my fault. I should've been more careful. I wasn't thinking at all."

Brooklyn sits up, rooting around for her discarded clothes and reaching for the tissue box at the same time on the end table. Making quick work of the clean-up, she covers her nakedness and stands. I don't move to help. In fact, I don't move at all, I just cover my eyes with my arm.

Not only has she flat-out knocked me on my ass, but I also don't know how to proceed.

Lucky for me, she reads through my bullshit and has concluded I'm an asshole and takes decisive action for the both of us.

"I'm turning in. I'll see you in the morning."

As she walks down the hallway, the sound of her bare feet slapping against the tile floor, she stops and leaves me with one final word.

"By the way. A Penelope Slattery called tonight. The message and her number are on the kitchen table. Goodnight, Garrett."

If I thought I was feeling uncomfortable the moment I came down from my orgasm, I was wrong.

This bit of news takes the cake.

The last thing I need in my life right now is the potential drama Penelope can bring into my world.

And to Caleb's.

Because whatever she's calling about, I know it can't be good.

18

BROOKLYN

I've never been the one to get possessive or weirded out after sex. To me, it's always been about chemistry, physical attraction and desire. Nothing more.

I'm not sure what's going on in Garrett's head after the sex and our brief exchange of good night's last night. The minute he pulled out of me and came on my belly, I sensed he got a little freaked out.

Which is fine. I get it.

I mean, that whole thing was unplanned, unscripted and completely unexpected. Maybe because of that, he got a little worried and compared it to what happened between him and Penelope.

Yeah, I don't know all the circumstances and facts behind it, but my Google sleuthing did account for a bit more information than I had before her call. It told me that Garrett knocked up someone that wasn't his wife before he was married and had a kid with her. Caleb. And that's definitely a story that leaves a lot to the imagination.

And believe me, I formulated lots of crazy stories in my head last night as I laid in bed, tossing and turning over the sudden mood swing from Garrett. Determined to find out the scoop this morning, I get up early to go take care of Caleb and find they are already gone.

Great. Just great.

Well, avoiding tough discussions is not my style and as soon as he returns, we're going to have ourselves a little come to Jesus discussion. He needs to know where I stand.

Just because we had sex, doesn't mean I want a relationship. Good grief, I don't want to be settled down at this age. While I really like Garrett – and let's be real – am super attracted to the man – I'm not here to find a boyfriend or future husband.

I'm here to do a job. And in my opinion, if that job can come with some fringe benefits, even better.

I make myself some coffee and then use the free time this morning to shower and run to the farmer's market, picking up some fresh fruits, flowers, and vegetables, and then call Peyton to tell her I'm on my way over with goodies.

When I let myself into my now subletted apartment, I find Peyton sitting on the kitchen table, her bare feet perched on the chest of a handsome guy in his early twenties, who I presume is the new roommate, Kyler. He's painting her toenails a bright aquamarine color and neither of them looks up as I walk in and drop my bags on the counter.

"Hey, girl." Peyton finally twists her head over her shoulder and gives me a proper wave. "Get your ass in here and meet my new boy toy."

I laugh, connecting gazes with the man in question, who lifts his dark brows and shakes his head.

"For the record, I am so much more than just a pretty boy. I have talents."

Peyton chimes in. "He's right! He took your place in the kitchen, Brooklyn. This man knows how to cook."

I give Kyler a stern look of warning. "You be careful, Kyler. She will soon be using you to do her laundry, grocery shopping, and future homework assignments, as well."

Peyton has the sense to look offended, leaning over and giving Kyler a shove across the shoulder. "Don't you listen to her, Kyler. She's just jealous that I'm getting all this attention from you and she's living with a man who is hands-off."

I clear my throat, stifling the truth. "Mmm-hmm. Tell yourself whatever you must, my friend."

Moving over to the table, I stand next to the two of them and offer my hand to Kyler.

"Hi, Kyler. I'm Brooklyn, this witch's former roommate. And it's very debatable whether I'll even come back with that sort of attitude."

I bend down and cover the side of my mouth with my other hand, speaking in a hushed, conspiratorial whisper. "Plus, she's a slob, if you haven't found that out by now."

Kyler busts out laughing and instead of shaking my hand, throws Peyton's feet over the side and jumps up to wrap his arms around me in an unexpected hug.

"*Umph*," both Peyton and I say at the exact same time. She grumbles at losing her balance when he let go of her feet. And I practically had the wind knocked out of me with his exuberant hug.

When Kyler lets go of me and stands back, he throws his arms out wide. "It's so good to meet you, Brooklyn. I've heard so much about you from this little chatterbox. She's told me some wild stories."

He waggles his eyebrows as a crease forms between mine. "I wouldn't believe any of the bullshit she's spilling. She's full of it."

We all laugh as Peyton runs to the kitchen (more like waddles on her heels to keep her painted toes from getting smudged) and pours some mimosas while Kyler and I get to know each other.

"Thank you so much for letting me crash here this summer. It helped me out of a tight bind. My ex and I broke up and he had the lease on the apartment, effectively kicking me out without any advance notice. And I don't have a lot of money for a place of my own because I'm working to pay for school. I honestly wasn't sure what I was going to do until Peyton offered this to me."

I frown. "That really sucks. I'm sorry to hear about your break-up. Were you together long?"

Kyler's vivid green eyes cloud over in a wash of sadness and my heart breaks for him. Regardless of whether I know him or not or his situation, we've all gone through complicated break-ups and sad relationship endings to empathize with each other.

The thought brings Garrett to mind. I feel like I still know so little about him or his life, even though I've lived in his house for more than a month now, and have now even slept with him. God, just the flash of memory has me clenching my thighs together from the tingles it evokes.

"Max and I started dating three years ago. I thought he was the one, ya know? He's older than me, more mature. Settled. Had a good job and had no problems supporting me while I went to school. But the things we used to enjoy together seemed to diminish, and he became distant the last six months. He started going to the gym a lot and for hours at a time. I liked his new buff body but found out he was sharing it with someone else he'd met. When I confronted him on it, he gaslighted me, and made me feel like I was insane and making things up in my head."

He waves a hand and straightens his shoulders, his smile apologetic. "I'm sorry, Brooklyn. It's so uncouth to overshare TMI after just meeting you. I'll shut up now and let you tell me something personal."

He playfully zips up his mouth with his fingers as Peyton

drops off the mimosas for each of us and then drapes her arms over Kyler's shoulders, joining in on the conversation.

"Yeah, girl. Let's hear it. Tell us about Garrett."

Oh geez. Nothing like being put on the spot the morning after you've just slept with your boss. I wiggle uncomfortably in my chair, trying to keep my poker face intact.

"There's really nothing too much to share. Except things are going really well and I absolutely adore Caleb."

I leave out the part about adoring my boss, too.

Peyton twists her lips in a scrutinizing gesture but then seems to decide to let it go.

She lifts her glass in a toast, and we follow suit. "Here's to summer Sundays and oversharing." She clinks her glass against Kyler's and mine, and we move onto other safer topics.

But that uncomfortable feeling remains, and I know I'll need to confront Garrett either tonight or tomorrow at some point. In the meantime, I enjoy my brunch with my good friend and my newfound friend, Kyler, and let all the other shit wait until I'm ready to discuss it.

———

"Oh my God, Brooklyn. Are you serious? He took you right there on the floor?"

Several mimosas and Bloody Marys later, and after a huge brunch Kyler made for us out of the farm fresh produce and eggs I'd picked up, I begin to spill the beans and share what happened between me and Garrett last night.

Kyler whistles from the kitchen where he's even cleaning up our dishes (yeah, Peyton really lucked out with this temporary roommate) and Peyton's mouth drops open at the acknowledgment of my confession.

I feel my face turn hot and flushed. "Yeah, we just went at it without really considering any of the logistics or ramifications."

"What ramifications? He rammed you to an orgasm. Nothing more to consider, if you ask me," Kyler muses without judgment from his spot in the kitchen. "I say, keep that shit going."

"Yeah," pipes in Peyton, who to my knowledge, is still a virgin at twenty-one. "I don't think there's enough sex in the world and you should get it where you can without overanalyzing or second-guessing a good thing."

I lift my eyebrow sarcastically. "Oh really? Don't over-analyze it? Just do it?"

She frowns. "What? I don't over-analyze things. It just hasn't happened yet. It's not my fault. Life just got in the way."

Kyler comes back in and refills all our drinks, patting a hand on Peyton's shoulder.

"It's okay, sweetie. It'll happen when it happens. There's no rush. But since you've waited as long as you have, you might as well find someone who checks off all the boxes, you know? You can be picky."

She nods and I add, "Absolutely. Find someone who gives you all the feels."

Peyton snickers. "Like Garrett gives to you?"

I roll my eyes and flip her off. "It's awkward now. I don't want it to be awkward. Plus, he's my boss. What if he decides this isn't good form and fires my ass?"

"Oh please. He wouldn't dare. You are irreplaceable. Plus, you're both single and it was consensual. While it might make it a little awkward at first, he'll get over it and you can move on."

There's a silent pause as everyone chews over Kyler's comment. And then he adds, "Unless neither of you wants to move on and you like playing house. Now there's a fun role-playing activity right there."

He chuckles and turns on the dishwasher as I feel the weight of Peyton's stare from across the table. Since first meeting her, Peyton has always had both a playful fun side and a serious side of her personality. She is adorably spunky, with a quick wit and devastatingly good looks, and dresses like a fashion model, which make her fun to be around.

She can be the life of the party. But she can also be intuitive, with a distrustful view when it comes to men.

She stares at me in thoughtful silence, questions floating behind her bright blue eyes and the black-framed glasses she wears.

"Go ahead, spit it out," I prompt.

"I know I teased you about the horny single dad and nanny scenario, but I'm also seriously concerned. It sounds like Coach Parker has some emotional baggage from what he's been through and I don't want you to get embroiled in that. You have a lot to accomplish in the next two years with grad school and your thesis. You don't need to take on some older dude's life's problems, do you, Brook?"

I give a humorless laugh, picturing Eros, the mythological Greek god, shooting his arrows of love and passion down at Garrett and me, tasing us with his potions and then leaving us to deal with all the conflict and chaotic aftermath.

I groan, throwing my head down dramatically on my hands on the table.

"I love what I'm doing with Caleb. I feel I've already made progress with him and I can't even tell you how happy it makes me. To see that boy smile is just...such an incredible gift. But then Garrett..."

Peyton leans her chin on her palm, sighing dreamily.

"Exactly," I point out, lifting my head and shooting her a grimace. "I don't know how I'm going to look at him again and not remember what he did to me. He turned me freaking inside out. But in the process, I think it freaked him out."

"Yeah, but it's not like you turned all clingy and possessive. That's not your style."

I shrug a shoulder, as Peyton and I head to the couches in the living room.

"I know. It's not me. It's whatever he's been through and experienced that's left him with a bad aftertaste."

"Well, maybe you'll have an opportunity to talk it through and he'll figure out what he wants."

Kyler plops down next to me on the couch, shifting on his hip to give me an appraising glance.

"Speaking of aftertaste," he coughs in his closed fist, his eyes lighting with a degree of mischief. "Let's go raid Peyton's wardrobe and see what we can do about this."

With a flourish of his hand over my athletic-wear covered body, he yanks me by the hand and drags me toward the bedroom, as I stare helplessly behind me at Peyton, whose only response is to throw herself on the couch and laugh.

Some friends I have.

19

GARRETT

My mother called me bright and early this morning informing me that she was at the airport and ready to be picked up.

What, now?

When I asked her what the hell she was talking about, she gave me the third degree over never listening to her and that she told me a month ago she'd booked her trip down to see me and Caleb. A month ago?

Okay, she was right. I checked my calendar and lo and behold, there it was. Honest to God, I've been so busy these past four weeks, with hiring Brooklyn, starting the summer training camp and keeping things moderated with Caleb, I completely spaced it.

And being as sleep deprived as I was after not sleeping a wink last night, and out of the blue call from Penelope, who could blame me for forgetting to pick up my mother? I was a little more than frazzled.

To add insult to injury, my lackluster greeting of my mother at the baggage carousel was met with a *tsking* noise, followed by a "*You look tired, Garrett,*" comment from mom.

As I load up her three bags into the back of my Range Rover, she kisses and hugs Caleb with her grandmotherly affection and leaves me with a pat on the back. Really, mom? That's what I get for scrambling out of bed to pick you up?

Let's just say our mother/son bond has been fraught with disapproval since I was a young boy. I could never do right in my mother's eyes.

"You really need to take better care of yourself, Garrett," she admonishes as I shift in reverse and we pull out of the airport parking, her judgmental tone already grating on my last nerve. "How else are you going to attract a lady friend looking like a worn-out old man? You're not making the big bank like you used to."

My patience is already wearing thin and she's only been here for less than thirty minutes. We're not too far out of Sky Harbor that I consider turning right back around and dropping her back off. But I take a calming breath, instead, because I know it will be good for Caleb to spend time with his grandmother.

I groan internally. I know my mother loves me, and I her, but our personalities couldn't be more different. In fact, she always had a softer spot for my younger brother, Thad, made only twice as evident after he died so young from spinal cancer. But even their relationship suffered when Thad, while still in college, married his wife, Addison. No one was good enough for her perfect, handsome youngest son. And then came the announcement she was pregnant, followed by the very fast death soon after their first wedding anniversary.

My mother is close to Addison and my nephew, Wyatt, though, even if Addison did move out to Boston around the same time Caleb and I moved down to Phoenix. I do feel bad about how my mom felt abandoned by her own family and '*never gets to see her grandsons.*'

A lump of guilt forms in my throat as I think about all the times I should've reached out and checked up on my former sister-in-law, Addie. We've both suffered such indescribable loss in our lives, and we are both raising our young boys single-handedly. If anyone understands the pain and grief I've gone through, and the discomfort associated with starting over, it would be Addie.

I don't blame Addison at all for the change in scenery she required during the darkest days of her life. In essence, I did the very same thing, moving from Indiana to Phoenix after Becca's death. And I do hate that it took us farther from my mother, but I've always insisted she could come down to visit whenever she wanted. Obviously, she has no problems with that at all.

"How have things been going this summer, sweetie? Is the new nanny working out okay for you?" My mother peers over her shoulder into the back seat, checking on Caleb and seeing that he's already dozed off.

I nearly swallow my tongue at the mention of Brooklyn. With a stealthy side-eyed glance, I wonder if my mom detects something is already up with us, wondering how I'll skirt around the issue with her while my mother is here.

"Yeah, she's great. Caleb loves her and we're seeing a lot of progress being made with her help. She's been working on speech and enunciation and even the speech therapist has noticed a difference. She's a great nanny."

Mom pats my hand on the steering column. "That's good, dear. You needed someone like your Becca to fill the void."

My eyes snap to hers in the passenger seat, confused by her comment. Does she think I'm going to marry my nanny? That Brooklyn will replace Becca as his mother?

"What the hell do you mean by that?" My words are acerbic, causing her to clutch her chest.

"Don't use that tone of voice with me, Garrett. All I mean is that without Becca, and with Penelope not involved with his life..."

"Her choice, need I remind you."

She chuffs at this remark and continues. "Anyway, I'm impressed with Brooklyn. We've had several good conversations and I think you made a brilliant choice. I can't wait to meet her while I'm here for the next two weeks."

I'd just taken a sip of coffee and choked, spewing the liquid all over my shirt.

"Two weeks?"

She tips her head and stares at me like I'm an alien from Mars.

"Well, technically not a full two weeks. I've made arrangements to take Caleb to Disneyland this week."

"Pardon? Did you just say you plan to take my son to Disneyland without consulting me first?"

She gives me a disgusted scowl. "Of course not. That's what I'm doing right now, silly. I'm letting you know I'm making plans."

I'm so thrown by this cavalier approach my mother seems to have about making plans for my son on a whim without considering all the things that go into it. She has no idea how difficult it will be to manage Caleb on her own.

"No, that's not going to work. You can't possibly do it by yourself."

My mother shushes me. "Oh, don't be silly. I know that. That's why I'm flying Addison and Wyatt out to join me. And Disney has a great program for disabled children. Caleb will have a wonderful time. Plus, I know you need a break, so I'm giving you one."

I'm about to go postal on my very own mother. Obviously, this little trip of hers was clearly planned ahead of time if she is flying Addison and Wyatt out and she took the time to research Disney programs for special needs kids. She's just now telling me about it because she knew I'd flip.

And she's right. I did. She no longer dictates my life or calls the shots about how I raise my son. I can just put my foot down and tell her no. She no longer has a say in those things that affect either one of us. My mother is a hard woman to get along with even on the best of days, but if I lose my patience with her now, she'll shut down and turn it around on me, making me look like the asshole.

So, I behave. I bide my time and remain patient, not allowing her to get under my skin.

As we drive past the security gate and into the drive, I notice a car parked on the side of the street, the shadow of a familiar profile sitting in the front seat.

My bullshit meter begins ticking loudly, as I start patching together all the things my mother has just mentioned, putting two-and-two together. Shifting the car into park, I glance in the rearview mirror, first seeing my sleeping boy conked out in the backseat, and then tracking out the back window at the woman I haven't set eyes on in over two years.

I breathe through my nose, my hands balling into fists as I watch her step out of her car and walk up to my drive toward us.

"Mother, what the fuck is going on right now?"

"Son, please don't use that language with me. You know how crude I think it is."

I stare incredulously back at her nonplussed expression, innocently blinking back at me.

My words are clipped. "Start. Talking."

"I received a call from Penelope a few weeks back and we got to talking. She was extremely remorseful for her poor judgment in giving up Caleb and knew you'd say no to visitations. I am simply brokering the discussion between you two today, in hopes of helping you come to some terms. For Caleb's sake. He needs a mother."

I now understand the meaning behind losing my shit. Because it's about to go down. My mother has finally crossed the line and I'm not opposed to throwing her out right along with Penelope.

"No. Nope. Absolutely not. That woman" - I jab my thumb toward the window – "gave up her goddamn rights two years ago in a court of law. She signed away her rights and a judge saw fit to allow it. And she was well compensated to boot, if you may recall. She didn't want to be a mother then, and she certainly hasn't earned the right to be called his mother now, dead parent or not. A zebra does not change its stripes."

My mother has the audacity to touch my exposed forearm and I flinch it away. "Honey, people do change. All I'm asking is for you to give her a chance to explain. That's all."

There have been times in my life where my temper has gotten the best of me and I'm not proud of that fact. The last time was when Becca and I argued over the phone prior to her accident. And the result was catastrophic, so I try to keep my temper from exploding at all costs.

But in this moment, as my life is being hijacked by the very woman who gave birth to me, I'm not acting like a rational man. My mother has jumped into a situation she knows nothing about. I'm sure somewhere deep in her heart she means well, but it is none of her fucking business.

I've been doing a pretty fucking fine job of raising my motherless son. I do not need her to run interference or insinuate that Caleb is not well-adjusted without a mother in his life.

I feel the walls of the car collapsing around me and I feel trapped, like a caged lion. Penelope now stands just a few feet outside my parked car and my mother sits next to me, stewing as if I've insulted her somehow.

And then, just when I think it can't get any worse, Caleb starts wailing, having been woken from his nap. As I turn my head to the backseat, out of my peripheral vision I see Brooklyn's car slowly drive into her parking space at the side of the garage.

This day just keeps getting better and better.

When I woke up this morning, my greatest worry was how I was going to handle the potential morning-after awkwardness with Brooklyn.

Now I have three women, and one cranky son, to deal with.

I take care of the easiest one first.

"Mother, please take Caleb, go in the house, and put him back down for his nap. You can at least do that for me since you've created this situation."

"But..."

"No buts. Just do it. Otherwise, I'm turning this car right around and taking you back to the airport this minute. And possibly running over Penelope in the process."

She turns ghost white and tight-lipped but says nothing more. She gets out of the front and opens the back door, removes Caleb out of his car seat and slams the door haughtily, leaving me in a silent car.

Sucking in the deepest, most calming breath I can manage, I open my driver's side door and walk directly over to Penelope, who plasters on a fake, contrite Botox smile. I don't reciprocate but instead, hold up my index finger for her to remain quiet.

"Stay here and don't say a fucking word. I will deal with you in a second."

And then I pivot on my heels, rounding the front of the car and stride toward Brooklyn, whose initial welcoming smile flips upside down into a look of confusion. The first thing I notice, however, is that there's something different about the way she looks – maybe it's her hair or make-up or clothes - but I don't have time to dissect what's changed.

Because right now, everything has changed. It feels like reality has slammed its fist in my face. First with my mother's arrival, her remarks about what she thinks I need and then the appearance of the one woman I can't stand who's made my life intolerable.

And now as I stand in front of Brooklyn, I realize she's the only one who calms me down and gives me peace. Provides a solace in my life when everything else storms like a cyclone around me.

I cup her cheeks in my roughened hands, bringing her gaze to rest on mine.

"You're going to have to trust me when I say that a shitstorm is brewing, and it started with my mother. I won't blame you if you choose to leave, but I would really love for you to stay. I need your support. I need you."

She blinks, pursing her lips and bending to the side to peer around me at Penelope, before straightening again and giving me a short nod of support. Exhaling all the stale air that was trapped in my lungs, I drop my arms and link my fingers with hers.

"Is that her? Is that Penelope?" she whispers, her eyes wide with guarded curiosity.

I tamp down the lump in my throat. "Yes. That's Caleb's biological mom."

Brooklyn straightens her shoulders as if preparing to go into battle for me. My sweet fiery warrior.

"Okay. I've got this."

She's about to turn and walk into the house when I pull her back with a quick tug and she topples into my chest.

Staring up at me expectantly, her lips part as I lean in and cover her mouth with mine. It's a kiss of gratitude.

Of apology.

A kiss to claim.

A clear statement to announce to Penelope and the world, that Brooklyn is mine. There is no one else. She's in my corner and I am in hers.

When I reluctantly pull away, my vigor is renewed and my conviction strong.

I don't know what's changed between last night and this moment, but it's as if that wall around my heart has crumbled and disintegrated, and I now realize I want this woman on my team going forward from this moment on.

She's my chance at a winning future. And I could definitely use a win after all the shit I've been through. Just one final shot to win the game.

20

BROOKLYN

Holy goodness, I don't know what I just walked into or what's about to go down or what happened leading up to the odd standoff I drove into, but hearing Garrett say he needs me by his side and that claiming kiss that left me breathless and with no alternative but to say yes is all I need.

The flash of jealous rage and hatred in Penelope's eyes when Garrett and I walked past her into the house was a little intimidating, I must admit. As a soccer player and former college athlete, I know a competitive woman when I see one. I've dealt with a lot of catty behavior out on the field and in the locker rooms and have managed to keep my head above the fray and not get into it with women who bring out their inner bitch.

But if looks could kill...*damn*, Penelope's eyes shot deadly daggers at me. Enough so that I will be watching my back and checking the doors every night to avoid getting stabbed.

"Does anyone want any coffee or water?" I politely offer as everyone files into the living room.

Corinne has already come in and given me a hug, stating how happy she is to finally meet me after the phone calls and Face-Time sessions I arranged between her and Caleb. Although I think she's a very devoted grandmother and a lovely person, it's clear there is definitely some friction happening between Garrett and his mother. The tension lines across Garrett's forehead are a clear indicator that he is not too happy with his mother at the moment.

Penelope chirps up. "I'd like sparkling water with a lime if you can manage."

It's an insulting dig of a request, but I oblige and respond with grace. "I think we might have some Perrier. Let me go check."

Turning to Corinne, I ask her if she'd like something, as well.

"Oh, thank you, my dear. Maybe some tea. My stomach is a bit off at the moment."

She glares at Garrett, who sits composed, but strung tighter than a bow, his lips in a flat line and a tick in his jaw demonstrating his brewing indignation, clearly ignoring his mother's remark.

Without looking at me, he waves me off when I ask him if he needs anything. As I walk back into the kitchen to locate the Perrier and brew the tea, I hear the stilted conversation between the three of them, Garrett's responses all clipped and abbreviated.

"How has Caleb been doing with his therapy?" Corinne asks, a slight hesitancy laced within her question.

"He's doing great. Thanks."

And then Penelope jumps in and I swear I think Garrett literally jumps down her throat.

"My baby's birthday is coming up soon."

His voice booms and quakes, shaking the room from its ferocity, extracting a squawk from his own mother.

"He is *not* your fucking baby, Penelope. He's my son and you gave up your rights to be his mother two years ago, in case you forgot. I'll gladly pull out the court documents you signed if you need a refresher on how easily you walked away from your *baby*."

I nearly drop the cup and saucer in my hand at this revelation. The last two days have been quite eye-opening as it relates to Garrett's life and Caleb's parental lineage. Up until last week, I'd only known Becca as Caleb's mother, and Garrett's wife, and knew she passed away in a car accident. But I had no idea of the back-story leading up to Caleb's birth or his first few years of life.

Holy baby Jesus in a manager. What a tragic story.

As I re-enter the living room, drinks in hand, both Corinne and Penelope are now in tears, small sniffles coming from Garrett's mother and Penelope's full-blown dramatical sobs filling the silence left between the three of them. What a circus.

I'm oddly at an impasse as to what to do with myself. Although Garrett specifically asked for my presence, to stay with him through this, I'm the obvious intruder in this very personal, very private family matter. I am not family. I'm not even at the level of girlfriend status.

I'm Caleb's nanny and care provider. Nothing more. And it's hella awkward.

"Garrett," I whisper, taking a place in the seat next to him, imploring him with my eyes in hopes he'll recognize exactly what I see. Realize that I'm out of place in this family dynamic. "I think I should..."

"Please stay, Brooklyn." With a pleading look from his anguished brown eyes, I comply with his request, folding my hands together in my lap and nervously pick at my nails, keeping my focus away from anyone else's censure.

Garrett's brittle voice breaks through the silence.

"Mother, I'll let you start out this conversation, seeing as you hatched this diabolical plan behind my back to take my son on a trip without my consent, and then encouraged this unwanted reunion with this woman."

He points an accusatory finger at Penelope, who dabs at her

tears in the corner of her eye with a tissue, looking up innocently with big blue eyes, like a Tweety Bird in a cage.

Either she's truly brokenhearted over losing her child and desperately wanting him back or she's giving us an Oscar-worthy performance, on par with Meryl Streep.

Corinne takes a sip of her tea before setting it down on her lap, a small frown pursed at her lips.

"Garrett, you know I worry about you and Caleb. Aside from Wyatt, you are my only family on this earth and I only want what's best for you all. You've all lost so much, and it pains me to know you're suffering."

"*Puh-lease*," he barks with grating hostility. "That's bullshit. This is not about me or your grandsons. This is about you and what you want and what you think *we* should want. We are fine, Mother. I have things under control and I don't need you meddling in my business or my personal life."

Corinne gasps, her hand flying over her heart as if it truly caused her physical pain.

"Garrett Allen Parker, I did not raise my sons to talk back to me like that. How dare you suggest I don't care about or love you or my family. You're all that matters to me. And children need their mothers. Wyatt has Addison and Caleb had Becca, but now he doesn't. I only want a woman in his life who will have his best interests at heart when I pass on and will be there for him when he needs a mother's touch."

I realize Corinne doesn't say this to intentionally insult me or diminish my role. She just doesn't understand the bond I've developed with Caleb over the last month and hasn't seen how I love and cherish her grandson.

The look in Garrett's eyes is close to murder. I've never seen him that close to losing his temper, except that night in the kitchen together.

"A mother does not abandon her child. She doesn't give him up and sever all ties in exchange for money, only to come back around when it's convenient for her. In fact, I should ask. Penelope, did you run out of the money I gave you? Is that why you're suddenly so interested in reclaiming your title as a mother? Because if so, that well dried up two years ago. There is no more. You don't deserve to know Caleb. You don't get to decide after all this time that you suddenly want to be part of his life."

He exhales loudly, the pain in his expression evident.

"Caleb's mother died. She's gone. No one will ever replace Becca in his life. She was the best woman and mother in the world, and he will never have someone like her again."

The words, although not directed at me or said out of cruelty, rip me to the core. I realize he's said them in anger, and they have nothing to do with me personally, but they hurt nonetheless. They've diminished my role with one fell swoop and cut me down to size.

Garrett doesn't see me as a qualifying substitute for motherly material. And he views me in exactly the role he hired me to be.

Just the nanny.

And nothing more.

21

GARRETT

It's late.

My head pounds from the tension headache that developed the minute I picked up my mother earlier this morning and grew as the conversation between Penelope, my mother and me exploded like a geyser from deep below and gushed over until there was nothing left. I am drained.

And somewhere in the midst of that circus of a conversation, I said something that rubbed Brooklyn wrong, but I don't know what it was. I only felt the shift in her mood throughout the remainder of the day, as she carefully removed herself from the discussion and kept her distance, leaving me to attend to my guests alone and locked herself away in her bedroom.

Penelope tried every possible thing she could think of to convince me that she's changed and to give her another chance. She said she was staying with a friend in Mesa for the next few weeks and she requested a few supervised visits with Caleb, which

I promptly denied because I don't have to grant her any such thing.

I made sure she left before Caleb woke up. I had enough of her drama for one day and didn't need her riling up my son.

In the end, my mother got her way, and I agreed to allow her to take Caleb to Disneyland, only for the sheer fact that Addison and Wyatt were already booked to fly out and meet them there and I didn't want to rain on their parade.

Needless to say, I let my mother have it, telling her in no uncertain terms that the next time she backed me in a corner like this I would not relent or give in. Fuck her and her manipulative tactics. I would block her ass from my life and Caleb's if she ever did something like this again.

After all the drama of the day's events, all I wanted to do was to find myself wrapped around Brooklyn so I could breathe in her feminine scent.

She's the balm to my soul and a light in my darkest corner.

My body still hums with arousal as I recall how incredible it felt being inside her warmth last night. It feels like it's been a year when in reality it's been less than twenty-four hours. My cock stirs just thinking about the haven her body provided me.

I'm helpless to resist going to her, as I open my bedroom door and pad down the hallway, past Caleb and my mother's guestrooms, who are both fast asleep, and around the corner to the guest wing where I find her door closed, a light shining beneath the crack at the floor.

I knock quietly three times. "Brooklyn. Can we talk?"

She opens the door, swinging it wide, inviting me in with the sweep of her arm.

Brooklyn is alarmingly beautiful, free of the make-up she wore earlier today and dressed only in her sleep shorts and tank. It dawns on me now what I didn't notice before.

"You looked really pretty today. Your hair was different. You were dressed up. I forgot to mention it, earlier, but I did notice.

You looked beautiful." I stop inside the doorway and wait for her to turn and face me.

When she does, I lift her chin with my thumb, so I can look in her eyes. "But then again, you look gorgeous like this, too. Naturally stunning. You take my breath away."

She turns away from me. "Garrett. Please don't say things like that to me. It's unfair."

"Why? They're true. I've been attracted to you from that day you barged in and took ownership of this household."

It's meant to be a joke, a funny quip but it falls flat.

"I'm your son's nanny. That's all."

Reaching for her wrists, I wrap my hands around her heated skin, holding her in place. Hoping she'll hear and see my sincerity and emotional conviction.

"Brooklyn, you are so much more than that to us. You must know that. Do you realize how much my son has improved since you've come into his life? He's able to do things he wasn't able to do before. Like using a utensil to eat by himself. His dexterity and motor skills are so much more refined now, more stable. I don't know what it is about you, Brooklyn, but you are the sunlight. You've brightened our lives. He adores you. And so do I."

As if biting into something sour, her mouth puckers with distaste and then she drops a bomb on me.

"I think it would be better if I leave."

The words don't seem to compute in my brain.

"What? No. Leave where? Why?"

My grip tightens until I realize I'm holding on too tight and I let go to drop my hand to my side. But I need to touch her. Know she's still here and in my corner. In Caleb's corner.

Her spine stiffens as I enfold her in my arms, clutching her to me. I'm a fucking grown man who has played against the world's toughest opponents in the game, but nothing is as imposing as the thought of Brooklyn leaving. Not when the game is going so well.

As a Coach, I keep what's working in my line-up. If a specific play works out on the court and gets points on the board, I continue to include it in the game strategy because that's how you win the game.

And we were winning this game up until this morning. Things were going in the right direction.

Until Brooklyn deviated from the winning strategy and gameplay.

"Brooklyn, please. Give us more time. In fact, my mom is going to be taking Caleb to Disneyland this coming week. Take the week off – paid, of course – to reconsider. Let me..."

I stop abruptly, uncertain as to where I was going with this. I still have my reservations about relationships holding me back, but if I want Brooklyn to feel valued, and not just as my son's nanny, then I need to step up and prove to her that I care about her. Not just in the professional role in our lives, but as a woman.

As a woman I care for deeply.

"Let you, what?" she prods.

I clear my throat, but my voice is still raspy and gritty with emotion.

"Brooklyn, will you let me take you out on a date?"

She's clearly caught off guard from my request, rearing back, her jaw dropping open until she snaps her mouth shut again, shaking her head.

"That's not a good idea. If I'm going to continue working for you, we should have separation. Not a romantic entanglement."

"I think it's a little too late for that, don't you?" I lift my eyebrows knowingly.

Her laugh fills me with some hope.

"Touché. But Garrett, how is this going to end?"

"What do you mean? You're an athlete. You understand how the game works. When you start gameplay, you don't question how it's going to end. You don't create room for doubt. You start the game with a mindset of winning. Not losing. You push hard and give 110%, but you don't ask yourself what happens if you fail. So, don't do that with us."

She lets out a resigning sigh but nods her head in agreement.

"You have a point," she whispers, a slight smile cracking at the edge of her mouth.

"Right?" I grin, cupping her cheeks in my hands and tipping her head back. "I thought that was a pretty damn good analogy I came up with on the spot. Now, are we in agreement? Will you go out with me and can I kiss you good night?"

I trace her cheekbones with my thumbs, and she lovingly obliges.

It's the first kiss in a game-changing play.

22

Every head seems to turn in our direction as we walk hand-in-hand into the restaurant. All the interest directed toward Coach Garrett Parker, Associate Head Coach of ASU men's basketball team and the mystery girl on his arm.

I knew this would be a bad idea, but he insisted. I refused on several occasions, suggesting we just stay in, but he wouldn't have any of it.

"I want to take you out on a real date. You deserve that, Brooklyn. And especially while Caleb's gone, and we have the whole house to ourselves."

"Exactly. We can just stay in and do whatever we want. I don't care about going out to fancy dinners or the movies. We can have pizza delivered and watch Netflix and chill."

"While that plan does have its merits – like eating naked in the living room - I still want to give you the whole experience. I promise, it will be great."

Corinne left with Caleb a little over a day ago and while Garrett and I haven't slept together again, he's been openly affectionate toward me. Kisses on the neck when I'm sitting on the chair reading, light touches as he passes me in the hallway, and even last night when we had a pretty hot and heavy make-out sesh on the couch as we watched a movie.

He's been the perfect gentleman, stating that he wanted to rewind and do things right. But in the meantime, he's gotten me so horny I haven't been sleeping very well. He's made it very clear that until I say yes to an official date, he wouldn't sleep in the same bed with me. I held out as long as I could, but the appeal of sleeping with him won out and I finally said yes to a date night.

As we wait for our table at the upscale restaurant, I notice a group of men in business suits talking at a table nearby, all of them staring at us with interest.

One of the men stands and waves us over. "Coach, come on over here."

Garrett glances down at me with a wary look. "Do you mind?"

I smile and shrug. "Of course not."

With the hand on the small of my back, he leads me over to the table where introductions are made.

"Hello, gentlemen. Good to see you all. Let me introduce you to Brooklyn Hayes. She's a grad student at the school."

I notice he steers clear of introducing me as his son's nanny.

The men rise to their feet, one by one, shaking my hand in greeting. Mike, Carl, William, and Lucas. The last one seems very familiar, but I can't quite place him. I think they're all faculty members at the university.

"Brooklyn, good to see you again. We actually met a few years back when you were interning for Professor Wilson. I'm in the art history department. I also happen to be this guy's friend."

Lucas thumps Garrett on the back with a large palm and it's then that I recall meeting him at an alumni dinner event where

Professor Wilson allowed me to tag along and gain exposure in the child psychology field by introducing me to a plethora of various people in the industry.

I shake his hand vigorously. "Of course, I remember now. Nice to see you again, Professor Mathiasson." He chuckles and throws a wave in my direction.

"Please. Call me Lucas. And how is my godson, by the way? I hear you're nannying for him this summer and doing a great job with it. That's not an easy task. That boy is rambunctious."

Caught off guard, I turn my head up to Garrett, who looks back with a slight hint of guilt as if he was just pinned with a crime.

"Lucas and I went to college together and we go way back. When I hired you, I mentioned it to Lucas here."

The three other men get back to their food and drinks, while Lucas remains to continue chatting.

"And whatever he tells you about his ball skills, is a bald-faced lie. He always thinks he was 'all that and more.' You know what they say, those who can't *do*, coach."

A grin splits wide across Lucas's mouth, expecting a retort from Garrett, who doesn't disappoint with his own lob back.

"Which is precisely why you became a *professor* and never turned pro."

"Oooh, burn." Lucas slaps his leg at the comeback and we all laugh at their friendly banter and juvenile behavior.

And then things turn a bit more serious as Lucas brings up the recent situation with Penelope and Corinne.

"Hey man, did things cool down after Penelope left?"

Garrett shakes his head, squeezing my hand reassuringly. Whether to bolster his confidence or mine is unknown.

"What a cluster that was. But I made it perfectly clear to Penelope that there was no way in hell I was ever going to reconsider my position."

Lucas crosses his arms and tips his chin introspectively. "You don't think she could try to contest the court decision, do you? Have it overturned and her parental rights reversed? Have you talked to your attorney yet?"

While he hadn't openly discussed it with me, I did overhear a small snippet of his conversation with his mom the other day about what rights Penelope could regain, considering the turn of events over Becca's death. He was naturally worried about anything that could alter Caleb's current living situation.

Garrett sighs. "Yeah, I need to call my lawyer sometime in the next week or so. I've just been so busy with the basketball program and just things." His voice trails off and he glances at me out of the corner of his eyes. I don't blush easily, but this particular comment has my face turning into a furnace.

"Well keep me posted. I'll let you two go, but let's catch up this weekend, okay? Just give me a call when you have a moment."

And then Lucas turns to me, offering me his hand to shake once more.

"I can't thank you enough for taking such good care of my godson. And if you can get this guy in line, you're a winner in my book."

"Thanks," I say, uncertain how to interpret his comment. "I'll do my best."

With a bro hug to Garrett, Lucas bids his goodbyes as the hostess comes over to direct us to our open table.

As Garrett pulls out the chair for me, he leans down to whisper in my ear. "I don't want you to think I went blabbing about us to Lucas, but I may have mentioned having a thing for you."

Did I mention furnace?

I gulp down some water to try and quench my thirst and cool me off some. This man seems to know the sexiest things to say to turn me on.

As we look over the menu, I notice a few gawkers staring at us but trying to go unnoticed. They're doing a horrible job of keeping their interest hidden.

"I think you've been spotted," I point out, nodding in the direction of the couple taking a photo of Coach Parker.

He just nods and holds his menu in front of his face, obscuring the onlookers' view.

"Does that happen a lot?" I'd never really gone out anywhere with Garrett and had no idea the type of hype and swirl it could create with the local basketball fans.

Dropping the folded menu on his plate in front of him, he reflects thoughtfully. "Not as much anymore, although I do get more and more ASU fans and alumni recognizing me now and stopping to ask for autographs as a coach, not just a former pro athlete. But there was a time I couldn't go anywhere without being recognized. Becca hated it."

His face falls. "Jesus. I'm such an idiot. Scratch that. Note to self. Do not bring up dead wife when on a date with a hot woman."

I take a sip of the wine that was delivered and wave my hand. "Garrett, I'm okay with you bringing her up in conversation. She was a huge part of your life and past. You can't just turn that part of you off. Just like you wouldn't stop talking about your college or pro ball careers. But my lord, can you please stop always bragging about your ball career?"

I give him a teasing wink and a roll of my eyes so he knows I'm only joking about that last part. Garrett laughs at my joke, reaching over the table to interlace his fingers with mine.

"Will you mind being seen in public with me like this?"

"Like what? Looking so hot in your dress suit?"

He waggles his brows suggestively. "You think I'm hot, huh?"

"Nah. My roommate was the one who thinks you look pretty handsome in your game day suit you wear on the sidelines."

He leans over the table, his lips teasing into a sexy smile.

"Just your roommate?"

I shrug nonchalantly. "I'll never tell."

"Maybe I'll have to get that suit out when we get home to see if it has any effect on you."

"Hmm, maybe you will."

23

Our first official date was everything I'd hoped it would be.

Brooklyn looked absolutely stunning in a sexy off-the-shoulder sundress that came to her knees and wedged sandals, showing off her athletically trim legs and smooth, sun-kissed shoulders.

The bodice hugged every curve and had my dick straining behind my zipper with the need to skim her bare skin with my tongue.

Brooklyn's dark blonde hair, normally pulled back in a pony or in a messy bun high atop her head, was left down and loose tonight, my fingers itching to wind through the strands and tug them in my fist. She doesn't try hard to look this beautiful.

"Did you enjoy yourself tonight?" I ask as the garage door closes and shrouds us in darkness, the only light coming from the small bulb above us.

She steps out of the red convertible sports car I drove tonight, hand clasped in mine as I help her to her feet and she places a gentle palm against my chest.

The moment our eyes meet, I know exactly where this night is heading. And I couldn't be happier. I've never shared my bed with another woman since moving to Phoenix. I've slept with other women, but they were when I was on the road and only one-night hookups.

Tonight, everything is different.

For me, everything has changed. I know I want this thing between Brooklyn and me to happen. It's the first time I've felt this way about a woman since meeting Becca. And even back then, it was different. This isn't a young or first love. It's a mature relationship where the stakes in the game are much, much higher.

Brooklyn's eyes turn silvery in the low light of the garage, hooded by her long lashes.

"I had the best time tonight." She licks her bottom lip and all I want to do is kiss her. Use that mouth to bring us both pleasure.

"I have an idea on a way to make the evening even better."

I quirk one eyebrow up. "Oh yeah? Does it require getting naked?"

She laughs, a smile breaking its way free with a sexy promise. "Well, maybe one of us."

"If it's you, I'm in." I can no longer stop my advances, her exposed skin at the base of her neck too tantalizing to resist.

I crowd into her, her back arching over the hood of the car, placing my lips on the sensitive spot at her throat. The vibration of her murmur I feel against my mouth as I nibble at her delectable taste. I allow my tongue to roam freely as she drops her head back against the hood.

Using the pad of my thumb, I stroke a line over her collar-bone, slowly mapping the expanse of skin that has been driving me nuts all night.

"You looked so sexy tonight. I was hard for you the second I saw you walk out in this tease of a dress."

Playfully I bite at the ruffle edging the top of her dress, pulling the material down with my teeth and a pinch of my fingers slowly...ever so slowly...to expose her perfectly round breast. She wears a simple underwire bra that I quickly unclasp, and her tits pop free.

When I plump the flesh of her breast in my hand, Brooklyn moans with closed eyes and I step into her body, wedging my thigh between her legs. The heat of her body mixes with mine and I know just how hot she'll be when our bodies converge.

"Can you feel this?" I ask through a husky filter.

My cock throbs at the juncture of her thighs, as I pant and rock against her, the friction creating sparks and flames.

"You do this to me, Brooklyn. You make me want you. I want nothing more than to be inside you again. But I can go slow. We don't have to do anything tonight if that's not what you want."

Brooklyn props herself up on her elbows, the movement lifting her head and also pushes her bare breasts toward me, as I swipe a wet path over the lush curves and valley of her chest.

"I don't need slow. I just want you, Garrett. Don't hold back."

She takes pity on me, dropping a hand between us and scoring her nails over my bulging length, increasing the level of pain in my balls, but sending pleasure rippling up my spine. I grit my teeth before I kiss her hard and deep, devouring her mouth in gratitude.

My tongue explores her mouth, lips sucking and licking her swollen lips, as she squirms against me, seeking friction against her sex. Lifting her in a swift movement, my hands cupping her firm ass, she clings to me with arms around my neck and legs wrapped at my waist.

Her teeth clamp down on my earlobe, the slick sound of her tongue tracing the shell of my ear. God, who knew the ear could be so erotic? The throbbing in my cock becomes almost unbearable, my balls are so full and hot with the need to spill myself inside her.

My hands seek the delicate flesh of her backside, fingers sliding over the smooth, round cheek and burrowing under the edge of her panties. I trace a teasing path over the wet center of her panties, wet with arousal, her gasp telling me she enjoys it.

"Lay back, sweetheart." As she lays out over the car, her legs spread wide, her dusty-rose nipples hard and pointing to the sky, I tremble with the need to taste her. To inhale her scent. To devour her skin.

I fling the dress skirt up over her knees, exposing her creamy thighs and giving me the perfect view of her sexy nude-colored panties. I dip my head and flick my tongue over her navel, then draw a wet line up the soft expanse of skin to her breast, taking a nipple between my teeth and sucking hard.

"Oh God, Garrett," she moans, arching her back. "Don't make me wait. I'm so wet for you. Take me now."

Jesus, this girl. This woman.

I watch in complete and utter awe as she slides her panties down her legs, kicking them off with a flick of her foot, and then slipping her own finger inside her pussy with a moan. I'm transfixed on what's happening, my eyes locked in on the action between her legs. She swirls her finger and bucks against her hand as I stare in a heated gaze.

"Fuck, you're so hot."

Her eyes peel open and she gives me a dirty little smirk. "I want to watch you, too. I heard you once before. That night outside your bedroom. It turned me on so much I had to touch myself."

I drop my head back, shutting my eyes at her sexy confession. Groaning at its implication.

"Like this?" I ask, ripping my slacks down and off my legs and palming my erection poking up through the waistband of my briefs.

Her breathy reply is my undoing. "Yes, just like that."

I can barely stand upright and consider for a moment picking her up and taking her inside to bed, but this is too hot seeing her across my car, finger fucking herself with a blissful smile across her parted lips. I want to fall to the floor in worship over this beautiful young woman who came into my life so unexpectedly and has turned my world on its head.

My mouth salivates with lust from her scent. I crave everything she has to offer – her wit, her intelligence, and her sex appeal. I yank at my own waistband, my cock springs free, as I begin to stroke hard and fast.

"Help me," she coaxes, reaching for my other hand not otherwise occupied by my dick.

"I want to make you come. Tell me what you need."

"I want you inside me." She demonstrates with the slide of her own finger through her slit.

I let my gaze wander down between her legs as she spreads her legs wider and my tongue lolls out of the corner of my mouth. All I see are pretty pink folds, glistening wet with her arousal.

With my cock in my hand, I lean over her body, the material of her dress rucked up around her middle, and I lick at her lips before kissing her deeply. Our kiss grows in intensity, savoring the sounds and flavors and tastes of one another, as I slide the head of my dick through her folds, grinding my pelvis over hers, creating erotic tension with our bodies.

"Brooklyn we should be more careful this time," I try to say with conviction, knowing we should probably use a condom this time, even though being bare inside her was so incredibly intense and fantastic.

"If you feel more comfortable with that, yes. But I'm okay if you're okay. I'm on birth control and safe."

The heat of her pussy beckons me, calls me in like a siren to a lost and weary traveler.

Brooklyn lays out before me now, gloriously ready, offering me her body and trusting me to do what's right.

I'm fascinated by Brooklyn's sensuality and the way she

responds without bashfulness or inhibition. With Brooklyn, she seems very open to it all. No fear or aversion to what might seem outside the boundaries.

"Oh, Christ," I sputter, my hard cock slicked from her heat, as I slide through her folds once again before positioning my cock at her entrance. And then I'm sliding into her heat and nearly black out from the pleasure.

Brooklyn tenses for a moment and I halt mid-thrust. "You okay?"

"*Mmm*, yes."

I'm lost in the sensation and the way her eyes narrow in lustful desire as I enter her.

With one hand on the car to hold me up, I circle her thigh with the other, locking her leg around my back and giving me leverage to fuck. I suck a nipple in my mouth, and on an upstroke of my cock, Brooklyn gasps loudly, wiggling her hips, thighs quaking. She reaches around and grabs my ass, running her hand up the curve of my glutes and digs in hard with her nails, positioning me where she needs it more.

"Yes, right there. Right th*e*...." And then she's moaning out what I presume to be a powerful orgasm, the sensations washing over her beautiful face, mouth lax and body rigid until all the tension leaves and her body succumbs to post-coital relaxation.

I give her a crooked sexy smile.

"You're looking pretty satisfied there, sweetheart."

She circles her hips, digs in her heels and presses them into my backside to push me deeper within her body.

Fuck, that feels good.

"I am pretty satisfied. Now it's your turn."

I bury my laugh in the crook of her neck. "As you wish."

24

Brooklyn

I wake from the most sensual dream I've ever had.

Rolling to my side, I realize it wasn't a dream after all, but happens to be my current reality and all the explicit images of what we did together last night flash through my thoughts, signaling the now tell-tale sign of desire and the pull low in my belly at how perfect it was with Garrett.

Our connection was frenetic, sparking potent and hot currents of electricity even now, without so much as a touch. In fact, my skin has erupted into feverish shivers where his mouth and hands explored me last night. My inner muscles clenching in recollection of the powerful orgasm he gave me. And one that I want again.

Garrett had never been more desirable to me as he was then, hair disheveled over his forehead, lips pursed firmly together, and head tipped back. Actually, no, I take that back. He's a different level of desirable when he's with his son when the love he has for Caleb spills over in his smile and soft brown gaze.

I can't help but think how lucky I am to have found someone like Garrett. A man so powerful, and sexy, who knew how to take care of me sexually, but doesn't ever walk over me outside the bedroom. He's exactly the man I want but haven't found before now.

As I lay in bed, curled up next to him as I watch Garrett sleep, my eyes scan across the smooth, broad expanse of his back, his body sprawled out on his stomach, taking up the majority of the bed, as I yearn to run my fingertips over his skin. With his face obscured by the pillow, head turned in the other direction, his soft snores erupt from his throat, like the sound of a far-off train, as he sleeps quietly, without a care in the world.

I don't know what his expectations are of me now that we've become intimate, but I do know I have some fears. Having sex with Garrett and sleeping with him last night isn't the scary part. What terrifies me, and has been ingrained in my head since childhood, is how this type of intimacy with a man could mean losing myself and my independence. I pride myself on being a strong woman who has worked hard for myself and others, but who doesn't lose sight of who I am and what I want. I won't allow anyone else to dictate what I do or how I get there.

Since the age of puberty when I became interested in the opposite sex, my very feminist mother continually reminded me (sometimes daily) that as a woman, I didn't ever *need* a man. It was okay and my prerogative to want one, to be attracted to and committed to one, and even to love a man. But I should never be dependent on them to make me feel secure or relevant.

It's been my guiding principle for as long as I can remember, and one that at times has really tripped me up when I became involved with a guy. It's the reason I've never been in a long-term relationship for fear of losing myself to a man. And to be fair, most of the men I've been with weren't looking for a relationship, either.

With Garrett, I feel like I'm on equal ground. Especially when it comes to working with his son. There have been no displays of machoism or male egotism. He's regarded me with respect when I've offered my suggestions and ideas and never made me feel inferior. Although, dammit, we still argue daily about the companion dog. He keeps dragging his feet over it, even though I site all the positive reasons on record for owning a therapy and companion dog.

Sweeping my feet out from underneath the sheet, I root around on the floor for something to wear. Finding Garrett's discarded shirt, I slip it over my head and tiptoe out into the kitchen, shutting the door quietly behind me.

Practically starving after last night's physical workout, I pull out a pan and the eggs from the fridge, as my mother's voice unconsciously filters through my head, her doubts she shared with me about this nanny job slipping in like a knife stabbing at my self-confidence.

"Darling, this role is such a waste of your intelligence and education," she'd said over the phone the day I accepted Garrett's offer. "You're a glorified babysitter and it could pigeonhole you into being this domestic house servant."

I grew irritated with her insulting description of my new job. "Mother, didn't you employ the services of nannies and daycare help when Brayden and I were children? You relied on them to make sure we were well-cared for and looked after while you worked with your patients nine-to-five every day. Are you that much of an elitist to believe that nannies are inferior to us?"

I knew my mom meant well and was only hoping I'd gain employment in a more clinical setting so I could learn more about therapy and child psychology, but her assumptions about this profession were inherently wrong and misguided, ultimately frustrating me.

But since then, she's changed her tune somewhat, as I've shared with her the things I've been able to accomplish through my daily one-on-one work with Caleb. His progress has been nothing short of amazing, even small things like his ablilty to pronounce simple words like *yes, no* and *fine*, allowing him a broader range of communication skills.

I'm so involved in my own thoughts that I don't hear Garrett come into the kitchen until the heel of his hand is between my legs, running a line up the inside of my thigh and skirting underneath the hem of the T-shirt. I love this part of a sexual relationship where this type of intimacy exists.

"Good morning, sweetheart." His words are as raspy as the scruff on his jaw that scrapes abrasively over the base of my neck.

The contact induces goosebumps over my flesh, and I shiver from the scent of his minty breath and spicy maleness filling the air around me. His hard erection nudges me from behind and I instinctively push into it, the rush of excitement radiating through every cell in my body.

"Morning," I respond, turning my head to the side so I can kiss him as I slide my hand down between us and laugh when I encounter nothing but his warm, smooth skin. "Are you naked?"

On an upstroke, I squeeze the crown of his cock as he pushes into my fist with a groan.

"Yes, I am. *My* kitchen, *my* rules. And yes, that means I'm naked. Which is exactly how I want you."

Opening my mouth wider, he fills me with his tongue, sweeping inside and thoroughly ravaging me with his demanding kiss.

When he pulls away, he clicks off the burner and tugs me to him with an arm wrapped securely around my waist, sliding it underneath the material. The hair on his arm tickles my tummy and I squirm into him.

"Do you know how many mornings I've walked into this very kitchen and had to fight myself not to walk right back out for fear that you'd notice how hard I was for you?" He emphasizes this with a thrust of his bulge into my crease.

"Hmm. No I don't. Maybe you should show me how hard you are for me, Coach."

A deep, ferocious growl fills the kitchen as he spins me around, lifting me off my feet and onto the granite counter. I giggle, admiring the powerful strength he uses to hoist me up without breaking a sweat.

"Oh, I'll show you all right. I'll demonstrate all the dirty, filthy things I want to do with you. You may just want to recant your request."

And then I'm on my back, staring up at that beautiful brass pot holder rack, as he places his mouth between my legs and begins to prove just how wickedly sexy his thoughts really are.

25

GARRETT

I was hard the minute I woke up and was on a mission to find her and bring her back to bed. But finding her in the kitchen wearing only my wrinkled shirt turned me savage to have her again.

My gaze fixes on her pink and wet opening, as I position my hands at the juncture of her thighs, plying her folds with my fingers, opening her up to find her wet and eager for me. Using the flat of my tongue, I lick up her slit, swirling her swollen flesh, tasting her sweet arousal and salty flavor in the back of my throat.

The sound of her intake of breath as I brush my bearded lips through her folds has my hips punching forward, seeking friction from something. *Anything.* It's excruciating to go slow, but I know that teasing her in this manner will get her there faster than diving right in.

Her eyelids flutter closed as I make a pass and swipe up her slit, circling my tongue over her sensitive nub. With a low growl of approval, I latch on to her clit and suck gently.

"Please...more."

As the lady requests, I give her more. I continue to sweep my tongue and increase the intensity of my suction, until I slide a finger inside, curve it upwards and find her spot.

"There..." she cries out, as I feel the walls of her pussy spasm against my fingers.

I don't wait another second. I slide her to the counter's edge, spin her around on her stomach and lift her hips so her firm ass is tilted up.

"This ass, sweetheart. It makes me want to do crazy things," I mutter into her ear, smoothing a palm over the taut skin of her butt, before taking my aching cock in hand and slamming inside with a long groan.

The momentum pushes her forward, as I pull her shoulders back in my grip, sending a gasp flying from her mouth.

"Oh," she moans, spreading her hands wide out in front of her, cheek flat on the countertop as I take control of our pleasure.

"That's right, Brooklyn. Take it all. Everything. I. Have. To. Give." I punch my hips forward, thrusting to mark each word I growl.

There's so much I want to give Brooklyn that goes so much farther than just sex. But right now, I'm only capable of loving her in this way. This burning physical promise of ecstasy and satisfaction.

Curling my hand around the front of her body, I zero in on her clit, rocking my rigid shaft at an angle that has me seeing stars.

I nearly come unglued when she moves her hand over mine, her fingers tangling together as we stroke her swollen flesh in unison.

She's wet and soft as satin. My restraint is limited, as the sense of urgency overtakes me, urging me closer to that precipice, my balls demanding release.

"Brooklyn, I'm close. Should I pull out?"

Her breath hitches as my dick hits a spot deep inside her walls. She lifts her head, body straightening, shifting back against my naked chest. A shake of her head as she twists her neck to kiss me open-mouthed has me nearly coming.

"Yes."

Being inside Brooklyn's pussy like this with no barrier is extremely dangerous and negligent on my part. While I trust her implicitly about being protected and safe, I'm more than a little skeptical after what I experienced with Penelope. Having an unwanted pregnancy flipped my world upside down and created a distrust that I can't easily change.

This situation with Brooklyn is completely different. I do trust her. I do care about her. I mean, for fuck's sake, she lives in my home and is sleeping in my bed. Should I worry about whether she's telling me the truth?

Slipping my other hand around her front, I squeeze her firm breast, plumping the flesh as she arches into my hand.

The moment I pinch her nipple, she goes off, trembling and quaking with mini spasms, her head dropping to bob languidly at her neck.

My own release is imminent, balls tightening, hips snapping erratically until I feel the start of my orgasm climbing, climbing, climbing up my legs, my thighs tensing and spine tingling.

My breath is labored and groans growing more and more desperate until finally, I tip my head back, pulling out from her tight heat and begin shooting hotly over her back and my stomach.

I'm absolutely spent, my arms looped around her front, holding her to me as our breaths slowly return to normal.

Reaching forward over her head, I grab the paper towel roll, tearing off a sheet and reaching between us to wipe up the sticky mess left behind over both of us.

"It's cool, I've got this. I'll just go take a shower."

"Mmm. That sounds good. Then how about we get back in bed? I think we should take advantage of the quiet while it lasts and snooze a little longer this morning."

Brooklyn turns with a mocking smile fixed across her red, swollen lips.

"Tired, are we, old man?" she snickers.

And as I chase her back down the hall, all I can think about is how fast I've fallen for this remarkable woman.

Damn. I've fallen hard.

26

BROOKLYN

Garrett and I spend the next three days in domesticated bliss.

We hiked up Camelback Mountain yesterday morning and then drove out to the San Tan Flat where we enjoyed dinner under the stars and even danced to a live band. For a tall white guy, Garrett brought out the moves and impressed me with his dance skills. Me, not so much. But I had fun because he made it fun.

The beauty of our alone time together was getting to know him on a deeper level. And honestly, I'd been dying to know the history between him and Penelope, and where Becca, Caleb and his change in career fit into the picture.

Over a margarita that was in a glass bigger than my head, I finally got up the nerve to ask him about his past.

"Obviously, I now know that Becca wasn't Caleb's birth mother, and I know a little about Penelope, but what exactly happened? Care to share the background on that story?"

The look that flashes across his face is riddled with guilt, sorrow and something else. Something enigmatic and bordering on tempestuous. But I patiently wait as he takes a long pull of his beer, staring off into the crowd around us.

"I was young and stupid."

I cover his knee with my hand, as we sit side-by-side in a booth facing the dance floor.

"We've all done dumb things, Garrett."

He huffs. "Not one that nearly ruins your life, your relationship or your career."

A pang of sorrow hits me square in the chest hearing the regret laced within his words.

"But look where it brought you? You have an amazing new career as a coach for one of the NCAA's best teams in the league and a wonderful son who you adore. And you were married to a wonderful woman."

I never knew Becca, but from everything he's told me about her, she was pretty damn great. She seemed to hold things together for him and stood by him during his darkest times.

"And don't forget the dead wife and gold-digging hoops honey who traded her son for cash."

I gasp on an inhale of my drink and choke out a cough. The bitterness in his words leave me speechless, so I say nothing, dabbing at my mouth with a napkin.

A few moments pass and he remains steely quiet.

"Garrett, I'm sorry. I know you suffered such a loss and it must have been horrible. And I didn't realize that Penelope..."

He heaves a sigh. "Was a fucking mistake. A one-night stand that I had on a road trip during my rookie year, right after Becca had broken up with me."

"Oh, wow. I didn't realize. I thought you were together at the time."

His look of disgust has me shrinking in my seat. "What, so all this time you thought I cheated on Becca? Thanks for that vote of confidence."

I swallow the lump in my throat because he's kind of right. Not knowing the entire sordid story, and only having partial facts, I did make an assumption that he stepped out on Becca when he got Penelope pregnant.

"You're right, I didn't have all the facts and made an assumption about how you ended up having a child with someone that wasn't your wife."

"Fuck," he curses, downing the rest of his beer and signaling the waitress for another one. "So, you've thought the worst of me this whole time, just like the media."

I shake my head. "No, that's not it at all. I just didn't know the circumstances surrounding Caleb's birth and the timing. Garrett, I've never thought poorly of you. I think you're an amazing man, coach, and father."

He stares down at the empty beer bottle, picking at the label while he waits for another.

"The media was fucking cruel and it was a shitshow for over a year. They created such sensational tabloid fodder. And of course, Penelope being Penelope, loved all the media attention and the limelight. I had just finally convinced Becca to take me back and marry me about a month before Penelope announced she was pregnant."

"Oh. How did Becca react?"

Garrett dips his head, hiding his eyes from my curious gaze. "Becca was unbelievably understanding. Which made it even worse because I knew how much it hurt her. My actions nearly destroyed us. It was such a slap in the face considering it was the reason she'd originally broken up with me."

I tilt my head to the side. "What do you mean?"

"Becca and I had been together for three years prior to that. I was faithful and monogamous always. But I was out on the road, traveling, becoming a rookie sensation, well, that drew attention from fans and the media. It attracted a lot of women trying to get a piece of me. Becca wasn't the jealous type. In fact, she was extremely mature about the whole thing. But during a home-stretch in Chicago, she came up for the weekend to visit and broke up with me. Told me she loved me, but she didn't want to live that lifestyle. And she wanted me to be free, in essence, to fuck around if I wanted to."

Garrett shakes his head. "She basically said, 'I don't want to stand in your way and have you live with regret. Go have fun.'"

I remain relatively silent, my hands in my lap, as our waitress returned, asking me if I want another drink, which I decline. Garrett hands over the empty bottle and takes a sip of the new one.

"The irony of it all," he chuckles darkly. "Looking back on it now, I wonder how I could've been so stupid. I was a fucking selfish asshole to let her go like that."

I scoot in closer so our hips and legs touch, and cup the side of his face, turning him to look at me.

"Garrett, you did what any twenty-four-year old rookie probably would've done. I'm sure she didn't blame you. It's better that way than to cheat on your girlfriend or wife."

"I never would've cheated," he says with conviction.

My hands still have their hold on his jaw, and I nod my head. "I know you. I know you wouldn't. You loved her."

I'll admit, I wanted to hear this story, but it doesn't make it easy to hear. I wanted to know about Garrett's life before I came into the picture. But it does hurt a little to learn about your lover's former wife and the depth of his love for this woman.

"I loved her, yes. But I ruined her life. I ruined everything."

"Garrett, life happens. You did the best you could under the circumstances. You can't blame yourself."

"Everything from that moment on was my fault. It was a chain reaction and took several years, but the night I slept with Penelope, it changed everything." He stands from the table then, grabbing the bill the waitress just left for us and looks down at me expectantly.

I feel awful now for starting this conversation. We were having such a great time together, dancing and drinking. And being that it is our last night before Caleb came back home, I'd hoped we'd spend the night together in bed, making slow love the entire night through.

Instead, when we get home, Garrett says he had some things to do to get ready for his team's basketball tournament the following week.

So, I lay in my own bedroom, wide awake for hours, the enormity of Garrett's situation crushing my heart and inducing a gut-wrenching pain over his loss.

27

I left on Tuesday for a road trip with my team at a tournament in southern California, leaving Brooklyn and Caleb back home to fend for themselves.

Brooklyn has been taking care of things in my absence for a month and I have no discomfort leaving my son in her care while I'm gone. But I miss being home with them both. My mother went off to Sedona on Monday, saying she had a wonderful time at Disneyland with Caleb, Addison, and Wyatt, but forgot how tiring it is to wait in such long ride lines with two young boys in the hot sun.

The timing of this summer tournament really sucks because I wanted to spend more time at home with Caleb. I missed his happiness, his laugh infectious, and I really needed his mood-lifting hugs after the heavy conversation I'd had with Brooklyn the other night.

It was rare for me to speak about the period of time before Caleb with anyone. Only in my appointments with my grief counselor did I ever share those feelings. When Brooklyn first asked me, I wasn't sure what I'd say. I know she's not like Penelope and wouldn't sell me out to the world, but there was a moment where I felt on guard and reluctant to share the truth.

But then I realized it was Brooklyn. She's proven her unyielding loyalty from the moment we met, not only with Caleb but with me, as well. So I opened up, sharing my most personal stories with her. And while part of it was liberating, it also reopened old wounds.

Reminding me of what I lost when Becca died.

"How's everything going, Coach?"

I look up from where I sit on the team bus to see Lance towering over me in the aisle, all six-foot-four of his lumbering frame taking up the entire space between the seats.

"Pretty good, bro."

There's a pile of papers on the seat next to me and I shuffle them together, picking them up to offer him a place to sit down. "Have a seat."

Before he sits down, he scolds two of the players sitting in the back of the bus.

"Yo, Donnell and Shane. Knock it the fuck off with that shit, otherwise, I'll have you scrubbing the bus floors tonight."

I quirk an eyebrow, peering over my shoulder to get a glimpse at the boys, who were shooting spitballs at one of the boys in the seats in front of them.

Boys.

I chuckle, turning back around as Lance sits down and I give him a side-eyed glance. "Look at you doling out the punishments like a hard-ass assistant coach."

He laughs boisterously. "Right? Who'd have thought I'd have it in me? Up 'til a few years ago, I was just like them. Getting in trouble all the damn time. Not caring about the consequences. It's a wonder I'm here today."

Nodding my head in agreement, I make some notes in my

iPad about some plays I want us to practice before our first tournament game.

"You're a great player, Lance, and have a good coaching career ahead of you. The boys really respect the way you give them advice on and off the court. You're doing great, bro."

I clap him on the shoulder because I am proud of how far he's come. It was a pretty big gamble hiring him for this gig, based on his downward spiral less than a year ago. Lance was dealing with some pretty deep emotional shit that affected his life, turning to drugs as a coping mechanism. Thankfully, he found a way through all that and dealt with it before it killed him.

"Thanks, Coach. I owe a lot of it to you. You're the only one who saw my potential and gave me a chance."

I give him a wave of my hand to dismiss his acknowledgment. "I offered you the chance, but it was you who did something with it. Speaking of which, I want to give O'Connell a chance to start at center. What do you think? I know you've been working a lot of one-on-one time with him these past few weeks. You want to give him a chance?"

Lance scrubs a hand over his chin thoughtfully. "Yeah, man. The kid has the power and speed but has really lacked aggressiveness. He guards and blocks like he's scared of the ball. But I found out while working with him that someone got in his head this past season, calling him names and it really messed with his mojo. But I think we conquered those fears. I'd like to see him start."

"Perfect. I'll add him to the starting line-up for tomorrow's game. Nice work with him."

"Thanks. Hey, I've been meaning to ask you how things are going with Caleb. Is Brooklyn working out for you?"

My heart skips a beat at the mention of her name. I've been doing my best to avoid thinking about her on this trip, but she's constantly there. I miss her in a way that I haven't missed anyone in a really long time.

I know this time away will be good for us, good for me, and I feel like shit for the way I left things the night of our talk, but I need that distance right now to figure out my headspace.

I'm not sure what I want with Brooklyn. It scares the shit out of me to know I've fallen for her so deeply.

I rely on her like no other in this world and I care about her more than I can admit. But after dredging up all those old memories and feelings the other night, it made me realize that I don't have anything to give her right now. I can give her sex, but my heart is still shaded too dark from all the trauma I went through. I'm just not in a place to be able to be in a relationship.

Not now, and maybe not ever.

"Things are good. She's doing great with Caleb. She's connected with him so well and has taught him so much. It's amazing to see how much Caleb has learned just from Brooklyn's tutoring this summer."

Lance grins. "I told you, man. I knew she'd be great for you guys. And you, too."

He winks and my hands twitch as I stare blankly at him.

Shaking his head and with a roll of his eyes, he deadpans, "Denial ain't just a river in Africa, Coach. I see it written all over your face."

"I have no idea what the fuck you're talking about. Nothing is written across my face except a desire to win this tournament." I draw a circle with my finger in front of my face.

He snorts. "For realz, Coach. I think you got it bad."

"Fuck you, Britton. Why don't you go toss some shit around with the boys back there? Have a little come to Jesus talk with them or something. Quit acting like you're a love-guru or Dr. Phil."

Lance stands from his seat and laughs. "Sure thing, Coach. Sure thing. But I'm on to you. You ain't fooling nobody."

Maybe not. Or maybe I'm only fooling myself.

BROOKLYN

"Okay, Caleb. Let's practice this again so when your daddy comes home, you can surprise him. He's going to be so proud of you."

I squeeze his shoulders in a side hug and hand him the iPad. Over the last three days, while Garrett has been out of town, I've been working with Caleb on using his iPad speech app, teaching him how to create sentences with the images on the app. He's been talking up a storm and it thrills me to know he's able to communicate so much more clearly now without having to rely on his own voice.

Caleb grins wide, letting out a little screech of excitement too. Then he points to the pictures on the app, spelling out his greeting for when Garrett comes through the door. I wanted to keep this a surprise until he got home, even though Garrett's been FaceTiming with us while he's been gone.

"Good job, buddy!" I give him an encouraging kiss on top of his head. I want everything to be absolutely perfect when Garrett gets home today, hoping that whatever slump he's been in emotionally will lift and we can continue working through this together.

He's been all too professional toward me when we've video chatted this week, whether that's for the sake of Caleb or he's trying to put distance between us, I'm not sure. When I mentioned it to Peyton, she suggested that it's *"just a guy thing"* and nothing to be concerned about.

But I'm not so sure. He's gone through a bevy of trauma in his life and the last thing he needs is to fall into a relationship with his nanny. So I've decided to just play it cool and focus on the one thing that truly matters, and that's Caleb.

And honestly, I'm not sure I am even ready for a relationship with Garrett. We fit together really well. I can see myself with him long-term because I understand who he is, what he loves and what he goes through on a daily basis with Caleb.

Yet, I have my own goals and dreams that don't include being his nanny forever. Once I leave and go back to grad school, what does that mean for our relationship? I'm not going to put my educational plans on hold for him.

Don't get me wrong. I've been enormously happy living with Garrett and Caleb this summer, and the icing on the cake is the personal feelings that have developed for Garrett.

But professionally, I want so much more. I don't plan on dropping any of those goals to remain a full-time nanny and live-in lover. In fact, my schedule for the fall semester just arrived in the mail this week. I'd dropped off Caleb at his occupational therapy appointment on Wednesday and then swung over to the apartment to have a quick coffee with Peyton.

"Are you excited about your last year of school?" I'd asked Peyton, who has one remaining year to finish her degree. I flopped down on the couch barefooted after filling my coffee cup with creamer to water down the extremely strong brew she always makes.

"Yes, although it's giving me pangs of anxiety. I have such a tough load this year. I really fucked myself over last year by taking so few courses. And now I have to add on my internship, to boot."

"You didn't really have a choice. You had to work and be there for your mother."

Peyton's mom went through a harrowing ordeal with her ex-husband, being sent to the hospital having been beaten nearly to an inch of her life. Peyton was by her side the entire time, taking a family leave of absence from school, but continuing to work to help pay her mom's medical bills and therapy costs after the event.

And it certainly didn't help her own health condition one bit. She admitted to struggling with her bulimia during that period of time and it broke my heart to know she will have to deal with that for the rest of her life.

"I know. It just really threw me for a loop and I still feel off balanced somehow, you know?"

Edging over to sit next to her, I placed my hand over her knee, patting it in a show of support.

"I totally get that. Who wouldn't? I feel off-balanced a little right now, too."

I shared my concerns about how Garrett was acting toward me this week, revealing all the naughty parts of our intimate relationship as she held her hand over her gaping mouth.

"See!" She pointed at me with a coffee cup in hand, index finger out. "I knew that panty and bra set would do the trick. What man could resist that hotness? Well, aside from Kyler, that is."

We laughed and had another cup of coffee before I had to leave to pick up Caleb, who was happy to see me, wrapping his tiny arms around my neck in a big hug.

And now, as we wait in the family room for Garrett, butterflies and nerves swarm my stomach, flitting around as if trying to escape. I've missed Garrett so much, but am scared to admit it to him, especially feeling like he's a bit uncertain of where things stand between us.

I suck in my breath, encouraging Caleb to get ready to surprise his Daddy, as Garrett appears from around the corner, dropping his bags on the floor, looking haggard and disheveled, but still utterly handsome.

The royal blue tie hangs loosely around his neck, his crisp white dress shirt unbuttoned at the top, revealing the sexy wisps of hair between his pecs. The gray suit jacket hangs over his forearm, which is exposed to the elbows under the rolled-up sleeves.

All my nerves take flight and I'm left staring at the man I think I've fallen in love with.

I lean down to whisper in Caleb's ear. "Are you ready? Go ahead."

The sweetest, toothless grin I've ever seen erupts across his face, as he turns to look up at me, nodding with eagerness.

Garrett stops, the creased frown at his lips unfolding into a beautiful smile when his eyes land on his son.

"Hey, buddy." He takes a few steps forward but I hold out my hand in the universal form of '*stop*.'

Garrett stops abruptly, a crinkle forming between his brows, but takes a started step back the minute he hears the robotic, Siri- voice from Caleb's iPad.

"*Hi, Daddy! I'm glad you're home. I missed you so much.*"

Garrett curses softly, blinks twice, stares at Caleb and then slowly, methodically, his gaze moves to mine.

No matter what happens between Garrett and me from here on out, nothing compares to this moment. The way he stares at me in wonder, and I feel the emotion welling in my eyes. Because the gratefulness and love that emanates from his expressive eyes at this moment is everything I'll ever need until my dying day.

In two large strides, he sweeps down to pick up his son, cradling him in his arms tightly, his discarded jacket landing on the floor next to my feet.

"Caleb, I've missed you so much, too. I can't believe you just spoke to me," he rumbles with unbridled emotion. I notice the tears welling in his eyes, but he blinks them away, holding Caleb at his chest so he can look him in the eyes. "You are the smartest boy in the world and I'm so proud of you for learning how to speak."

Caleb coos and babbles then holds his arm out to me. At first, I think he wants the iPad to converse some more with his dad, so I pick it up from my lap to hand it to him, but he shakes his head.

I cock my head with a frown. "What do you need, buddy?"

He squirms in his father's arms and reaches out both hands, opening and closing his fists at me.

"You."

I slowly rise to my feet with trembling legs and step forward. I'm gifted with the scent of baby soft skin of a boy and the masculine, spice of a man.

Caleb flings his arms wide, tugging me into him as Garrett embraces me in his arm, as well.

"That was incredible, Brooklyn. Thank you," Garrett whispers in my ear, kissing my temple, as I smile through my tears.

We hug for a few moments until Caleb gets restless and wants down. Garrett bends down and places him on his butt on the floor, as we watch his quick scoot over to his trucks and toys in the corner, leaving Garrett standing at my side.

"Brooklyn, look at me."

He turns to stare down at me, cupping my jaw tenderly in his warm, powerful hands and an ache forms in the center of my chest. Suddenly the distance that grew between us over the last few days disappears and ceases to exist.

"You gave me something today that I will cherish forever. I love you, sweetheart. I fucking love you so much."

29

GARRETT

We made slow, passionate love that night, taking our time to get reacquainted with each other's bodies and needs. Goddamn, I missed this girl with a ferocity that I didn't even know existed until I left and came back.

Over the next several weeks, things seemed to fall in place for us. The summer basketball camp ended, and I was back at the university reviewing the lists of our incoming freshman and meeting daily with our coaching staff, including my boss, Head Coach Welby. Preparing for a new season and a new team is always an exciting time, but also takes me away from home more hours than I spent away during the summer.

Thankfully, I know Brooklyn is at home, taking good care of my son. And when I come home in the evenings, she takes care of me, as well. It's a win-win situation.

In fact, with only a very limited amount of guidance and help from me, Brooklyn planned the entire birthday party for Caleb this past weekend. His fifth birthday was August second, and

Brooklyn made sure it was a well-attended, kid and family-friendly event. Lots of balloons, cake, train and car decorations, and a Spiderman impersonator that gave each kid a Spidey-bracelet that would shoot out silly string. My mother had even flown down again for the weekend, but I specifically stated that Penelope was not invited and if she showed up at my mother's request, both would be booted out.

Thankfully, it was only my mother who arrived, with gifts galore. Caleb was the happiest little boy ever and by the time Brooklyn and I landed in bed last night, we were exhausted but thrilled it all went so well.

"If I haven't said so already, you're incredible." I nuzzle her neck with my lips as I rub her shoulders from behind her. "Everything was perfect today."

She turns her head to look over her shoulder, smiling and kissing my knuckles. "You're welcome. I had so much fun. I've never planned a five-year-old boy's birthday party before. It was a new experience, for sure."

Too tired to start anything I might not be able to finish, I continue to massage her muscles as her body sinks into the mattress, her moans of pleasure sending mix signals to my interested cock.

"I really like your friends."

"Who? Peyton and Kyler? Yeah, they're pretty great. I don't know Kyler very well since he just moved in this summer, but he's a great guy. Talented artist, that's for sure."

My fingers gentle their strokes as I feather them over the sweet curves of her backside, humming as I do.

"Looks like he and Lucas seemed to strike up a pretty passionate conversation. I saw them speaking intently over near the pool shed earlier. It's great Luc had someone here who he could talk art history with. Lord knows I'm not that person."

I chuckle, but get no response from Brooklyn, as I angle my neck to see if she's still awake. Sure enough, she's fast asleep. My lips caress her neck with a soft kiss as I say goodnight and turn out the lights, a feeling of contentment washing over me like a wave in the ocean.

───────

We woke refreshed this morning after a good night's sleep and made quick work of getting each other off in the joint shower we shared. Now as I sit in my office reviewing some recruiting reports that just landed on my desk, the image of Brooklyn down on her knees in the shower, water sluicing over her wet hair as she gazed up while she sucked me off, has my dick thickening behind my zipper.

I glance over at my desk clock, wondering if I have time to run home for a quickie during Caleb's afternoon nap time. Adjusting my dick in my pants, I'm just about to grab my keys to leave when our team admin, Chey, knocks on the door.

"Coach Parker?" she asks, peeking through the opened doorframe.

"Yes, what's up, Chey?"

She shuffles her feet together, clicking her heels like she's Dorothy in *The Wizard of Oz*.

"There's someone here to see you." She gives a side-eye glance down the hallway, as if to ensure she wasn't followed, and then frowns. "A Miss Penelope Slattery."

Everything in me deflates, including my semi that was hoping to get taken care of over lunch. My distaste must be obvious as Chey pipes in intuitively.

"I can tell her you're in a meeting or busy at the moment if you'd like." And then, as if considering whether she should say anything or not, she adds sheepishly, "She wasn't very nice to me, so I'd be happy to show her the door."

I choke out a laugh because I'd love to do just that. But I know it's my fault that Penelope is here because I've been ignoring her calls since she left town. She's left me several messages requesting that I call her back and asking to set up a time for her to see Caleb. She'd specifically asked if she could visit over his birthday.

With how well Caleb has been improving over the summer, I'm not interested in upsetting the apple cart. My boy is becoming more and more independent, finding his voice through his speech app, and increasing his mobility with the help of his walker. In fact, this past month when we went in for his check-up, the doctor gave me the most positive news I'd heard in years.

"Mr. Parker, Caleb is progressing increasingly well. Whatever you're doing is helping tremendously."

And in my heart of hearts, I know we owed it all to Brooklyn and her magic.

To screw with that dynamic by adding Penelope into the picture was not something I was about to do. And legally, I didn't have to. My attorney had assured me of that.

"I appreciate the offer, Chey, that's very sweet of you. But I owe Penelope a conversation. You can show her in. But give us only ten minutes, please. Then you can barge in here and boot her out." I give her the *wink, wink* sign and she leaves with a chuckle.

I exhale a long, exasperated breath, hoping to inhale some patience in the process. "Time to find your balls, pal."

The *click, clack, click* of Penelope's heels echoes down the short, wood-floored hallway and I fix a tight smile on my face as she walks in.

"Now I see why you wanted to work at a university." Her voice is brittle with jealousy and sarcasm.

I give her the *'what the fuck are you talking about'* look. She waves a manicured hand behind her. "Your cute little receptionist. Robbing the cradle, if you ask me."

I roll my eyes and sigh. "Hello to you, too, Penelope. For the record, I didn't hire Chey, nor am I *'robbing the cradle'* by doing anything with her." I use air quotes. "Jesus, you're a piece of work."

I take a seat behind my desk, watching with guarded interest as Penelope lifts a bony shoulder and takes a tour of my office, which isn't much. I finally unpacked all my boxes that had been lingering around unopened for over six months, placing my trophies on the shelves, hanging framed pictures of me from my college and pro ball days on the walls, and displaying my signed NBA basketballs and books on the bookcase.

Penelope flutters her fingertips over my *Rookie of the Year* award and sighs wistfully.

"I remember your rookie year, Garrett. I remember watching you play and thinking to myself, 'Oh my God, that man is everything I want.'" She tilts her head to the side, looking at me over her shoulder as if I am some pet or trophy she won. "And I got what I wanted."

"Jesus Christ, Penelope. It was one night. One fuck. If that's all you ever wanted, that's pretty pathetic."

There's a flash of something cruel and calculating in her eyes and then it's gone, as she sways her hips, clad in a tight pencil skirt, over to the side of my desk. She leans over to trail a finger along my jawline. I flinch, pulling just out of her reach.

"I was so in love with you, Garrett. I still am. But you're right. I didn't get everything I wanted." She dips her head as if saddened by this fact, then returns her blue-eyed gaze to me, innocently blinking her long, fake lashes. "I gave you a son and you went and married your sweet little barren Becca, who couldn't give you *anything*."

My temper seethes underneath my skin, itching and clawing to get out. Ready to strike her down like an angry lion. But I won't allow her to provoke me, or get me to react. That's exactly what she wants me to do.

I clutch the armrests of my chair with my fists, so tight my knuckles turn white. Breathing sharply through my nose, I count to ten, much like I have to do when Caleb pushes my buttons during his meltdowns.

I'm the one about to have a meltdown right now, though. I try to teach my kid to turn the other cheek when he's provoked. I need to take a dose of my own medicine.

Pushing the chair away, I shoot to my feet and posture myself over her, causing her to lean back against the desk demurely, until a manipulative smile curves at the corners of her mouth.

Realizing I'm giving her exactly what she wants, I step back and cross my arms over my chest, which heaves with pent-up rage.

"If I recall, Penelope, that son you gave me? You gave him up for fucking money, you greedy, whoring bitch."

She covers her mouth as if I've just slapped her. I'll admit, that was the lowest, harshest thing I could say. Tears well up in her eyes and shame washes over me.

I catch myself before reaching out to comfort her. "I'm sorry. I didn't mean that. But you can't speak ill of my dead wife, Penelope. That's not fair. She was a really good mom to Caleb, regardless of whether she could bear children or not."

Penelope straightens her shoulders as if finding her resolve.

"I know she was, Garrett. But she's gone. And I want to be back in my son's life. He deserves to know his mother. And I realize, I was so stupid when I signed away my parental rights. But it was only because I knew you and Becca would be good parents to Caleb. You would give him everything I couldn't. And I did it for his benefit. I didn't want to confuse him by being a weekend or every other month mother. I stand by that decision. I know you don't believe me, but I wanted what was best for him at the time."

I wasn't born yesterday. After the messy battle we had in court, and finally settling on a ridiculously high payout settlement, I don't trust one lick of what she's spewing.

Shaking my head, I snort. "You're right. I don't believe you. And while I appreciate the fact that you did him a solid by staying out of his life, I'd like to keep it that way."

Penelope's face falls and she is wide-eyed, and panic-stricken. She takes two steps forward, placing her hand right above my heart, which beats erratically as my blood runs cold and my blood pressure rises.

"Garrett, please. I am Caleb's own mother. He needs me. I want to prove to you that I've changed and can be a good mother to *our* son."

I remove her hand from my chest, holding it for a moment too long, as her facial expression turns to hope. And then I fling it off me and drop it to her side, then turn her shoulders around toward the door. The open door that I want her to leave through.

"Thanks for stopping by, Penelope. The answer is no. He is doing just fine without you in his life. It would only cause him confusion and could possibly stunt his emotional development, which has been flourishing as of late."

What I don't mention is why I believe that's happening, which has everything to do with Brooklyn. But saying that would only add gasoline to this already raging fire.

Penelope spins around but doesn't speak. Like a chess game, she's figuring out her next strategy to achieve checkmate with me.

But she won't outsmart me.

I've played one too many of her games in the past and know when to stand firm.

Especially when it comes to my son.

30

"A wedding invitation came in the mail for you today. It's on top of the stack on the hall table."

Garrett enters the bedroom from the bathroom, where he'd just brushed his teeth and threw his clothes in the dirty hamper. He comes toward me, chest bare, wearing nothing but his gray boxer briefs, his package giving shape underneath the cotton material.

He lifts his eyebrows suggestively, noticing where my eyes have drifted. He strokes a palm over his hardening flesh, and I part my lips, my mouth suddenly going very dry.

The bed dips under the weight of his body as he places a knee at the end of the bed, his hand running the length of my leg from my ankle to my shin. I squirm at the touch, because I know what it means, and I like where it's going.

I've been sitting against the headboard, laptop across my legs, reviewing my class schedule for the fall semester that starts next week. I'm both excited and nervous about how this will change the dynamic between Garrett and me. And Caleb.

Just last week, I went with Garrett to attend the private school's open house in Scottsdale where he'd enrolled Caleb in kindergarten. He asked me to come along to meet with the Principal and teacher, as well as his case manager, therapists and school psychologist to review and add input to his initial Individualized Educational Plan. With all the work we put into Caleb's learning this past summer he has grown leaps and bounds and is ready to be educated properly.

Which is exactly, it seems, what Garrett has in mind for me right at the moment, as he removes his underwear before prowling up the bed, his taut abs sliding over my legs. He leans on his side, propping himself up on his elbow, running his fingers up and down my legs and between my thighs.

"Whose wedding is it?" he asks casually, keeping up with his torture by sliding a finger under the edge of my panties. He lifts his eyes to me when he finds me wet.

Knowing it'll be useless to try to get anything more done tonight, I close the lid, and set the laptop on the bedside table. Then I scoot down and face him, mirroring his stance by propping myself on my elbow.

"Lance and Micaela Britton's."

Garrett begins trailing wet kisses down my arm, the hair on top of his head tickling under my chin, as I drop my hand to encircle his cock in my fist, giving it a nice, tight stroke.

"Ah," he says before latching on to my nipple through my tank top. I arch into him on a moan. "But aren't they already married and having a baby together?"

He grips the top edge of my panties and slips them down my legs, as I kick them off the edge of the bed. I jack my leg up and over his hip, as Garrett throws an arm behind my back, pressing me into the curve of his body. His girthy cock, now very hard, nudges into my middle. He continues stroking my bare leg, as I luxuriate in the sweet tease of his fingertips.

With one swift move, he flattens his back against the mattress and swings my hips over to straddle on top of him. His knowing smile is devilish because he knows how much I love being on top. The quickest way to get me to orgasm is to let me ride first.

Experimenting with a few grinds of my pelvis, I rotate my hips seductively, stretching my torso up, as Garrett works at my tank, yanking it over my head and arms. Garrett loves my breasts. I've never paid them much attention or flaunted them, mainly because sports bras aren't very sexy.

But the way Garrett worships them, with his mouth, hands, and tongue, has made me realize how important they are to my sexual satisfaction. He even got me off the other night just by playing with my nipples. He wouldn't touch my clit or even let me touch it, but relentlessly sucked, licked, and teased my nipples so thoroughly, that he had me screaming out my release in no time, before he slid inside of me to enjoy the ride.

"Well yes, technically they are legally wed. But I guess Mica's family wanted to do a big reception and invite all their friends and family to celebrate both their marriage and the baby. It'll be fun. And we'll get to see all the guys again from school."

Garrett's hands have been plumping my breasts, his mouth poised to suck a taut, sensitive nipple into his mouth when he stops, his eyes drifting up at me with jealous concern.

"All what guys? Did you...were you ever involved..."

I grin, quirking a brow and rubbing my mound over his erection. "Are you asking if I ever fucked any of them?"

His reply is a ragged growl. "Yeah."

I join my hands with his, helping him to squeeze and knead my tits in his hands, enjoying the sensation of working together to achieve mutual gratification. Such good teamwork.

"No. Never. I kissed Lance Britton once at a party our

freshman year. But nothing happened. He got wasted and blacked out before anything became of it."

"Good," he bellows. "Well, not that he got wasted, but that it stopped him. Because you're mine. These are mine." He demonstrates with a swipe of his tongue over both breasts.

"This is mine." His hands land on my bare ass and he squeezes, then one hand swats a cheek, as I buck against him.

"And this..." His thumb circles over my clit, swirling and dipping inside the wetness. "This, sweetheart, is all mine. All fucking mine."

"Yes," I cry out, as he swiftly enters me and we both shudder at the sensation.

And then there's no more discussion about the past.

Only the here and now.

31

GARRETT

Staff meetings in any business setting can be boring, tedious and a waste of time. Luckily, today's coaching staff meeting centered around our incoming team, as we sift through and analyze each of our kids' strengths and weaknesses to determine how we'll work with them individually throughout the season.

As I enter the conference room in the athletic building on campus, laptop and a stack of analytics I'd printed out earlier, I notice my colleagues, Jon Richman, the Director of Team Operations, Byron Hope, the other assistant head coach, Lamar Press, the team's Strength & Training coach, as well as our administrative assistant, Cheyanne, already in the room.

"Morning," I nod in greeting, taking a seat at the first open spot.

Jon is talking with Byron about his new '67 Mustang he bought over the summer and is restoring, showing him pictures from his phone. I lean to the side to get a good look at his new 'baby.'

"Nice."

Jon doesn't seem to like my 'mid-west compliment' and grunts. "Just nice, bro? Nah, man. She's fucking beautiful."

Lamar casually glances up from his laptop to comment, a bit of sarcasm lacing through it. "Put you back a pretty penny, though, didn't *she?*"

"Hell, man. She's worth it." He side-glances toward Chey, covering his mouth to whisper conspiratorially. "And this beauty doesn't talk back like my wife. Only purrs when she's happy."

Yep, just like it is in a locker room, except we're wearing business casual attire in the conference room.

"Okay then, Jon. Enough with the inappropriate female references." I give him a stern glare to ensure he knows I mean it. "Anyone know where Coach Welby is?"

I look down at Chey at the far end of the table. She's tapping away at her laptop with her black raven hair falling over her eyes. Her head pops up, then diverts down to her phone, checking the time. "He'll be here shortly. He's running just a little late finishing up an interview with *Sports News Radio.*"

As we wait for our Head Coach to arrive, we talk shop, discuss some of the other things we did over the summer, games we took in, vacations we went on. I steer clear of my personal life but do mention that Caleb is starting kindergarten.

"That's great to hear, G. That kid of yours is pretty inspiring. He doesn't let anything slow him down." Byron shoves a hand out to fist bump me.

Jon joins in. "I'm telling ya, bro. It feels like it was just yesterday when Kristin and I walked Amelia into her kindergarten class. Then I blinked and she's already a junior in high school this year. I don't know how that happened. And she started seeing a boy over the summer that she worked with and they're getting serious."

He shakes his head. "I'll tell you what. Having *that* conversation with your seventeen-year-old daughter is about as fun as getting all your teeth pulled without the Novocain. It's painful, uncomfortable and has you gripping the arm chair hoping it'll just end."

Lamar mutters, "I bet she knows more about sex than you think she does. Just tell her to remember to wrap it before she taps it."

"What the hell, man? That's my daughter you're talking about."

Lamar can be a little dense and rough around the edges at times, but I'm sure he doesn't mean any disrespect by his comment.

I'm about to jump in to smooth things over when Coach Welby flies through the door.

"Sorry, I'm late. Let's get started."

That's what I like about Coach. He's no-nonsense, direct and can be blunt to the point of caustic at times. But he's a good leader and has turned out some really great players over the years. Most recently, we had a handful of players get drafted into the NBA, including last year's senior, Carver Edwards, who's now up in Seattle playing for an expansion team.

The only problem with the current coaching dynamic is it leaves me little room for advancement. Coach Webly isn't going anywhere anytime soon, which leaves me with wanting something more in terms of responsibility and authority over my coaching decisions. I know I have room to grow in my coaching skills, but I am competitive, and always aim for the next big achievement.

I sigh wistfully, recalling my early days out of college when I was young, free and loving life. I had no mortgage, no responsibilities and certainly no disabled son to worry about.

The whole kindergarten situation really freaked me out. As a basketball player and coach, you need to display mental toughness – both on and off the court. Toughness and resilience are needed strengths in order to win the game. And if you show any sign of weakness, you'll be eaten alive by your opponent.

In this case, my opponent seems to be life in general. If I let down my guard for one second or lose my grip on the ball, it'll have me beat.

And I'm too competitive to lose at anything.

———

We've been at this for two hours now and I can tell we're all getting a little antsy for a break. But Coach Welby doesn't seem to notice.

"Okay, let's talk about Tyus Washington."

I shuffle through my stack of print-outs, all alphabetized and in order, and pull out Tyus's stats.

"His last year in high school he averaged 22.3 points, 3.8 assists and 2.2 steals per game as the point guard. He was a McDonald's All-American and received the MVP for being the leading scorer at the Proviso West Holiday Tournament." I continue reading through his long list of achievements when there's a knock on the conference room door.

All heads turn toward the door, which is closed but not locked. I'm closest to the door and rise from my chair to go open it.

There's an older looking gentleman, with a gray-white tuft of hair in a comb-over, a wrinkled plaid suit and a folder in his hands standing on the other side of the door.

"Yes? Can I help you?"

He clears his throat, his eyes darting around the room behind me before landing back on me.

"I'm looking for Mr. Garrett Parker."

My forehead crinkles and I tilt my head. I have no idea who this guy is. I'm not saying I'm the most recognizable former player in the world, but my face has graced a lot of national magazines and TV sports commentary. I find it odd he doesn't recognize me if he's looking for me.

"I'm Garrett Parker. What can I..." I don't get a chance to finish my sentence.

"Mr. Parker, you've been served. Have a nice day."

The next thing I know he's shoved the folder in my hands and spins on his heels, practically sprinting down the hallway whence he came.

A silence fills the room as I pick my jaw up off the floor, staring down at the ominous folder in my hands.

I don't even have to open the envelope to know exactly what it is and who it's from.

"Goddamn, Penelope," I curse loudly. "Goddamn her."

32

BROOKLYN

It's been two days and Garrett won't talk about it.

He came home the other day after his staff meeting irritated and grumpy, slamming doors and mumbling under his breath about his "mistake" and "why can't she just leave us alone?"

After I fixed dinner and cleaned up, he gave Caleb a bath and put him to bed, while I got situated on the couch with some newly assigned coursework from class. I'm taking three courses this semester, one of them related to clinical psychology. Even as I read through the first chapter of the textbook, my brain is working to diagnose and breakdown the distress and dysfunction that seems to be sidelining Garrett this week.

I, of course, am fully aware of what's gotten him in such an uproar and know all about Penelope's lawsuit. Her petition is to have the original parental rights reversed so she can seek joint custody.

It's the most absurd thing I could ever imagine. Penelope

wanting to share custody of her disabled son that she gave away two years ago. What the hell is she even thinking?

What's even more disturbing is that I overheard Garrett on the phone in his office with his attorney last night. His lawyer apparently explained that in many cases like this, where a mother has given her child up for adoption, the judge can overturn the original verdict in favor of the biological mother's request.

I could offer no words of encouragement to Garrett, because really, what good would it have done? It doesn't change the situation and certainly can't prevent the potentially life-changing decision from happening.

All I could do was offer up my body in hopes of sating his frustrations with the world. I knew he'd just received a devastating blow and he was a desperate man in need of some relief, in whatever way he could get it. Even if only a physical and temporary solution, it was something.

When I heard him hang up and silence descended over the house, I slowly crept down the hallway, knocked quietly on his door and walked over to his desk, where he was hunched over like a sad and dejected Quasimodo.

I stood behind him and slid my hands over his bunched shoulders, squeezing and manipulating the straining muscles of his tightly corded neck and back with my ministrations. His lips parted on a pained sigh, as I trailed my fingertips down the front of his chest, lifting the material of his tucked shirt from inside his shorts.

He leaned his head back, flopping it to the side, as I kissed the rough texture of his scruffy jaw, using my tongue to lick over the taut, throbbing vein in his thick neck. I felt the current of vibration rumble from his throat, sucking a spot in the hollow of his throat that I knew he found sensitive.

"I need you," he murmured with a gravelly voice, lifting his arms behind his back to pull me closer.

Without a word exchanged between us, I stripped off my

shorts and T-shirt, removing my bra and panties, as he unbuttoned and unzipped his shorts. My gaze drifted to the fat bulge in his underwear, the tip of his erection straining to punch through the edge. He grabbed the elastic and pulled it down, allowing his cock to spring free.

I was about to kneel in front of him and take him in my mouth when he reached for my hips, spinning me around to bend me forward over the desk. The warmth of my breasts touched cold, hardwood and the contradiction sent shivers down my spine and had me gasping, as did the forcefulness by which he spread my legs and speared me from behind with his tongue.

Crying out something altogether unintelligible, the tip of his tongue slipped through my wet folds, his hands roughly holding me open for him. I could feel the wetness dripping from my core, my hardened nipples pebbling with every sweep of him between my legs.

Suddenly, his tongue disappeared, replaced by the wide, straining head of his cock as it surged inside me.

There was no time to even adjust my stance, as one of his palms securely fitted over my hip and the other pressed into the top of my shoulder, anchoring me into the desk and to him. And then he was slamming into me in a frenetic pace, no sultry rhythm or calculated tempo to his pistoning hips. It was just pure, unadulterated rutting.

Dewy sweat beaded my back, my thighs rubbing against the smooth edge of the desk, as Garrett breathed and panted like he was running with the bulls, focused only on finishing.

And then he came, long and hard, with a groan that mixed satisfaction with agony. Pain with pleasure. Love with lust.

My pussy flooded with his spend, as he pulsed and pulsed out his release. It was a long silent moment until the pressure of his hands left me, the spots where he had touched me now cold and marked from the roughness of his grip.

No words were exchanged, no terms of endearment or gratitude given. As he slipped out of me, leaving me empty and bereft, I felt the dynamic shift between us.

Something foreign and strange, full of censure and distaste, crept up my spine as Garrett quickly stuffed his dick back in his pants and zipped up.

He reached over my shoulder to hand me the Kleenex box, which I accepted with a soft, "Thanks."

As I cleaned myself up, he picked up my discarded clothing, hanging them over the arm of the chair, before turning toward the door.

"I'm going to bed." And then he paused, a heavy stone of guilt being hoisted above him, ready to be flung over a wall that was just built between us. It was a battle cry. A testimony to his anguish and torment.

"I think it's better if you sleep in your own room tonight."

And then he was gone, leaving me naked and alone.

Now just feeling like an intruder and interloper in his life.

An unwanted nuisance.

Feeling like just another frustration for him to contend with.

33

GARRETT

Everything I had, I gave it all to her.

My rage, my sorrow, my despair. She took it all from me. She wrapped me in her arms, gave me the shelter of her body and soothed my aching and beleaguered heart.

And what did I do for in return?

I gave her the cold shoulder. I iced her out.

I am a motherfucking asshole.

But I couldn't stop myself. I was so angry over what I'd learned from my lawyer, Bob Guthry, about the possibility a judge could just snap his or her fingers to overturn the original judgment, that I think I temporarily lost my mind.

I allowed my frustrations over this Penelope situation to deconstruct and tarnish everything Brooklyn and I have been building together. I took advantage of the situation and Brooklyn's kindness. And now I'm hiding out – from her and myself.

When I left Brooklyn in my office, I went straight to the

liquor cabinet, pulled out my Scotch and returned to my bedroom, in hopes I could drink myself to sleep.

No such luck.

Instead, my past is catching up to me, haunting me with a vengeance. It has my thoughts gripped in its steely tentacles, holding me hostage as I play out every stupid mistake I've ever made on loop like one of those gif videos.

Over and over again, including that night five years ago when I got that fateful call from Penelope.

"Hey babe, do you know where my razor is?" I call to Becca from the bathroom of our new house we'd just moved into a month earlier, just twenty-minutes out of Indianapolis.

I'd just returned from a grueling ten-day road trip, leaving Becca, my new fiancée and future wife to do all the heavy lifting, unpacking and organizing. Though if you asked her, she doesn't mind. She was just thrilled to finally be settling into our new life together.

I was just thrilled to be able to fuck her in every room and surface in our new house. It was a win-win in my mind.

Becca rounds the corner of the master bath, tipping her head and rolling her eyes.

"My mom was right," she muses, opening up a cabinet and pulling it from the top shelf to hand it to me. "Men really are blind to anything in plain sight."

I smack her ass, a 'yipe' exhaling from her parted lips.

"Hey, it's not my fault. I just didn't know where to look."

I extract the razor from her hand but grab hold of her wrist to pull her into me. She is soft and warm, and I've missed her so much while I was gone. She is my home and my rock, and I was a mess while we were apart.

We'd just gotten back together two months earlier, after a little over a month-long separation, which Becca insisted we take.

"Not because I don't love you, Garrett," she'd confirmed the night she broke it off with me three months earlier. "But I don't want you to live with regret or be tempted to cheat on me. It'd break my heart. I'd rather you figure it out on your own terms without me tying you down."

I tried reasoning with her, explaining and pleading my case that she was the love of my life and I didn't want anyone else. But she stood firm and gave me no choice. For some reason, she had this idea in her head after hearing all the stories about other male pro-athletes who weren't faithful to their wives and girlfriends, that I would become like them.

A dirty statistic and scandal of infidelity.

Becca was a small-town girl with small-town ideals, pragmatic to the core. I couldn't convince her otherwise.

I'd tried to get her back by making an ass of myself by groveling and leaving her drunken fool-hearted voice messages for the better part of two weeks. But she wouldn't respond. So, I finally said 'fuck it' and stopped protesting over my freedom.

My teammates were all on board to help me out, introducing me to tons of 'hoops honeys' along the way. Like a kid in a candy store, I ate it up. The attention of all these hot women flocking to me. My head got big and I turned into a jackass.

And then one night on a road trip to Pittsburgh, after I played like shit, only scoring three points and one measly rebound, I went out to a club and got wasted with my friends. I'd drawn the attention of a tall, confident cocktail waitress named Penelope, who told me to wait for her at the end of her shift. Which I did, because why not? We went back to her place and fucked.

And then I passed out.

I couldn't even recall if it was good or not. Or if she had fun because I was a serious headcase. All I know is when I woke the next morning, there was a used condom, thank God for that. I called an Uber and left without saying goodbye.

She wasn't the only one I slept with during that period of time, but the only one that had life-long consequences.

"Hey Bec, maybe I won't shave, and I'll let my beard grow out. What do you think?" I ask her, scrubbing a hand over my neck and jaw, staring in the mirror at the dark five o'clock shadow worn by a content man.

I tilted my head to check her expression.

"Hmm," she says, thoughtfully considering the change.

I'd always been clean shaven. In fact, it got me a lot of magazine covers and exposure with journalists comparing me to a "tall, strapping Calvin Klein model." Which, come on, did wonders for my ego.

"I guess we could try it out. I've never kissed a bearded face. Unless you count Santa Claus when I was five."

I drop my mouth open in an expression of horror.

"You little hussy!" I tease, stalking toward her as she backs up against the glass of the shower door. I playfully rub my stubbled cheek over her face and then down to the top of her cleavage.

She latches onto the top of my hair, pulling tightly, her breasts heaving with every panted breath.

My phone gave a shrill ring from the bedside table, stopping any further exploration of Becca's body.

I stood tall and looked down at the smiling and loving face of my fiancée, not knowing then that it would take a long time after for that smile to return again.

"That could be my agent with the specifics on my new contract."

She waves me off. "Go. Take it. I'll jump in the shower and meet you in bed."

I give her a loud kiss on her cheek and sprint to grab the phone. But when I answer it, the caller is indeed not my sports agent, Cristopher, but instead an Unknown Caller.

"Yo, this is G. What's your business?"

There's a slight pause of silence before a female voice responds. A voice I don't recognize but would soon hear a whole lot more of.

"Is this Garrett Parker?"

Something in her tone spells out doom. It's hesitant. Clear. But crisp. It sounds like a knife slicing across a knife sharpener. I glance over my shoulder into the bathroom, where Becca stands under a stream of warm water, her head tipped back and arms raised to her soapy hair.

Protect her, my heart screams.

My own voice sounds weak and inept. "Yes."

"Garrett, this is Penelope Slattery. We, uh, met in Pittsburgh a few months ago. Do you remember? At Storie's Nightclub?"

Tension already bombards my temples, as I drop my head, my free hand massaging my forehead.

"Yes. How'd you get this number?"

She doesn't answer right away. And something about that pause ignites a rage inside me for no reason other than that someone sold me out.

"It doesn't matter. What matters is the reason I'm calling. Garrett, this is really hard for me to say, so please just hold your judgment for a second before responding, okay? Do you promise?"

"No, I don't promise. Now, what do you have to say? I'm busy."

I've channeled my inner-asshole because I've been stuck in these situations before, where someone wants money from me. They give me a sob story and request help. Normally it's family or distant relatives, not strangers, though.

"Please." *Her tone is so desperate, as the line is flooded with the sound of muffled sniffles from her tears.*

"Fine, I promise. But you've got thirty seconds before I hang up."

I sit down on the edge of the new Cali-king Becca and I had just purchased, the firmness underneath holding me up and keeping me from hitting the floor when she drops the bomb in my lap.

"Garrett, I'm really sorry. This wasn't supposed to happen. I didn't mean for it to happen, please believe me."

A worm wiggles inside my stomach, like the bottom of a Tequila bottle, inducing fear and nausea.

"What. Is. It?" *I practically shout, the simmering boil ready to explode under the lid that contains it.*

"I'm pregnant, Garrett, and you're the father. We used protection that night, but it's not 100% effective, obviously. And the baby is yours. I just hit twelve weeks."

"Jesus fuck."

The bed didn't hold me. I slipped off the edge and landed on the floor.

Just like my life, it hit with a thud and I couldn't seem to get myself back up.

34

BROOKLYN

I've packed an overnight bag and have decided to go back to my apartment to stay with Peyton and Kyler for the short-term, to give Garrett some space. It's pretty obvious that Garrett needs some time to sift through all the legal matters that will ensue related to Caleb and he doesn't need me - in his house or in his way - clouding his focus on the bigger picture related to his son.

Plus, this nanny gig was only supposed to be a full-time summer job, anyway. It's now August, I'm back in school and Caleb is adjusting extremely well to all the plethora of changes to his schedule and life. Garrett will only need me here part-time after school and some evenings.

This decision to leave weighed heavily on my mind as I lay awake in my room last night, leading up to the conclusion I finally landed on.

I will move out and back home for at least the foreseeable future. I just need to run all this by Garrett this morning.

In fact, he seems to be running late this morning. I glance

over at the stove clock to find it's after eight-thirty, the time Garrett is normally out the door. Caleb needs to be at school in thirty minutes.

"You all done with your breakfast, buddy?" I ask him, where he's playing with a toy truck on the kitchen table. He grins and goes "*zoom zoom*" – or at least, his version of it, anyhow.

"Okay, then. I'm going to go check on your dad. I'll be right back, okay?"

I ruffle his hair as I walk by and head down the hallway toward Garrett's bedroom. The door is closed, and I can hear him on the phone, sounding agitated.

"I'm not sure, mom. It's all uncertain. I just heard from them this morning and I have to think about the offer and get back to them by the end of the week."

I know I'm eavesdropping and it's an inconsiderately rude thing to do, but I can't help but overhear what he's saying. I wonder if the offer he's referring to is a deal between Penelope and his lawyers. Maybe they've reached an agreement or decision already.

There's a pause and then he responds again, a little more gruffly and to the point. "Yes, I know you'd love having him closer. Yes, family is absolutely important. But this is happening so fast. I hadn't expected it."

Another pause and my brows form a crease, as I'm trying to decipher what it is he's talking about. Why would Corinne be closer to Caleb? Is the family he's referring to the three of them? Is Corinne moving down here to be closer to Caleb?

My head spins with possibilities, and then it's as if the floor drops out from underneath me when I hear him say the last thing before I run back into the kitchen, covering my sobs in a towel at the sink.

"Yes, I realize that means I'll need to let Brooklyn go."

———

In the end, I couldn't face talking to Garrett this morning. Instead, I finished getting Caleb ready for school and left a note on the table that I was dropping him off and that I'd talk to him later.

That was three hours ago, and I've been crying uncontrollably since then. Poor Kyler skipped out the minute I walked in, claiming he had an early class to get to. And Peyton, thank God for best friends. She held me in her arms on the couch and let me sob and sniffle all over her cute jumper, while I babbled endlessly about the truth behind love and the merits of remaining single.

"I let my guard down, Peyton. I fell for him and look at where it got me. I'm such a fool. He just wanted the convenience of a live-in summer lover. God, I was played so well. I might as well been a Steinway. And he was my Elton John. *Played*, dammit."

Peyton tries to stifle her chuckle but fails miserably. I give her a bitchy side-eyed glance.

"What?" she asks innocently. "I'm sorry, I was just picturing Garrett in those funky get-ups and glasses that Elton wore in the seventies. He'd look ridiculous."

She strokes a warm hand down my back, rubbing it reassuringly and coo'ing softly.

"Honey, you'll be fine. Whatever happens, you were a strong, independent woman before meeting Garrett, and you'll be even stronger after whatever" – she flutters her hand in the air – "happens, happens."

"But he told me he loved me, and I love him. And I love Caleb. I didn't go looking for this to happen, it just did. And now I feel like I can't breathe. Like this boulder-sized rock is lodged in my chest, squeezing off my airways." I heave a dramatic sigh.

Peyton scoots on her butt around on the couch, facing me with crisscross legs, leaning forward with her elbows on her knees, chin in her hands.

"Brooklyn, I can't imagine what you're going through or what you're feeling right now because honestly, I've never been in love like that. But I know what it feels like to have the bottom drop out in your life and be unable to control anything. To feel like somebody up there," she points a finger toward the ceiling, "has you on puppet strings and is dancing and flinging you around haphazardly, laughing at your misfortune."

She reaches a hand out and pats my thigh. "But that doesn't mean you can't move forward. It just might mean cutting the strings to do it."

Her mouth turns down in a pout, her bottom lip tipped in an empathetic frown.

"This is exactly why they always say it's never a good idea to get involved with an employer. God, I'm so stupid!" I jump to my feet, pacing back and forth, muttering incoherently and whining about how unfair life can be.

And then realization dawns as if a bolt of lightning from heaven above comes crashing through our third-floor apartment. My voice shakes in a panic-stricken timbre.

"Oh my God, Peyton. What if...what if Garrett is going back to Penelope? Holy shit. That's why he was talking about family on the phone. He wants Caleb to live as a family with both his real parents."

I fall flat on my stomach onto the couch, my head squishing into the pillow, my hands punching into the feathers, as I scream out a long, tortured cry. Had anyone been recording me at the moment, they'd have thought I was a sick cow dying a painful death.

Peyton kneels down on the floor beside me, shifting the hair out of my face, smoothing back the wet mess stuck against my cheek.

"I'm sure that's not the case at all. He despises that woman. But listen, girl. If that's the worst possible thing to happen and he does get back with Penelope, you still have a life ahead of you. You're going to finish school, study hard and get your Masters degree. And you have great friends and family who love you and will be by your side the entire way. Your life does not need to revolve around some man to make this happen and you know it."

She's right. I know she's right. And if the tables were turned, I'd give her the same exact *Girl Power!* pep talk.

But it sure as hell doesn't help much when you're heartbroken and heartsick over the man you love who might be going back to the mother of his child.

Regardless of what we may have shared or become to one another this summer, that's the one thing I can never be to Garrett or Caleb.

35

GARRETT

I'm going through the motions to get through this day and hoping it'll end soon so I can go back to bed and forget everything.

I wish I had a magic wand to wipe away everything that happened in the past and start fresh. Start new.

Which is what's so appealing about the offer I received this morning.

The day began with a call from the Athletic Director at a small university in Franklin, Indiana, just outside of Indianapolis. Their former Head Coach passed away unexpectedly over the summer and they were in a search for a replacement for the upcoming season. The Athletic Director quickly confirmed I was on top of their short list and he wanted to see if I'd consider the position.

My head was spinning, stomach roiling and my mouth felt like someone stuffed cotton in it after the amount of booze I drank the night before. But it blurred and dulled the recollection of the way I handled myself with Brooklyn, just a little. What didn't help was the reminder that there was still a chance that I could lose Caleb if Penelope gets what she wants.

The minute I was served the petition yesterday from Penelope's lawyer, it was like the walls started caving in on me and the earth gave way under my feet. I was in a free fall and being boxed in at the same time if that's even possible.

What is possible, my lawyer said, is the likelihood that I could be in for a long battle with Penelope over Caleb. He told me to schedule a meeting this morning, and that's where I was heading first.

Needing someone to vent to, I called my mom to let her know of the petition and then told her about the job offer to get her opinion on things. Of course, she had mixed feelings about Penelope, believing that she should have a right to see her child, and wears rose-colored glasses when it comes to the belief that Penelope has changed her ways.

I vehemently disagreed that point and said I'd fight it 'til the bitter end with everything I had.

Regardless, my mother was thrilled to hear there was a small chance I might be moving back home to Indiana. I told her not to get her hopes up, but I was strongly considering it. This role would be great for my career.

Although the school is a Division-Three and as far from the Pac 12 as I could get, securing a Head Coaching job could be a big stepping stone for my career. The first step would be to fly up to Indiana and meet with the AD, see if the program would be a good fit for my coaching style, and then figure things out with Caleb.

He obviously factors a great deal in me accepting any offer to move. The idea of uprooting him, especially since he's doing so well and just started school, weighs heavily on this decision. Caleb is my number one priority, and nothing or no one else, comes close.

Except my feelings toward Brooklyn – which are right now all over the fucking board.

After hanging up with my mother, I took a shower, reviewing what I would say to Brooklyn when I saw her this morning and how I would apologize for my behavior last night. But by the time I made my way into the kitchen to speak with her, she and Caleb were already gone. She'd left a note on the table indicating she was dropping him off at school and she would see me later.

The ground beneath me seemed to shift and tilt even more. Is this what vertigo feels like?

How could I possibly choose between a job and the woman I loved?

Wasn't this exactly how it happened with me and Becca? But in that situation, Becca gave me no choice. She took the decision out of my hands.

This time, I need to stand up for what I want. If I end up taking this job and moving, I want Brooklyn with me. Not just for Caleb and consistency in his life, but for me.

I've fallen for her and can't see my life without her in it.

Resolving to take one step at a time, I pick up my keys and head out to my car.

First things first, head to my lawyer's office and deal with this absurd petition.

———

"Listen, Garrett. Technically, Penelope has a legal right to petition to reinstate her parental rights, but that doesn't mean the court will grant it. She has the burden of proof here and will have to prove that when she willingly and voluntarily terminated her parental rights to Caleb that she did so under duress."

My attorney, Bob, leans forward over his desk, elbows flat, fingers steepled together. Nothing he's said so far has really reassured me that this thing will go away easily.

"What does that mean, under duress?"

Leaning back against his high-back leather chair, he appraises me with an inquisitive stare.

"Since I wasn't your attorney for the original proceedings in Indiana, we'll, of course, need to request the transfer of jurisdiction to Maricopa County to get the ball rolling on this. As soon as I receive and review the previous court documents, it will help explain the reason the judge made their decision. It's not often that a court will grant termination of parental rights at all unless Penelope had issues and that's why she had to give him up at the time. Was she an addict? A pedophile? Mentally unstable? Was she in jail?"

My face contorts in a confused look. "No. I don't think so. All I know is she said she couldn't raise a child and didn't have the money or the inclination to handle a lifetime of child-rearing work. Mentally unstable, maybe. I did get a restraining order against her initially because she would not leave me alone. Would show up unannounced. Call me and leave me crazy-long, rambling messages about why I didn't love her. She's nuts."

Bob nods his head. "Hmm. Okay. Maybe there is some psychiatric condition present. Or maybe she was just a young woman who wasn't ready to be a mother and you and your former wife were the perfect solution. Has she been stalking you recently?"

I think about her calling my mother. Coming down to Phoenix unannounced. Calling me out of the blue.

"I guess, maybe. She's been in contact with my mother. And then she showed up at my home about a month ago. Oh, and then at my office before she filed this petition."

A calculating smile tips across Bob's face, his dark green eyes lighting up as if a light bulb just turned on.

"That's good. Very good. We'll establish that she's crossed the line and is a potential threat to you and your family."

I sigh, conflicted over what the right thing is to do. "I don't know, man. I don't fear her or worry that she's going to kidnap my boy or anything. I'd hate to accuse her of something that she didn't do."

A slam of his hand across desk startles me and I jerk back in my chair.

"Garrett, this is exactly what I'm talking about. It's this type of behavior that she's exhibiting that will only get worse unless you put a kibosh on it now. Stop it before it becomes a problem. If she's done it in the past, she's absolutely capable of doing it now. And you," he points a long, gnarled finger at me, his eyebrows threading together gruffly, "need to establish boundaries right the fuck now. Be careful. Women like this...desperate for attention, money or love...will not hesitate to push the envelope, even if it means doing something extreme."

I swallow the lump that's formed in my throat, rubbing my palms, now clammy from sweat, over my thighs. Shit, this is the last thing I want to think about.

I make a mental note to remember to change the password for the security alarm tonight when I get home.

Because if anything ever happened to Caleb or Brooklyn, I'd never forgive myself.

Just like I haven't forgiven myself for Becca and the part I played in her death.

36

I haven't heard anything from Garrett today except a brief '*Thank you*' text earlier this morning which I assume was for taking Caleb to school. Other than that, he hasn't reached out, which speaks loudly to where his head is at with me.

Everything that went down between us last night and the call I overheard this morning sits like a lead balloon in my gut.

I've never given myself to a man like this before. Lost myself in him and allowed him to lose himself in me. And look where it led me.

Maybe I should have listened and heeded my mother's warning. Then I wouldn't be in this predicament.

"*Don't ever give up your dreams or anything else for a man, Brooklyn. Giving away your heart is the first step in giving away your independence.*"

While she and my dad were great parents to me and Brayden, they divorced when I was young and lived separate lives.

My mother once told me that she married my dad because he

"didn't smother me." I didn't truly understand what that really meant at the time until I started dating and got involved with a few guys who constantly needed my attention, barely leaving me time to breathe.

Because of that, I've kept myself guarded against the possibility of falling in love and relying on him and vice versa. And now as I ruminate over what transpired this summer between me and Garrett, that's exactly what I've done. Unintentionally or by default, our lives became intertwined, mostly due to Caleb. It turns my stomach inside out to think that Garrett may not truly love me or want me, but simply needed me to care for his son.

Someone who is his round-the-clock support. Is that all I am to him? Just a live-in nanny and instant onsite booty call?

Garrett has some pretty heavy shit to deal with right now and it makes sense he doesn't want me to be an interference. And I won't be an afterthought, either. It's a hard lesson to learn, but one I'd rather learn now than later.

God, I feel sick.

Now that I've stepped back and begun peeling back the onion layer, it screams the tenants of human behavior and psychology – the very same thing I'm studying right now as I sit in the library. Garrett is using me in his own way – intentionally or not – as a distraction. Maybe even as something to hold onto like an anchor or buoy. I was convenient and easy and now that he's gotten what he needs from me, I can be replaced.

But they can't be replaced for me. Not after how my heart reacted this morning when I dropped Caleb off at school. I watched him from the window behind the doorway of his classroom, sitting at his desk and listening intently to the teacher in the front of the class. He wore a big, baby-toothed grin at whatever he heard, as he raised his hand to answer, using his iPad to respond.

It made me so proud in that moment, knowing I had something to do with that. Losing him would hurt like hell. It worries the living daylights out of me to think of what might happen if Penelope has her parental rights re-established. I've seen enough of her behavior to have legitimate concerns over her ability to parent him properly.

Which makes me torn between wanting to be there for Garrett and stepping away so he can figure it out on his own. And maybe that's what he's already doing and the reason I haven't heard anything from him. But the idea that this is how it will end between us pierces my heart in two, slicing my chest open like an Exacto knife.

"Hey, Brooklyn. Can I grab a spot at the table with you?"

I must've been staring into space as I lift my gaze to the sound of the voice. My head rears back as I look up to see Kyler, both hands latched around the strap of his backpack, a friendly smile perched on his lips.

"Oh, hey, Kyler. Of course, be my guest." I gesture toward the chair across from me, moving my laptop and books out of the way to make room. "What are you doing here?"

He glances around the room, his eyes filled with mischief. "Wait, this isn't the gay bar? Dammit. My GPS screwed up again!"

I choke out a loud laugh, getting evil glares from the students at the table next to me.

"Oh my God. You're so funny. I needed that, thanks."

Unzipping his bag, Kyler sits down and pulls out some study materials, as well as a bag full of chocolate chip cookies.

"Shh," he says, putting his finger to his lips, shoving the bag toward me. "We don't want to get caught with contraband. Who knows what those evil librarians do to criminals like us. But feel free to help yourself."

I lean forward, taking a whiff of the cookies. "Are these homemade?"

My mouth salivates from the smell of fresh baked chocolatey goodness.

Kyler winks. "It's either bake or make really bad life choices when I'm stressed. At least the baking keeps me out of trouble."

"Oooh...sounds interesting. Are you going to fill me in on this naughty side of you?"

I take a bite of a cookie with a waggle of my brows as he snorts out a laugh.

"Yeah, nope. Not unless you share yours."

I shake my head. "Touché, guess we're at a stand-off then. But I will find out. It's only a matter of time."

Kyler snorts out a grunt. "You might be waiting awhile..."

He trails off as he stares at something, or someone, behind me. I spin around in my chair, intrigued by what's caught his attention when I see Lucas Mathiasson walking toward us. Professor Mathiasson.

"Brooklyn, I thought that was you," he greets, placing a hand at my shoulder before stepping to my side, glancing at both me and Kyler, before hesitating a moment on Kyler. "Good to see you again. Kyler, is it?"

There's a fraction of a second when I feel like an intruder between them. I think they may have met at Caleb's birthday party, but the connection is palpable. Definitely feels like they may know each other in a different way.

Lucas returns his gaze to me and smiles. "How are you doing? How's Garrett and my godson doing? The last time I saw them was at Caleb's birthday a few weeks ago."

"Um, they're good. Caleb started kindergarten last week. He's doing so great."

"I had no doubt." Lucas pinches his lips together and then turns toward Kyler, who I noticed seems rather flushed.

"I'm sorry. I'm so rude. How you are doing, Kyler?"

Lucas holds out his hand to Kyler, who seems to be twitching nervously in his seat.

"Uh, good. Busy with school, work, that kind of stuff." Kyler practically chokes out his words, his gaze quickly retreating to the table. And is that a blush I see creeping up his neck?

I jump in, adding, "Kyler, Lucas is actually an art history professor at the university. You two have a lot in common. In fact, my guess is you'll have one of his classes at some point since you're studying art and design."

Kyler's hooded eyes track the tall, towering body of Lucas, starting at the floor until they reach his head. "Perhaps. And yes, I recall Professor Mathiasson mentioning that."

"Funny, I don't recall you mentioning anything about that when we met," Lucas adds, his comment laced with a suspicious tone.

As if someone just lit a fire under his butt, Kyler jumps up from his seat, sending the chair tipping back on its back legs before hitting the ground again. Kyler begins throwing his stuff in his bag before haphazardly zipping it up and throwing it over his shoulder.

"So sorry, Brooklyn. I just remembered I have to be somewhere. I have a...a meeting. I'll catch ya later."

He turns swiftly around ready to leave before throwing a glance back over his shoulder. "Nice to see you again, Professor. Catch ya on the flip side."

And then he's gone and even as I stare at this retreating form, I don't miss the way Lucas's lips curve into a saucy smirk.

When he notices me staring at him, he blanches, before resuming his casual stance and crosses his arms in front of him. He's wearing a crisp white shirt and tie underneath a dark navy sweater vest, his gray slacks perfectly pleated in the front. I nearly laugh at how very different he is from Garrett.

"Would you like to have a seat?" I ask, pointing toward the empty chair where Kyler just sat.

Lucas glances at the chair, with a look of forlorn, and then returns his gaze to me, smiling once again.

"Nah, I should really get going. I just finished up a study

session with a few of my students and saw you over here. Wanted to say hello. Everything going okay?"

I consider his question and really don't know what I'm at liberty to tell him. Garrett and Lucas are close friends, and I know he knows about everything involving Caleb's mother, but I don't know if he's up-to-date on any of the recent drama.

I pin my lip between my teeth and give a half-hearted shrug. "I guess things are okay. Caleb is doing awesome in school. I'm so glad Garrett decided to put him in kindergarten this year. He's loving it and thriving in the program."

Lucas grins. "That's my boy."

It's so sweet how Lucas views Caleb as his own family. And Garrett, for that matter.

He tilts his head curiously. "I hear a *but* hidden somewhere in this conversation."

Letting out a long heave, I fold forward, elbows on the table, my hands covering my eyes in uncertainty. Lucas crouches down on his knees at the end of the table, leaning in with folded hands, elbows facing out, staring me down for a response.

When I'm finally brave enough to look at him, I slowly peel my fingers from my eyes and sigh.

All I have to say is the one name that conveys everything.

"Penelope."

37

GARRETT

I arrive home later than normal tonight, mostly due to the extra time spent squeezing in the meeting at the attorney's office and then some errands I had to tack on at the end of the day.

Walking into the house, I smell something delicious wafting through the kitchen and am greeted with the sound of Brooklyn's singing. The initial glance around the room provides sight of Caleb sitting at his chair eating what looks to be SpaghettiOs and chicken nuggets, red sauce smeared all over the table in front of him, as well as on his mouth, hands, and bib. But he looks happy.

I don't see Brooklyn at first glance, but I know she's here because the sound of her tune carries throughout the kitchen, indicating she's close. And then she pops in my field of vision, her back to me on the other side of the island as she extracts something out of the oven.

When she stands and turns, she nearly drops the casserole dish out of her hands, her mouth dropping open in a silent scream.

"Oh my God, you scared me," she yelps, placing the hot dish on a trivet. "I didn't hear you."

And then her gaze drifts to the bouquet of flowers I have in my hand. The flowers I stopped by specifically to bring home to her. Mostly as an apology, but also out of thanks.

I lift my eyes to hers, my lips forming into a slow smile. "These are for you, Brooklyn."

She stands still for a few moments, eying the arrangement, which is full to the brim with all sorts of beautifully colored flowers, their long stems of green looking like a painter's palette.

When she finally drags her silvery-green eyes to mine, she wears a wary look.

"Wow. Um, thank you. They're beautiful."

Taking two steps forward, I hand her the bouquet. "Not even close to as beautiful you are, Brooklyn. Inside and out."

She clears her throat, as the sound of Caleb's iPad voice interrupts us.

"Pretty, daddy," the automated voice says for him, my heart swelling up like a balloon from his comment. Not knowing if he means the flowers or Brooklyn, I respond from my gut without turning to look at him. I keep my gaze glued on Brooklyn, who chews her lip doubtfully.

"She sure is, buddy."

Waving a hand in the air and sidestepping me, she takes the bouquet over to the sink, unwrapping the packaging covering the stems and finds a vase from the top shelf to fill with water.

"Brooklyn, I'm heading out of town tomorrow and will be gone overnight."

The thought of telling Brooklyn about the possibility of this head coaching job seems a bit premature, so I leave out the reason I'll be gone. I walk over to Caleb and kiss his head, steering clear of the mess in front of him.

"Oh, okay," Brooklyn says as she places the flower vase on the table, just out of Caleb's greasy reach. "That's not a problem. But I do need to speak privately with you before you go."

There's something in her voice that seems tentative and so unlike the Brooklyn I've come to know and admire. She speaks her mind. Doesn't take no for an answer. Is usually right about any topic she's speaking about. It makes me wonder what it is that has her uncomfortable. Probably how I've been acting so icily toward her.

"Of course. That's good because I want to talk with you, too."

Grabbing a wet dishcloth from the sink, I wipe away Caleb's food splatter and sticky hands, before helping him down from the table to his walker.

I swear, the kid has improved so much in the last three months, I'd bet he'll be walking on his own in no time. Maybe even running by the end of the year.

Which only leads me to second-guess the idea of accepting this job and moving away. It could derail all the work and effort he and Brooklyn have put into his progress this summer. And then I'd be right back to square one.

Obviously, the decision to move would be made conditional upon finding a good private school, as well as therapists and programs just as good, if not better, than what he's been involved in down here.

The future is all up in the air right now, like a juggler managing four balls at once, but tomorrow will tell if the opportunity is right. My mother plans on meeting me in the afternoon to help me tour the area. I'd love to include Brooklyn this time around, but there'll be time for that once I have an offer in hand.

In the meantime, I'll wait to see what she wants to discuss and hopefully get back into her good graces so we can resume where we left off before the shit hit the fan with Penelope.

———

"I don't understand. You're moving out?"

We'd already put Caleb to bed and are sitting down in the family room with a glass of wine, the TV on low, set to some Entertainment television program. When Brooklyn said she wanted to discuss something with me, I had no idea it would be her living arrangements.

"But I need you here." My voice sounds panicked as if I were saying, "*Iceberg, dead ahead.*"

Perhaps I should clarify that what I mean to say is I *need* her, *need* her. Personally. Because I love her not just for Caleb's sake. But I'm too stunned and in a state of shock to think clearly right now.

"Garrett, I love being here with you and Caleb. This summer has been nothing short of perfect. But now that Caleb is in school, and I'm back in school, I think it would just be easier that we separate our time."

She quickly looks down at the floor, as if there's something extremely interesting on the carpet near her feet and more important than the topic at hand.

"Hey," I demand rather crisply. "Don't do that. Look at me, please. Does this have something to do with me acting like a world class asshole the last night? If so, I can't apologize enough. I was just…"

She takes a sip from her wineglass and shifts on the couch, our eyes meeting and locking in on one another.

Brooklyn stares me down as she speaks. "It's just that you have a lot going on and it made me realize that I'm just a complication in your way."

She's about to say more, but I stop her, reaching for her wrists and tugging her close to me. So close our noses nearly touch and my knees connect with hers.

"Brooklyn, you are not now, nor have you ever been a complication. You've been the exact opposite of that. You're not the complication, it's this damn lawsuit. It's just really difficult not knowing how this will end up. You and Caleb are the only solid things in my life right now."

I frame her jawline with my hands, fingers spread wide, my thumbs stroking just underneath the buttery soft skin of her chin.

"Please, sweetheart. Stay with me. Stay with us."

Her eyes close as if it's too much, and I watch the flutter of her eyelashes against her cheek. But when they open again, her eyes shine bright with steely resolve.

"I'm going home tonight, Garrett. I'll stay over with Caleb while you're gone, but otherwise, let's just give this a break between us. You have a lot to work out and your priority should be on Caleb."

My head spins not only from the words she chooses, but the implications behind them. They are almost verbatim to what Becca said to me that night so long ago when she broke up with me. Before we were married.

Something inside me snaps. Breaks free, as if I'd been housing a block of ice inside my chest and it just began to thaw and defrost, icicles that had formed now chipping free and melting. Snapping apart like broken ice chunks.

The melting of the ice only secondary to the crack of pain, like a whip across my chest, that flays me wide open.

I drop my hands from her face, uncertain what I should do with them. They feel foreign to me. An unattached body part. Just like my heart feels at the moment.

"I won't argue with you to stay, but I will say this for the record. You are not, nor have you ever been, in my way." Standing, I move to the fireplace, where a framed picture of me, Becca and a very young Caleb sits, adorning the mantel.

I pick it up, running my thumb over the ornate silver décor, shutting my eyes against the onslaught of emotion that wants to well up and spill out.

"Brooklyn, I messed up so much when I was with Becca. Maybe I was young, or just stupid, but I was a worthless prick who didn't deserve her. She knew it and that's why she left me when she did. But I turned things around. Refocused my energies on winning her back. Proving to her that I could be a good man and earn her trust back. And things were great for a long time. We were a good family and she was a great mother."

I hesitate before returning the photo to the mantel but place it upside down. I turn to Brooklyn, pledging my vow.

"It's time I finally let her go. By holding on to her the way I have, I've not given you much room in here, have I?" I thump a spot above my heart.

Brooklyn purses her lips, a crease forming in between her light brown brows. "I...no...that's not it."

It's all become very clear to me now. The realization of what Becca's death did to me. My therapist has been telling me for years that unless I forgive myself and let go of the guilty conscience over Becca's death, and the horrible fight we'd had over the phone that night before she was killed, then, in essence, I'm just dying by living in the past.

I step in front of her and drop to my knees, sitting back on my heels, toes digging into the floor.

Holding out my hands palms up, she places her small hands in mine.

"Brooklyn, it's okay. And you're right. I have a lot of shit to deal with and I understand that you have to do what's right for you. I may be a selfish bastard and want you for myself and for Caleb, but you have to live your life. So, I won't stop you from this. Let's talk when I get back and we can figure things out from there."

She nods her head and seals the deal with a quick kiss on my cheek before she leaves me, sitting alone on the couch, wondering when my life will finally settle down.

38

BROOKLYN

"Slow down, girl! I'm about to die from heatstroke here."

I come to a skidding stop, bending at the waist to place my hands on my knees, catching my breath that has been sucked from my lungs from running at such a fast pace.

"Sorry," I sputter, gulping in large inhales of air. "Didn't realize I was sprinting so fast."

Peyton catches her breath next to me, panting hard and mirroring my stance at my side.

"Was the devil chasing you down, or what?"

An hour earlier, I'd been sitting at the library working on a paper for my clinical psychology class and needing a break, hoping to shut off some of my thoughts whirling around my head with a good run. I sent Peyton a text to ask her to meet me at the track where I could let off some steam. And pent up frustration.

I hadn't seen or spoken to Garrett in over a week. The day after our conversation, he'd texted me to tell me there'd been a change in his plans, and he'd decided to take Caleb with him on his overnight trip. I still didn't know where he'd gone or why, but it didn't really matter.

When he returned, he'd called and left me a voicemail giving me the week off, stating he had some time off before the basketball season started and he was going to spend it at home, doing some cleaning and hanging out with Caleb in the evenings.

None of it seemed too strange, but I was curious as to what he wasn't telling me. Maybe I was reading between the lines and there was something else going on that he didn't want me to know about.

Maybe I'm PMS'ing, but my thoughts fluctuated all week, flipping back and forth between standing my ground and maintaining my independence, to wanting to rush back into Garrett's arms and stay there forever.

Each time I was ready to pick up the phone or hop in my car, my mother's words would echo in my ears.

"Brooklyn, don't ever lose yourself to a man."

Dammit, mom. Get out of my head.

Suddenly, I'm exhausted – emotionally and physically – as I drop to the park bench behind us, as Peyton follows suit, eying the donut truck across the grassy knoll from us.

"I see you drooling over those donuts. You don't fool me behind your sunglasses and ASU ballcap."

She gives me a wide-eyed, innocent look and slaps a hand over her mouth.

"Me?" she objects dramatically. "I would never."

We both laugh at her obvious joke, but there's always an underlying concern over how she really is doing with her food demons. She once admitted to me that there had been a time in her life when she inhaled an entire box of glazed donuts before purging it all and then doing it all again because she'd failed a biology test in high school.

I guess we all have our own set of demons that we live with. Mine is the voice inside my head, preventing me from going after

Garrett. Logically, I know I shouldn't. That I really need this time to resolve the issues and complications that could prevent us from being together long-term. If that's even what he wants.

Or what I want.

I've fallen in love with Garrett. I have no confusion over that, whatsoever.

And of course, I love his son, too. With everything I have inside me.

But committing to them both now, while I'm young and have my whole future and career in front of me, I wonder if it's the right thing. Am I even ready for that level of commitment?

Garrett's older. He's lived and experienced things I haven't yet. He's traveled the world. He's started a family. And he may want to begin adding to that family sooner rather than later.

Do I want that?

Or do I need to experience life on my own terms, start a career that might take me who knows where?

Peyton taps me on my temple with her knuckle. "Earth to Brooklyn. Either you're seriously zoning out about donuts the way I am, or your faraway expression is about a very tall and very handsome coach."

I give her a sheepish grin and she laughs.

"That's what I thought," she clucks, shaking her head. "Which means I'll have to eat donuts all by myself for the rest of my life because my friend is head-over-heels in *loooooovvve*."

I playfully shove her in the shoulder, and she topples over on her side across the bench, catching herself with a hand and laughing with her unique high-pitched laugh. No one can outlaugh Peyton. When she does, it's with verve and gusto and an absolute impossibility to resist laughing with her.

"You're a shit," I gripe, a smile twitching at the corners of my mouth.

Peyton jumps to her feet, grabbing my hand in hers and linking our elbows together.

"That's a distinct possibility, but I'm still your friend. And you're my friend. And friends don't let friends eat donuts by themselves. I did you a solid by going on this godawful run, so you get to make it up to me with greasy, fattening donuts."

She smirks and gives me a wink, adjusting the bill of her hat while dragging me toward the mobile truck parked near the lot. I suppose she has a point. What kind of friend would I be if I didn't go along with all her crazy-cockamamie ideas?

39

GARRETT

I received the offer for the Head Coach position and accepted it.

I'd have been a fool to refuse because it comes with some pretty huge dollar signs and perks that I'm not receiving where I'm at right now.

The only problem now is how I'm going to break this to Brooklyn that we're moving right after the Labor Day holiday.

But that's the smaller problem compared to how I'll convince her to move with us.

Once I signed the offer, I started getting my ducks in a row, beginning with Caleb's school. The beauty of moving from one private school to another in different states is that the school in Franklin, Indiana won't begin their fall session until after Labor Day, which is perfect timing.

There's also the housing arrangement in my offer. The university has a home on campus reserved for incoming faculty in the athletic department, so I'll have time before I need to find a home to buy. And as far as daycare is concerned, my mother has already offered to stay with us for as long as we need her, to allow Caleb to adjust to his new surroundings and schedules.

What's left unsaid is the part about "without Brooklyn."

But I'm hoping I can change that tonight.

I'd called Brooklyn and invited her over for dinner tonight telling her Caleb had something very important he'd been working on in school that he wanted to show her. Which is indeed the truth. His class had been making a family tree, and when I asked who the obviously female stick figure was in the picture, he said it was Brooklyn.

I was going to leverage the shit out of that picture as a means of getting an affirmative answer about moving with us.

I wasn't above using underhanded tactics to get what I wanted.

Just like the first time Brooklyn ever showed up at my house, all hell seems to break loose in the kitchen just as I hear the doorbell ring in the entryway.

The oven timer goes off, buzzing obnoxiously loud, the scent of Brooklyn's favorite pizza wafting in the air, and Caleb begins screaming in an overly-hangry temper tantrum for his own dinner.

"Calm down, buddy. You have to wait for just a few minutes. Let me go get Brooklyn and then we can eat."

Part of his irritation is from over-stimulation and a lack of a nap. When I told him Brooklyn was coming tonight, he refused to lay down and that's where things went rapidly downhill from there.

Using the potholders, I slide the pizza stone out of the oven, but when I turn around to set it down, I misjudge the distance and instead of landing it on the counter, it slides off the oven mitt and onto the floor with a *schlop*.

"Shit," I curse loudly, the stonewear crashing to the floor and pizza sauce splattering every direction. "Goddamn it."

There's a second delay and then Siri's voice admonishes me. "Daddy said a bad word."

And then on repeat, "Shit, shit, shit, shit."

Laughter rings out from the other side of the kitchen as Brooklyn stands in our midst, looking like a ray of sunshine with her golden hair tied back into a knot and a bright smile painted across her wide, lush mouth.

"Caleb, that's an adult word that only adults can use. It's a bad word for kids."

She steps in and gives Caleb a hug, who adoringly hugs her back. Returning her attention back toward me, her eyes lift as if to say, "*what now?*"

"Hey, *sweet-*" I stop myself from using the nickname I've been calling her for months. "Brooklyn. As you can see, we might need to call out for delivery. I'm pretty useless tonight."

She laughs, mirth ringing through the sound. "I can see that."

Without thinking through the implications, I throw off the oven mitts and open my arms wide to offer her a hug, which she accepts willingly.

With her soft, sweet linen scent surrounding me, I couldn't care less about the ruined pizza. My hands shake with the need to hold her tighter. Longer. Without ceasing. If I could, I'd never let her go.

But she finally steps back and out of my arms, as I take a look around the open kitchen, filled with memories of Brooklyn from the past three months. Memories I cherish and that will be with me for a lifetime to come. And hopefully, if all goes to plan, memories we'll continue to make together in a brand-new kitchen elsewhere.

She takes a seat next to Caleb as I place a quick text order to the local pizza shop a few miles away.

"How are your classes going?" I ask just to fill the silence and hear the sweet melody of her voice.

"Really good. I had a paper due today. Oh, and I've been in the library a lot lately and ran into Lucas the other day."

"Yeah, I've been a horrible friend. He's been trying to get in touch with me but I haven't had much time to return the call. If you see him again, tell him I'm sorry."

"I will. And how are things" – she glances quickly between Caleb and me - "with you?"

Grabbing the back of the kitchen stool, I pull it out to sit down.

It's now or never.

"Can we dispense with the small talk for a second? I need to tell you something, Brooklyn. I've been offered a job as head coach."

Watching her face light up with enthusiasm for me is akin to seeing the Eiffel Tower at night, sparkling and shining brightly for all the world to see.

"Really? Garrett, that's amazing! Wait, what happened to Coach Welby?"

Clearing my throat, I shift to the edge of the chair, placing my folded hands on the table between us.

"I don't mean here at ASU, Brooklyn. The job is in Indiana. That's where Caleb and I went last week on our trip. I went for the interview and checked out the area. Got the offer yesterday. It's a really fantastic opportunity for me."

Just like a bubble bursting, her excitement dissipates, disappointment coloring her cheeks and lines across her face. I want to reach over and erase those lines with my kisses. Drag my hand through her hair and pull her into my lap, holding her in my arms so she has no question how good it will be if she comes with us.

"Oh, wow. Indiana. That's...*wow*." It's said very unconvincingly, which makes me chuckle. "So you're, like, leaving soon?"

I nod. "Yes. We need to be there over the long holiday weekend. I'm putting my house on the market tomorrow."

She swallows audibly. "I see."

Caleb decides to join in the conversation on his iPad app. "Nana live with us."

Her eyes snap from me to him, then back at mine.

Pain. Sharp and crisp filters through them.

Through a tight smile, I add, "Yes, buddy. Grandma will live with us for a while, at least."

I reach for Brooklyn's hand, but she snaps it away as if I've struck her.

"That's good that you have family there to help. For Caleb's sake."

Placing my hands in my lap, I lean back in my chair, closing my eyes momentarily in search of the right words. Opening them again, I stare into her marble-colored eyes, swirling with silver. "Brooklyn, there's something else. I want to invite you along. To come with us. What I mean to say is..."

Brooklyn pushes back in her chair, shaking her head adamantly, her hand telling me to stop talking.

"Go with you?" Her voice skyrockets to break the sound barrier. "To Indiana? Are you joking?"

A frown forms along my lips and my first response is to take offense at the tone she uses in reference to the state I grew up in. But I know it's not about that or that she has anything against the state itself.

"No, I'm not joking. I want you to move with us. I love you. Caleb loves you. I don't want to lose you."

Brooklyn nervously paces back and forth taking large inhales and letting out long exhales of breath.

And then she turns on me, pinning me with a scolding look. "You do realize that my life is here, right, Garrett? That I'm in the midst of my first semester in grad school. That I have a lease on an apartment. That I can't just uproot my life on a whim." She ticks all of these things off on her fingers as if I hadn't thought about them before now.

"Let me get this straight. You just expect me to leave everything behind to relocate for you so that you can have a live-in nanny and a beck-and-call girl service at your disposal. Did I get that right?"

I've never heard Brooklyn raise her voice in this manner. Apparently, I've never provoked her enough to warrant such ire. Tension drips from her biting words, her body coiled in an unfamiliar resistance.

Instinctively, I reach for her, hoping to temper some of the maelstrom in her vitriolic comment.

"Brooklyn. Please," I offer lamely. "That's not why I want you to come with us and you know it."

"Don't touch me, Garrett. This whole decision of yours, while it's great for you, is not for me. I'm not moving to Indiana and I'm sorry if you thought otherwise. You obviously haven't heard a thing I've said over the last three months if you just expect me to drop everything to chase after you."

My neck snaps back as if she's thrown a vicious punch with her statement.

"That's not what I thought at all. You have it all wrong. I don't want to lose you and I've done some research on the school and your program. I wouldn't expect you to stop pursuing your dreams of finishing your degree. I love that about you, Brooklyn."

Not wanting to encroach on her space, but needing to touch her in some way, I let my pinky feather over her knuckles, her hand hanging at her side. She doesn't pull away, but it isn't a warm reception and she certainly doesn't reciprocate the affection.

Caleb's comment seems to throw a little levity in this tense argument and has us both gritting our teeth to keep from laughing out loud.

"Daddy, Brook mad. She very mad."

"Oh, buddy," she responds, her tone bathing him in feminine tenderness. She places a hand on top of his head, gently soothing him with a rub of his neck, in which he literally turns into putty in her hand.

"I'm sorry if I sound angry. I'm not mad at you or your dad. I was just taken by surprise." Her eyes flit to mine and I know what she means without saying it. "I'm just sad about the situation. It's grown-up stuff and doesn't mean we're mad at you. Okay?"

He nods and asks to get down to play until the food arrives, which I hope is soon. Food always helps diffuse anger in any situation.

Caleb goes off to play in the family room while we both watch him make his way there. She slowly turns to me again, folding her arms across her chest.

"Garrett, I think I should say goodbye. This summer has been amazing. You are an amazing man and father, and I do love you. But I can't go with you. This is where our lives go in divergent ways. I think your opportunity sounds wonderful and I'm so happy for you. Really, I am."

She unlocks her arms and wraps them around me in a tight hug, as she whispers in my ear. "I hope it's everything you want it to be for you and Caleb. Goodbye, Garrett. I'll miss you."

And then with a brief kiss on my cheek, Brooklyn drops her hands, walks slowly into the living room where she crouches down next to Caleb, gives him a hug and kiss, and then walks out the front door as I just watch her go.

It's only as the door closes that I hear, "I'll always love you."

40

BROOKLYN

I had no idea that your heart can actually hurt from heartbreak.

My chest feels like it's been ripped open, my heart yanked out with pliers, thrown on the ground, mowed over with a lawnmower, cleaved and chopped to pieces with a meat grinder, and then returned to the empty cavity in my body.

Drama queen, much?

Maybe a little, but this has been a living hell.

There's been no consoling me the last four weeks. And believe me, there's been plenty of attempts by Peyton, my girlfriends, my mother, and even Kyler, who is a staunch oppositionist of love and relationships. He's even been kind enough (okay, I made him) to stay with me today and watch *Gone with the Wind* in its entirety.

It's one of my all-time favorite classic movies because of the character of Scarlett. I love her transformation in the film and the book because she goes from this meek little brat, who thinks she has to have a man, to dealing with some of the most horrendous things a woman must live through. On her own.

She deals with the loss of parents, her child, a freaking Civil War, the death of her best friend and then her husband. But she comes out tougher and stronger than she was going into it all and that's why I love the movie.

"You do realize, Manhattan, that you're exactly like Scarlett."

I make a face at Kyler, who is sprawled out across the one long couch we have, turning to glare at him from my pretzel-like position on the loveseat. He's been calling me by the moniker of Manhattan instead of Brooklyn recently for no other reason than he thinks it's funny and is being ironic.

When I moved back into my bedroom, we offered to let Kyler stay with us until the furnished studio apartment on the first floor comes available in October. It's actually been great having him stay with us, and especially having a male opinion on matters of the heart.

"I'm nothing like her. She was a brat with no warmth or empathy toward anyone but herself. She used people and played games to get what she wanted. I've never done that."

Kyler rolls his eyes at me. "Right. You *never* play games."

I sit up from the couch, throwing off the blanket I'd been cuddled in for the last hour and hit the Pause button on the remote.

"You got something to say there, Kyler Scott? Say it to my face. What kind of games do I play?"

He repeats my actions and sits up off the couch, swinging his legs over so his bare feet hit the floor, thrusting his arm out at me.

"Give me your phone," he demands.

"What? No. Why do you want it?"

I lift it from the coffee table, cradling it in my hands, protecting it by cradling it to my chest like it's a baby or a precious object.

"Give it to me." He flaps his hands and I grunt with displeasure.

"Fine, take it."

Curious as to what he's doing, I watch him swipe the screen lock and open up my texts. He scrolls through the log.

"One. Two. Three," he counts, pausing to look up at me as he says, "And that's just on one day last week."

He resumes scrolling and counting until he gets to ten. Then he stops, carefully placing the phone back in my hands as I snatch it back.

"Brooklyn, Garrett has tried so many times to get in touch with you and you've ignored his calls. Not only is that fucking rude, but it's a game to bust a guy's balls like that."

I snort. "I'm not ball-busting anyone. I've been busy when he's called and by the time I'm free, it's late."

Out of the corner of my eye, I see a pillow whizzing toward my face and I duck to avoid being hit.

"What the hell?"

"You're so full of it, Manhattan. You're avoiding him and because of that, he's had to hand in his man-card because he's being such a pathetic loser."

Growling, I throw the pillow back, which he catches and places over his lap.

"Garrett is not a loser."

In the few short months I've known Kyler, I've found him to be oddly full of wisdom and a really great listener. Plus, he's funny, sarcastic and a whole lot of fun to be around, but he also has no problem giving it to you straight. Which seems to be the case now.

"Let's put it this way. Girls like to be chased. I get it. And men, because of all that prehistoric cavemen shit, enjoy chasing because when they get their prize, it makes them beat their chests like King Kong. It's good for the ego and increases our testosterone levels. But going through the motions and never getting what they're after? Well, that's another story. And let me tell you, I'm feeling pretty sad for poor Garrett's ego right now."

"Pfft. He has no problem in the ego department, Kyler. The

man was an NBA superstar and a player in his time. And honest-to-God, I'm not doing this to hurt him." Kyler's eyes narrow on me.

"Well, not too much. It's more or less out of self-preservation. That first night after they moved, and he had me FaceTime with Caleb? I cried myself to sleep after that and decided from then on, I just couldn't do that to myself. It was too much. I can only be strong up to a point."

Kyler chews his bottom lip and then scrunches his face. "So, how are you going to handle seeing him at the upcoming wedding reception? Aren't they mutual friends of you both?"

I nod. "Yeah, Lance Britton. He was one of Garrett's players last year and then he coached with him this summer. It was actually Lance who brought us together."

"Aw, sweet story," Kyler coos, making kissing noises. "How cute."

"I actually ran into Lance on campus that other day. He was hired as an Assistant Coach to cover for the vacancy when Garrett left. I may have asked him if Garrett would be there."

Kyler nudges my shin with his bare toes. "Well, there you go. It'll be the best time for you two to talk things over. Even if it proves fruitless and you don't get back together, you can still fuck each other's brains out because everyone does that at weddings."

"You're a perv. That's not gonna happen." I give him a wink and a nudge back. "But I like the way you think."

41

Garrett

I always want things I can't have. Isn't that our constant human condition?

I'm an unwitting victim of the grass is always greener effect.

It's been that way my whole life. I see something I want, I work to get it. Once I have it, I want something else.

My life is full of decisions based on this way of thinking. In fact, after Becca's death and the trauma with Caleb, I started seeing a therapist at the suggestion of my coach, to identify what I was doing and why.

My therapist called it self-sabotage. I called it stupidity. The moment something is going well or right in my life, I do something to fuck it up. Case in point, taking the job in Indiana and ruining things for me and Brooklyn.

I'm telling this all to Lucas as we sit in a bar and commiserate over this most recent stupid decision.

"Nothing turned out the way I expected it to," I lament over the third bottle of Stella I've had since landing in Phoenix. I'm back for the weekend to attend Lance's wedding reception.

"Oh yeah? What did you expect?" Lucas gives a sarcastic quirk of his brows as he tips back his martini.

"Well, I didn't expect that my mom would get sick almost immediately upon our arrival in our new home. So sick, in fact, she wasn't able to take care of Caleb after school or in the evenings, so I had to find a sitter service who specialized in special needs kids. Talk about looking for a needle in a haystack. And then there's the part where I realized I was scammed about this new job."

"The ol' bait and switch, eh?"

"Exactly," I bemoan, sliding my fingers through my hair with a sigh. "Everything they promised I'd have in this basketball program had been compromised by the dirty coach who I come to find out the NCAA was investigating under claims of recruitment violations with incoming freshman. While I'm not being incriminated for any of the scandals, it still sheds a poor light on my program and doesn't leave me much of a chance to turn it around."

He tips his head thoughtfully. "I've seen you pull out some pretty fucking big miracles from your players, G. And even more so with Caleb."

God, Caleb. Have I ruined him?

"That's the worst part, Luc. Caleb's progress has been thwarted by this move. He'd been doing so well with his walking and communication, but his moods turned sullen and depressed. I had no idea a kid his age could have these types of emotional breakdowns, we're talking Def-Con 5 levels. But he's definitely reverted back to his old behaviors."

"Well, what were you doing before that was working and helping regulate those moods?"

I stare blankly at Lucas, giving him the '*Do I have to spell it out for you*' look.

As if the light dawns on him, his mouth open in an O. "Brooklyn. Right."

"I'm telling you, the only bright spot to all of this is that I just heard from Bob Guthry yesterday about Penelope's lawsuit. The petition has been dismissed by the judge who wouldn't consider reversing her parental rights petition. I about shit my pants, not gonna lie."

Lucas claps my shoulder hard. "That's wonderful news, bro. I'm so happy for you and Caleb. This is definitely cause for a celebration."

I thought so, too. But even with that great news, I still found myself at my wits end the week leading up to this trip back to Phoenix. I was ready to throw in the proverbial towel and give up and go back home.

Home is where Brooklyn is.

All I can think about is how or what I can do to win Brooklyn back.

And then an idea landed in my lap and I was smiling the rest of the week.

As I walk through the massive party tent, decorated with silver streamers and white shimmering twinkle-lights strung from the rafters, I see the familiar faces of former ASU basketball players all mingling about.

Heading to a large bar at the back side of the tent, I weave through the room and scoot around large groups of people, many speaking Spanish, a language I don't know. It makes sense since this reception was put on by Micaela's family, specifically for her family. As I pass, many look up and wave or nod and I return it in kind.

"What can I get you, sir?" the bartender asks.

"How about a Corona?" He nods and swiftly bends to pick up

a beer bottle from the ice-filled tub near his feet and hands it to me over the bar top.

"That'll be four-dollars, please."

I pull a five-dollar bill out of my pocket and slap it on the counter. "Thanks, man."

Turning to survey the crowd, I hear him say "*De nada*" as he moves to the other people waiting for their drinks. My back is partially to the side when I feel a large, meaty palm slam down on my shoulder.

"Hey, Coach Parker. Good to see you here, bro. I thought you left town."

I spin around to come eye level to Carver Edwards, a former ASU player who graduated a year before I took on the coaching spot, and who is now playing for the pro team up in Seattle.

We shake hands and he *clinks* my beer bottle with his.

"How's it going, Edwards? Yes, I'm back for the weekend. Didn't want to miss out on Britton's party. I'm surprised to see you here, too. I'd have thought you'd be playing this weekend."

Carver tips his head in a nod. "The team played last night so I hopped a plane down so I could celebrate Lance and Mica. Me and the missus fly back tomorrow morning."

As if summoned, a beautiful, tall blonde steps into view, as Carver grins broadly, opening his arm to cradle her into his body.

"Garrett Parker, this is my wife, Logan."

We greet with a shake. "Great to meet you, Coach. Carver and I watched all the ASU games on TV last year when he was home. We're big fans of our team."

Carver interjects, bending his head down to be heard over the noise.

"Coach isn't at ASU anymore. He took a head coaching job in Indiana this year." He stands to his full height and meets my gaze. "Did I hear that right? Lance mentioned that's why he got the spot on the coaching staff."

I scan the crowded area around the three of us, checking to

see if anyone is within earshot or listening. Seeing it's safe to talk, I fill them in on the news.

"Well, that was true up until two days ago, when I gave them my resignation." Carver's eyes grow wide and I lift a finger to my lips to signal the secrecy. "That isn't common knowledge yet, so please don't mention it to anyone. Especially the press."

We laugh at the reference, as we have a mutual dislike of the press as it relates to our personal lives. I recall Carver battled quite a bit of media interference a few years ago regarding an adopted son.

"Of course, your secret is safe with us. But what happened, if I may ask?" Logan says, peering up at us both.

"Let's just say the grass wasn't greener. My home is here and that's where I want to be. There might also be a woman who drew me back."

Carver chuckles, pushing his hand out to fist bump with me in acknowledgment.

"Isn't that always the case?" He smiles down at his glowing wife.

"Congratulations on your marriage, by the way. Now, if you'll excuse me, I'm going to swing through the crowd to see if I can find the woman I'm here for."

"You got it, Coach. And good luck with that."

I glance back at the happy couple, lifting my crossed fingers in the air. "I'll need it!"

42

BROOKLYN

"God, this is such a bad idea. How could I let you con me into wearing this tonight?"

I grouse at Peyton, who just smirks at me with her know-it-all grin, as I wobble on the heels and try to walk upright in the tight slip of a dress she made me wear.

"Girl, you will thank me later after you get some, because you look hot as fuckity-fuck. Garrett Parker is going to take one look at you and..." She stops short.

"And what?" I prod, giving her a *'go on'* stare.

She clears her throat and backs up two steps, causing me all sorts of confusion.

"I have to go...to the restroom..." Peyton points a thumb in the opposite direction behind her, turns and skips away, leaving me gaping at her sudden disappearance.

"Wait, I'll go with you."

"Hello, sweetheart."

My tongue swells and throat tightens, my tummy dropping to

my toes and my heart shimmying in some weird Latin-style dance move at the sound of Garrett's deep, resonating voice. It sweeps over me like a paintbrush and colors my cheeks with a bright pink flush.

I'm stranded and stuck, watching Peyton run for the door of the tent and turning to find Garrett standing in front of me, looking all too gorgeous decked out in his gray suit and blue tie. Damn him for being here and looking so fine.

Just, damn him.

I breathe in his sexy, spicy scent and lift my hand in a tiny wave. Using my purse as a protective shield, I clutch it against my chest, as if it'll be the barrier between us and will keep me firm and resolute in my aim to steer clear of him.

To not fall in bed with him tonight.

His eyes flash darkly and flicker appreciatively as they scan down my body. The way he's devouring me with his eyes right now could be my breaking point.

S.O.S. I might not make it out of here alive.

We both try speaking at the same time.

"You look amazing, Brooklyn."

"I'm not going home with you tonight," I blurt, his subsequent chuckle is low and filled with amusement.

There's a tease in his voice. "I didn't expect that you would. That's not why I'm here."

"Oh. Fine. What are you here for, then?"

Garrett's lips twist in a devilish smile, sending my pulse hammering and clamoring underneath my skin. My body reacts to his hoarse and gruff laughter. The tips of my nipples puckering hard against the tight bodice of this too-restrictive dress.

"Can we?" He points toward the outdoor area where there are tables and chairs and several fire pits blaze hot and red against the pitch of night.

In hopes of finding someone I know out there to join us, I lift a shoulder in agreement, as he places a hand at my elbow to guide me outdoors.

His grip is gentle but warm and solid. It reminds me of where his hand has been on other parts of my body. Intimate parts he made warm and glowing from his touch.

I give myself an internal scolding to stop thinking about that and pull my shoulders back in a stern, poised fashion. Unfortunately, by doing so, my breasts thrust out in front of me, drawing attention to the tight buds of my nipples, poking through the material.

It draws Garrett's attention, for sure, which he quickly diverts like a gentleman.

We stop over on the far end of the courtyard, near some sand volleyball pits and a Bocce ball court, empty now that it's after dark. The peals of laughter from kids in the background have me looking around in hopes of seeing Caleb.

As if reading my thoughts, Garrett says, "He didn't come with me. I needed to have a grown-up conversation with you. *Alone*."

His last word is promising. Sensual. A claim.

And it sends shockwaves scattering through my blood.

Garrett stands just a few inches from me, the hand on my elbow skimming over my bare arm, up and down. Up and down. My skin breaks out in goosebumps.

"Are you cold?"

"No. Just sensitive."

He sighs. "Brooklyn, I'm here tonight for you. To share something with you. Something I've never told anyone else before, except my therapist."

My lips form a silent O.

"God, I don't even know where to start."

Even in the dark, I can see the tremor in Garrett's hands, which he's dropped in front of him, nervously fidgeting with them like he's rolling a snowball. This man doesn't ever get nervous.

Even when confronted with the things Penelope tried to pull, he was a rock.

Oh shit. Did something happen with the lawsuit? Did he lose Caleb?

My heart hammers loudly. So loudly it drowns out everything else around me.

But what he shares with me has nothing to do with Penelope, not much at least.

"I love you with everything I am," he begins, immediately thawing my icicle heart. "But I have a shit way of showing it. I made assumptions about what you would want to do when I told you I was moving. I assumed you'd be like Becca and would just automatically come with me. But you're not her. And that's what I love most about you.

"You see, I came to realize after Becca and I got married and we fought for custody of Caleb, that I didn't love Becca the way I should have. I did love her, but not with everything in my heart. I should've wanted to have done anything for her, the same way she did for me. She loved me selflessly, as well as my son. But two years into our marriage, and a year after she adopted Caleb, things started to unravel. I was on the road so much of the time, and when I'd return home, I was useless and self-absorbed. I devoted my time to anything other than being a good father and husband."

I scrunch my nose, his words repelling and rancid. "I find that hard to believe. You are a great father, Garrett."

He lifts a shoulder. "I am now because I was given a second chance to figure out my shit. To learn what it means to really spend time with and care for a child. It didn't come naturally to me and it didn't happen until after the accident."

I'm too stunned to say anything, so I just stare at him with unblinking eyes, trying to reconcile the old Garrett to the one I know.

"The night of the accident," he swallows thickly, his voice gruff. "She was leaving a friend's house, after getting advice about what she should do. She called me on the road, crying, and told me she wanted a divorce."

I gasp. "What? Why? You loved them both."

Garrett's gaze flits down to the ground, his eyelashes fluttering to avoid eye contact.

"That night, we argued. Hard. Yelling, screaming, name calling. It was ugly. I was defensive and told her she was making drama out of nothing. But she made points I couldn't refute."

My head swims with all the questions I want answers to. It's as if I'm standing over a table full of puzzle pieces and something's missing. I can't quite put it all together to make sense of it.

He stares at me for a long minute before speaking again.

"She told me the distance was too hard to deal with. Which it was. She was at home in Indianapolis with a young child, without any family around, and she was so lonely. I was barely ever there. And when I was...well, she felt it. Felt my distance. Knew that I..." Garrett clears his throat with a cough.

"Becca said I didn't love her enough or the way she needed me to. And that by not loving her, it was killing her inside. That she would rather die than be in a loveless marriage."

Tears sting my eyes and I gasp through a sob. In fact, I'm crying openly, over feeling the pain this man and the woman he married had experienced. Reaching out, I cover his fist with my palm.

"I'm sorry, Garrett."

"She literally died believing that death was better than staying married to me."

His body jerks in a silent sob. "She'd been so distracted by her tears and our argument, that she took a curve too fast, veered into the other lane and the truck coming from the other direction smashed into the driver's side. But I am the asshole who killed her. It was my deeds that killed her, killed my dog and hurt my son."

We're both quiet for a while, as I internalize and digest everything he just shared with me. His anxiety from a tragic event that's shaped the way he loves, redirected his son's and has changed the course of his life extensively.

I'm at a loss of what to say or do, so I gather my courage and wrap him in my arms, humming into his chest that 'It's okay' and 'I love you' and meaning it.

This man is not guilty of any crime. He didn't kill his wife. He didn't cheat on her or abuse her. He wasn't violent or reckless. His only sin is carrying around the weight of this guilt for all these years and hurting himself in the process.

Murmuring into the broad expanse of his chest, I say, "You are a good man, Garrett Parker. And don't you ever forget it."

43

Garrett

We talked on and off for three hours until the party waned, people said their goodbyes and the waitstaff began cleaning up the catered food and beverage leftovers.

Our conversation was interrupted several times with friends stopping over to bid their leave, including Peyton, who found someone to take her home. As well as a lot of kissing and snuggling under the stars.

By now, I'd already told Brooklyn that I was moving back to Scottsdale and the reason for it.

"I've made so many mistakes in the past, sweetheart. And leaving you for a job was the top of the list. Brooklyn, you are the very best thing that has ever happened to me or Caleb. You're exactly who I want to spend the rest of my life with, but I understand if you don't feel the same or aren't ready for that. I can wait. I'm moving back for you and for Caleb, but I want you to have all the time and space you need to come to your own conclusions. When and if you're ready, I want this to be an equal partnership.

Because if it's one thing I've learned the hard way, it's that there has to be balance and equity in a relationship. One person can't carry the entire load."

A touch of fall is in the night air, cool and crisp, with a soft breeze that swung through the branches in the tree above us. My arm perched on the back of the outdoor sofa, my fingers idly stroking her dewy, soft skin. Her head rests in the crook of my arm, and I can feel her breath in the hollow of my throat.

"Do you still want me to be Caleb's nanny?"

"Not as much as I want you to be my girlfriend. I want you to be part of our lives in whatever capacity you see fit. Until I find a new job, I'll be home with my son and when needed, I can hire out for daycare after school for Caleb. You're going to be busy with your class schedule. But I'd love to have you spend time with us. With me."

Holding her like this again makes me want to do everything with her. But she already told me she wasn't going to go home with me tonight, so I have to be content with just snuggling until she's ready to leave, breathing in her light feminine scent, kissing her perfect lips, and exploring her mouth with my tongue.

"Get a room, you two," Lance teases, as he and Mica approach us hand-in-hand. "But when you do, kids, make sure to use protection, otherwise you'll end up like this."

He jokingly strokes a hand over Mica's swollen pregnant belly, larger than her small frame can handle. Something inside me sparks to life. A desire to someday see my girl pregnant. To start a family with her. But not before she's ready and has accomplished everything on her bucket list.

I throw my head back in a fit of laughter, at the same moment Brooklyn leans over to whisper in my ear. "I'd like that someday."

White-hot need surges to my balls as if they are gearing up for the challenge and I jump off the couch, tugging her hand in mine to bring her to her feet.

"Okay, then. Congratulations to you both. We need to go now."

We give a speed round of kisses and hugs and thank them for inviting us, letting them know to keep us posted on the impending birth of their child, and then we run-walk out to the parking lot.

When we get to her car, our hands have minds of their own, stroking, grabbing, pulling at each other with desperation. I get to the point where I'm about to make a fool of myself from how hard I am for her.

My body is tight and ready, yet I feel lighter than I have in ages. Perhaps it's that weight that's been lifted by sharing my most intimate of secrets with Brooklyn. Breaking down that final barrier and opening up to experience redemption and forgiveness.

My heart is light, my dick is hard, and I am holding onto the love of my life.

Nothing could be better than this.

Except maybe one thing.

"Garrett, take me home."

Yep, there it is.

EPILOGUE

"Oh my goodness, just look at how handsome you look!"

Caleb comes bounding into the family room, his little bow tie askew, the suit jacket and slacks that I bought him just a tad too big and hanging over his feet, but with enough room to grow into, with a broad grin on his face.

Today is his kindergarten graduation and afterwards, we are going over to Lucas's house where he's hosting a little party in honor of our newest graduate.

Caleb stops in front of me, his wiggly body still in motion, and hands me a piece of folded up notepaper.

"What's this, buddy?" I ask, flipping it over in my hand but finding nothing to indicate what it's about.

"Daddddddy...he help writed it."

The words are punctuated and slow to come, but Caleb has progressed incredibly well in his speech performance this year. Even the doctor and trauma specialists are astounded by the miraculous ability of his to show this much progress.

Of course, Garrett is Mister Overachiever, so why wouldn't his son be the same?

Speaking of Garrett, I look up from the mysterious note in my hand to find him ambling down the hallway, hands in his pockets, his effortless male sexuality on full display, making my body come alive at his presence. A small smirk plays at the edge of his mouth, as I flap the folded paper at him.

"Exactly what is this about?"

He sweeps his son up into his arms, who squeals in delight, as they stand in front of me eying them dubiously.

"Open it and find out."

"*Owenitup*," Caleb demands.

The note is folded in quarters, as I lift and separate each flap until it's open in my hands. It's a Caleb original piece of art. There are three stick figures, similar to the one I received last fall. One tall man wearing a gray T-shirt and a whistle around his neck. No pants, which I snicker over. Underneath it says DAD in Caleb's handwriting.

Then there's a kid-sized Caleb with his arms raised high. His name is spelled underneath.

And finally, a female stick figure, with a pretty pink dress and long yellow-blonde hair and a gigantic smile. Underneath it doesn't have my name, though.

I look up at where Caleb is playing with Garrett's beard, running his hand over the stubble and laughing from the scratchy texture.

"This is beautiful, Caleb."

"'Nuther one." He pokes at his dad, who extracts another folded picture and Caleb takes it from his hand and shoves it in mine.

I open this one and it's a picture of just the man and the woman, holding hands.

"Aw," I sigh. "That's so sweet. Is that me and your daddy?"

When I look back up, both Garrett and Caleb are no longer standing, but on one knee in front of me.

"Last one," Garrett says, a gleam in his eye, as he hands the note to Caleb and we go through the motions again.

This time, when I open it, I see a few differences from the other pictures. In this one, there's still three of us, but a fluffy dog has been added next to Caleb's likeness. And then under my figure, he's written the word MOM and there's what appears to be a diamond ring (not to scale) on the left side of my hand.

My eyes connect with Garrett's, before dropping to see his hand, which holds a blue ring box in his palm. "Um..."

"Brooklyn Renee Hayes, we're going to keep this short and sweet, because we have a kindergarten graduation to get to. But I know without a doubt that it wouldn't have even been possible had you not entered our lives. You make everything better, sweetheart. You've helped both of us become better men. You're smart and beautiful, have the biggest heart, and maybe not the best singing voice or dancing skills..."

He grins broadly and I thump him on the chest with my palm, blinking back the tears in my eyes that threaten to let loose.

"Brooklyn, will you do me the honor of becoming my wife, and becoming Caleb's mom, and making us the happiest two men in the world?"

Garrett opens the box, a beautiful solitary diamond sparkling inside, along with a small paper-made ring, which if I had to guess, is a handmade Caleb work-of-art. He reaches for my hand and slides the ring on my finger, as happy tears storm down my face.

My voice wobbles a little as I throw my arms around them both, squeezing and shouting my reply. "*Yes, yes, yes, yes!*"

When I pull back and Garrett kisses me, Caleb tugs on my shirt to grab my attention.

"We make you cry?" he asks, his voice this sweet, but sad little whimper. Then he turns to Garrett, an angry scowl across his face, scolding his dad. "You no make my new Mommy cry!"

I dab at my eyes as I laugh through the tears, my body quaking with joyous laughter.

When I finally gain my composure, I tug Caleb into my arms and place kisses all over his adorable face as he squirms in my hold.

"Sometimes when the people we love make us really, really happy, we cry."

My lips tremble and I turn my gaze up to Garrett, who seems to share the same expression. "And I'm really, really happy."

And then Garrett flicks his head toward the patio door, nudging Caleb to go open it. Caleb giggles, looking expectantly between his dad and me, Garrett nodding again with a *'go ahead.'*

Without his walker, but with a slight gimp in his stride, he heads to the backdoor, reaching on tiptoes to unlatch the door and slides it open.

"Come here, Teddy!" his little voice calls out and I hear a scampering of paws on the patio floor.

My eyes turn into saucers because I can't believe what I'm seeing.

"Did you get a dog?" I exclaim, my gaze locked on the big, fluffy giant Golden Retriever being ushered into the house by his new best friend.

"Not just any dog. A companion service dog for Caleb."

I watch in awe as Teddy, who stands just as tall as Caleb, licks his face generously, Caleb laughing and wiping off the slobber with the back of his hand and groaning happily, "Gross!"

This is all news to me, and I had no earthly idea Garrett had even been considering this addition. I've been throwing out the idea since the first week I moved in and he always had an excuse as to why it wouldn't happen.

But now, Caleb has his dog, and I couldn't be happier for him. Garrett must have been working on it for months because service animals do not get acquired quickly.

"When did you do this? Oh my gosh, this makes me so happy for Caleb!"

Garrett lifts a shoulder, a small smirk playing at the edge of his mouth.

"After Caleb's last seizure, I realized my grief over losing Ollie was holding back Caleb. And I eventually listened to what my beautiful girlfriend had been telling me all along. It's only through your love and support that I am finally able to let go of that loss. Now I'm ready to remake a life, kids, dog and all, and the only one I want to do it with is you."

He kisses my lips, exchanging our first touch as an engaged couple. It sparks a promise of everything I could ever want, with a man that believes in me, inspires me, encourages my independence and empowers me to reach my goals.

"And I want to do it all with you, too. I love you, Coach Garrett Parker. Now and forever."

COURTING LOVE AVAILABLE NOW

If you enjoyed Coach Parker, Lance Britton and some of the ASU basketball crew, read the Courting Love series now!

Courting Love (A College Sports Series)

ACKNOWLEDGMENTS

To my sister, Jen, for all her feedback related to working with and educating special needs children. It takes love, patience and a big heart, and she has it in spades.

To my friend, Kayla, paralegal extraordinaire. Thanks for all the answers to my 'what if' questions relating to parental rights and legal standards regarding child custody laws.

To my editor, Debbie and proofreader, Virginia, thank you both for catching all my manuscript and story mishaps. You ladies rock!

Thanks also to my beta reader, Cristina, and my friend, Jen Nathan, for the comments and suggestions early on in this writing process.

To my local Emerald City Author Chicks - I was so inspired by all of you during our May Writer's Retreat in Port Townsend. You are all superstars and I'm so glad I could spend those three nights with you writing, drinking, learning, walking, and talking shop.

And lastly, thanks to my Sexy Swooners and ARC team for taking the time to read my books and share the love of my characters' stories.

ABOUT THE AUTHOR

Sierra writes new adult and sizzling hot contemporary romance. She's written and published 20 novels, including the award-winning series, ***Courting Love*** (college sports) and the erotic ménage serial, ***Reckless – The Smoky Mountain Trio***.

Sierra lives with her husband and dog in the Seattle area. She is a sucker for cheap accessories, loves anything dark chocolate, and enjoys attending live concerts.

Subscribe to her email list here: www.sierrahillbooks.com or find her here:

ALSO BY SIERRA HILL

The Physical Series

Physical Touch

More Than Physical

Physical Distraction

Physical Connection

Standalones and Flirt Club stories

One More Minute With You

The Reunion

Character Flaws

His Fairytale Princess

Whipped: A Second Helpings Story

Resolution: Road Trip (A Resolution Pact Story)

Be Patient – The Waiting Game (An Escaping the Friend Zone Novella)

Spring Break Navy Seal (A Spring Breakers story)

Courting Love (A College Sports Series)

Full Court Press

The Rebound

Pivot

Fast Break

Jump Shot

Reckless – The Smoky Mountain Trio serial

Reckless Youth

Reckless Abandon

55751233R10144

Made in the USA
Middletown, DE
21 July 2019